Evernight Publishing

www.evernightpublishing.com

Copyright© 2014

Jenika Snow

Editor: Karyn White

Cover Artist: Sour Cherry Designs

ISBN: 978-1-77233-177-6

ALL RIGHTS RESERVED

THE GRIZZLY MC: VOLUME TWO

DEDICATION

Thank you readers for all of your continued support, and thank you Evernight for being such an amazing publisher.

THE GRIZZLY MC: VOLUME TWO

ONE NIGHT IN THE OUTLAW'S BED

The Grizzly MC, 3

Jenika Snow

Copyright © 2014

Chapter One

She shouldn't watch him. She shouldn't even look his way. All that accomplished was seeing the skanks rub themselves all over him and the other MC members like they were cats in heat. Maggie Drake looked down at her fruity drink that was half full, picked up the glass, and downed the rest of it.

"Whoa. Looks like someone wants to get trashed tonight?" Mora, her best friend since they had been twelve years old, was grinning.

Maggie shook her head and breathed through the burn of alcohol. The drink wasn't even that potent, at least it shouldn't be, but clearly the bartender had felt generous when filling it with liquor. Well, better for her because she was feeling pretty shitty.

"Yeah, and I'm getting another one. I don't even want to be able to see straight by the end of the night." Mora's grin fell, and she gave Maggie a sympathetic look.

"Honey, getting laid off isn't the worst thing to happen."

Maggie shook her head again and played with the rim of her glass. "Maybe not, but it sucks nonetheless. Oh, and let's not forget about the fact I moved back to this shitty little town after that douche-bag John broke up with me for some big, fake breasted bimbo." She held up three fingers to Mora. "I also get to work for my dad in an automotive parts store of all places, too." It sounded even worse when she said it aloud. "And living in his basement at the age of twenty-three isn't humiliating at all." The last was said thickly with sarcasm. "That kind of brings the whole sucky thing full circle."

"Ever hear the saying 'Everything happens for a reason'?"

Maggie gave Mora a bland look. "Seriously? You do realize people hate that saying?"

Mora shrugged and tried to offer another smile, but it wasn't as peppy as it was moments before. Mora stared at her for a moment and breathed out. "Ok, let's get you another drink then."

Maggie gave her a thumbs up, and watched as Mora left their pub table and headed to the bar. Maggie looked over at Diesel, against her better judgment, but shit, she couldn't help it. She had known the man for as long as she could remember. But he was this feared outlaw in Steel Corner, associated with The Grizzly MC, and she should run in the other direction, not want to gravitate toward him. He was over ten years older than she was, was the freaking vice president of the motorcycle club, and was a bear shifter on top of that. To say he was dangerous was an understatement. Although she wasn't privy to club business and didn't know the members on a personal level, she knew enough. Like every other Steel Corner resident, she knew that the Grizzly MC was badass, did illegal activities, and had a very violent nature. People steered clear of them, and just a look at their leather and cut wearing appearances scared the shit out of people.

Although she might not be "friends" with the club, she probably saw them on a more personal level than most of the town's residents did. That was a given when her father owned an automotive parts business and the MC members came to him several times a month. So getting involved with Diesel, in any shape or form, would be bad for her. Not to mention he had been a man-whore before she moved out of Steel Corner, and after seeing three women walk up to him and rub themselves all over his leather-clad body, it was clear he still lived that lifestyle. But even knowing all of that, and telling herself that she most definitely did not want a man like Cane "Diesel" Marsh going anywhere near her in a sexual way, she couldn't help but stare at him. Watching his thick, muscled forearm flex when he lifted his arm up to bring his beer bottle to his mouth had her wet between her thighs.

She wanted him, had wanted him since she was seventeen years old and she had been working the weekend at her dad's shop. Even years later she could still picture that day so clearly. Diesel had come in with a bunch of the other MC members, and that was the first time she had been so close to him, had smelled the leather, sweat, and motor oil that had surrounded him, and knew for the first time in her life what hardcore lust was. But he hadn't noticed her other than a glance and a chin lift her way. She would have lain on the counter naked for him if he ordered her to do it. That was how much she had wanted him. She had been dumbstruck by the dangerous aura that came from him—from all of them. All it had taken was that one moment for her to know that she wanted Diesel to *own* her—even if at the tender age of seventeen she hadn't even known what the hell that truly meant, but she knew she wanted it. Maggie wanted him to make her feel what it was like to have a real male fuck her.

A shiver worked over her body at that thought. That seemed like ages ago now, but even moving away hadn't done anything but push those carnal desires deep down inside of her. Now being back in town had everything rushing forward. All it took was the sound of motorcycles coming down the road, and the sight of that metal glinting under the sun as they passed through town, for her to feel that hardcore desire she had whenever in his presence. And now, seeing Diesel in the flesh after so many years, yeah, she was wet and wanted him, and knew that he was the only man that could give it to her.

She glanced at him again. He wore a short sleeved shirt, and the tattoos that covered his entire right arm from wrist to under his shirt were so damn arousing she actually clenched her thighs together. She could overlook the slut currently perched atop his lap, could even ignore the way she had her arms wrapped around his neck and played with the light blond hair tied at the nape of his neck. But what she couldn't ignore was the pounding of her pulse between her thighs every time she looked at him.

Get a grip. You're back home for less than a week and already you are fantasizing about Diesel?

She glanced at Mora at the bar, but she was too busy flirting with the bartender to worry about bringing the drinks back so they could get good and sloshed. Maggie looked back at where Diesel and a few of the other bikers sat. Diesel's expression was stern as he leaned forward and rested his forearms on the table—slut-free, she noticed—and spoke to Court. It was like she had never left, and all these years hadn't passed. Being away from Steel Corner had been good for her, at least that was what she thought, but as soon as she stepped back in this town all of her old feelings resurfaced. And those old feelings had to do with Diesel currently looking right at her. Maggie's mouth went dry, her heart started to pound fast and hard, and she swore Diesel could tell she was on edge even from this distance. His light blue eyes watched her with this knowledge that had always made her feel twitchy, as if he could see right into her soul. His mouth moved, and she realized he was still talking to Court, but kept his attention right on her.

God, he was still so big, maybe even more muscular than the last time she had seen him, and those muscles were clearly visible under his shirt and leather cut. Maggie tore her eyes away from him, because even though she had a nice buzz going on, she wasn't nearly drunk enough to let her thoughts go to where they were trying to go: her under Diesel's huge body, both of them naked, and him pumping into her like he was staking a claim. Her cheeks heated, and fortunately Mora came back, slid a big-ass margarita in front of her, and started talking about the bartender. Maggie grabbed the drink, sucked down half of it, and waited for oblivion.

"Girl, you okay?"

Maggie looked at Mora who watched her intently over the sugar-coated rim of her glass. She hadn't told anyone about this carnal need to have a man that was so, so very wrong for her. But she had just enough alcohol in her bloodstream, just enough liquid courage pounding through her veins, that telling Mora now about something that she had kept deep down inside of her didn't sound like such a bad idea.

"This about the fact you've been eye-fucking Diesel since he walked in?"

Maggie didn't respond right away, just grabbed her drink and tipped it back, taking in a mouthful and swallowing it until her throat grew numb. She may not have ever told anyone how she felt for the biker, but Mora had lived in Steel Corner her whole life, too.

"You do realize that your silence is confirmation enough?" Mora lifted a blonde, arched brow at her. "And you do know that you can't lie worth a shit, and I'm pretty good at reading people?" Mora smiled widely. There was a chorus of deep male laughter, and they both turned and stared at the four MC members sitting around the table. The bottle of whisky between them was nearly gone, but it was still pretty early in the night, and she knew that bottle would be replaced as soon as it was empty.

"We should have gone someplace else." Maggie looked over at Mora, who was still staring at the bikers.

"Why? Everything else in this town is so lame compared to this place."

Maggie did agree with Mora, but it was also a bar owned by the Grizzly MC, one that was currently filled with many of said bikers. The energy in this place was intoxicating, if not a little dangerous. She looked around and saw several of the club members she recognized, but many that she didn't. They all had a common denominator, and that was the fact their cuts stated they were part of the Grizzly MC. There were a few men that didn't have cuts on. They played pool or sat at the bar, and she had to assume they were passersby. The residents of this town tended to stay away from anything that had to do with the Grizzlies for obvious reasons.

"Besides, the eye candy is pretty spectacular here."

"Yeah, I can't argue with you there, but you notice we are the only women here fully dressed, and the only ones that don't look like we are about to kick someone's ass?"

Mora chuckled and went back to drinking her margarita. "You know what I think you need?" Mora paused. "I think you need to do something to get out of your funk and make this homecoming a hell of a lot better."

Uh oh, she could only guess what her friend without a filter was about to suggest, but Maggie had a pretty good guess when Mora looked over at the MC members at the table again.

"Don't even say it."

"Say what?" Mora was still looking away when she answered. "I just think if you want Diesel so bad, which I can't blame you by the way, I think you need to do it. What do you have to lose?" Mora looked at her again. "I'm being serious right now, Maggie."

Yeah, she could tell that, and there weren't many times that Mora was serious. She was more of a party all the time kind of girl. "What am I supposed to do, Mora? Go up to him and tell him that I want to have sex with him?" Mora opened her mouth, but Maggie shook her head. "Don't answer that."

Mora smiled.

"You know I'm not outgoing like you are. Heck, I've only been with two guys sexually in my life, and even that a lot left to be desired."

"That's my point, Maggie. You're twenty-three, moved out of this crappy town after high school, got a degree, and did something with your life."

Maggie snorted.

"I'm serious. So what if shit didn't go the way you envisioned? Everything happens for a reason, right? It isn't like you don't know those guys. I mean your dad owns the shop they come and get a lot of their parts for their bikes for. And they have known you guys for years, have even drunk with your dad before."

"Mora, they are bikers, lead a dangerous life, and are so not what I should get involved with. I'm trying to get my life in order, remember?" Maggie swallowed another mouthful of her drink. "Yeah, my dad might be close with them, but I never was, not like that, and besides," she leaned in a little closer, "I've been gone for five years. He probably doesn't even remember me."

Mora shrugged but didn't respond.

"Besides, he would eat me up."

Mora chuckled and looked at the bikers again. Maggie followed her gaze and saw a busty brunette now giving Diesel a little lap dance. Ugh, that girl had it going on in the body department, that was for sure. Her big fake breasts were all jiggling around in that loose top, her flat stomach was on display with a little belly button ring punched right through it, and those jean shorts were so minuscule every time she bent over to shake her chest in Diesel's face Maggie could see the crease where her thigh and butt cheeks met.

"That girl would eat me alive." Maggie had meant to keep that to herself, but the alcohol was making her blurt things out she normally wouldn't have said. "Even if I had the balls to go up to Diesel, you think he'd pick chubby Maggie over that skanky thing?" Maggie was short, on the thicker side, and her long brown hair never did what she wanted it to. She didn't have the long legs that the scantily clad woman now currently straddling Diesel had.

"Come on, girl. Let's dance."

Maggie sucked down the rest of her drink. Yeah, she had nothing compared to a lot of females, Mora included. John had broken up with her for a woman that had more going on for her in the looks department than Maggie could even compare with. If those thoughts weren't enough to put her in a slump she didn't know what would. Mora grabbed her hand and hauled her to the small dance floor that was currently occupied by a few couples moving to Aerosmith. The song ended, and another one began. It was slower, kind of sensual, and Maggie was feeling more than loose enough to let go and enjoy herself for once in her life.

THE GRIZZLY MC: VOLUME TWO

Chapter Two

Diesel lifted the shot Court handed him and tossed it back. Drevin and Court were currently having an argument over who had gotten their dick sucked more times in the last year. Dallas seemed to be sulking, and he had been that way for the last week. But he didn't offer up any information, and Diesel wasn't the prying type.

"Dude, what about you?" Drevin tried to get Diesel in on the conversation.

"Man, don't get me involved. I'm not talking about my dick with you assholes." He grinned at them. Although they kept trying to bring Diesel into the conversation, he was more interested in something else. Not even the barfly, who was also a club whore, could distract him from the curvy brunette dancing. What he should have done was haul Maggie Drake out of there and taken her back to her father's place. This bar wasn't a place for her to be hanging out in. Hell, she should be at home under a blanket with a mug of hot chocolate in her hands, not at a place owned by and filled with Outlaws. Diesel was happy he was who he was, but that didn't mean he wanted to see a young girl like Maggie here, getting drunk and checked out by a bunch of motherfuckers. And that was exactly what was happening. As soon as he had entered the bar with the other club members he had instantly seen her. He wasn't going to lie and say the human part of him didn't get hard as a rock at the sight of her almost modest attire. Diesel was so used to seeing females flaunt their shit around, barely covering their pussies and tits up because they thought that was what a male wanted to see. Some may very well like no mystery at all, but Diesel, no, he wanted to have to imagine what a woman looked like under her clothes. The bear side of him had risen up, too, scenting out the familiar part of her, and the fact she was a grown woman now. It had been years since he had seen her, five to be exact, and although he was aroused to see her now, back then she had just been the daughter of Brian Drake, a close friend of the club and the guy The Grizzlies got a lot of the parts for their Harleys from.

"Dude, I'm telling you that female sucked my cock like she was a Hoover." Court leaned back in the seat and slammed his hand down on the table. The beer caps that littered the scarred wood jumped from the action. "She sucked my cock for so long my shit got numb."

"Man, you're insane if you're trying to play it off like you could last that long," Drevin said with a chuckle. "I know for a fact I saw you go into one of the backrooms with a club whore, and no more than twenty minutes later she was coming out wiping her mouth like she had just eaten dinner, and you followed behind stumbling to put your belt back on." Drevin was outright laughing now, Court had a scowl on his face, and Dallas still wore this perpetual stoic expression. The two prospects that had joined them out tonight, Dark and Tore, laughed their asses off.

Diesel turned his attention back to Maggie and watched her sway her hips to the music. He had felt her eyes on him, and when she wasn't looking he was the one staring at her. He shouldn't, and not because he was thirty-nine and far too old for her. He should stay away because compared to him she seemed like this innocent virgin, and he was this vicious bear starving for fresh meat. He was a dirty bastard with filthy sexual needs, ones that would have marks on her pretty cream colored flesh, and leave pain resonating throughout her body. When he found a female to relieve himself with, he liked things rough, liked to be in control. As much as Diesel wanted Maggie, wanted to feel himself push deep inside of that tight little body, wanted to feel her come from the force of him fucking her, and wanted her nails digging into his back until he hissed out in pain, he knew he couldn't have her. She was too good for the likes of him, that was for fucking sure.

The female currently on his lap and grinding her shit all over him had clearly thought his erection was for her and from what she was doing, because the low hum of approval that came from her told him as much. When she reached down and attempted to slip her hand down his pants, he stopped her with a firm hold on her wrist. He turned his head to look at her, but all there was reflected back at him was the look of dirty need. He hadn't slept with this particular female before, and although a lot of the MC members had a favorite club whore they slept with on more than one occasion, Diesel was a one woman kind of male. He didn't like to double dip and didn't like sloppy seconds, but females that hadn't been with any of his MC brothers were far and few between, especially ones that liked his dirty kind of sex. He lifted the female off of him and set her aside. She huffed out and pouted in disappointment, but he still had his focus on Maggie. Fuck, she had blossomed from the short and chubby girl he had seen at her dad's shop to this curvy woman that had nice, wide hips and big fucking tits. Her thighs were thick enough to hold onto him as he fucked her against the wall, her hips went on for miles, and her ass had him imagining spreading those round cheeks and licking her tight hole between them. He looked at her breasts again and nearly groaned aloud. The mounds were so big, so naturally bouncy, that his cock jerked as he watched them move up and down and from side to side while she danced. He should really look away, find a female to screw nice and hard, and put his thoughts of having Maggie out of his head. But he was also a masochistic bastard with sadistic tendencies, and wanting a female like Maggie, knowing he couldn't have her because he was so very bad for her, was as masochistic as it got. But the things he wanted to do to her, the pleasure and pain he wanted to give her, were all sadistic, and so damn hot as the images played through his head.

"D, hey man, you going after something?"

He looked over at Court who spoke. The female that had been all too willing to stroke Diesel's cock was now working herself all over Court. But the biker wasn't interested and pushed her away. Drevin was right there, grabbing her around the waist and pulling her on his lap. Yeah, Drevin was a newly patched in former prospect, and wasn't picky on what he stuck his dick in, or if he got sloppy ass seconds in the very same night.

"You like something over there?" Dallas said in a low, deep voice and tipped his chin toward the dance floor. "You scoping out that hot piece of ass out there with the jeans on?" There was a slight slurred quality to Dallas's voice, and it was clear the male was drunk.

Although Diesel knew who he was referring to, he still looked in Maggie's direction. Her eyes were closed and her arms were up in the air as she moved slowly to the music. Her friend was dancing the same way, and he could see the redness tinting Maggie's cheeks. She was drunk, which he would have known even if he hadn't been close enough to smell the alcohol coming from her pores. He was a bear shifter, as were all the Grizzly MC members, but there were a lot of bullshit ideas on what a shifter could and couldn't do. They didn't heal instantly when injured, and although they had heightened senses and strength when in their bear forms, when they were humans they still had weaknesses. And Maggie Drake was one fucking weakness for Diesel, but he couldn't quite understand why. His bear was pacing back and forth inside of him, needing to be released, and for the first time in his life he had never felt so pulled in two different directions. His pulse beat in his dick, and the longer he looked at her the more he wanted her. She had been cute back in the day, and the last time he had seen her was when she was only seventeen. She had been just a kid, and he wasn't some sick fuck that wanted any part of that, but now? Now she was all woman, and as much as Diesel knew he shouldn't even tempt that darker side of him, he honestly didn't know if he'd be able to be strong and stay away from her.

"Man, I'd fuck that girl two ways to Sunday."

Diesel snapped his head toward Dallas and bared his teeth, but the other male was still looking at Maggie.

"Fuck, she sure has grown up since the last time I saw her." Dallas was a newly patched in Grizzly MC member. He had been a Nomad for more years than Diesel could even remember, and had hung around Steel Corner for extended periods of time. So his knowing Maggie and recognizing her wasn't too much of a surprise.

Still, hearing Dallas talk about her like she was another club whore had this fiery rage burning deep inside of Diesel, accompanied by the need to knock Dallas's teeth in.

"Shit, look at the ass on her. And she's shaking that shit like she wants me to go over there and fuck her."

Something snapped inside of Diesel, and he swept his arm across the table, sending the empty bottles scattering to the floor and scaring the piss out of the females that hung around them. They scurried back, and although the music was still loud overhead, the noise from the people had dimmed and he felt their eyes on him. Dallas was still in his seat with his beer bottle resting on his thigh. Diesel was fuming. He felt his muscles grow under his skin, and knew that the scent of his anger was clear, yet that son-of-a-bitch Dallas just sat there with this stoic expression on his face.

"Say something one more time, Dallas. Say one more thing about fucking her ass, touching her, or even look at her and see what I do."

Dallas cocked a blond brow. "Is she yours?"

For a moment Diesel didn't respond, but then gritted out, "No."

Dallas didn't say anything for a few seconds, but then the corner of his mouth kicked up. "So you're confronting me about a random female?" He brought his beer bottle to his lips and took a long drink. He set it down on the table and stared at him with red-rimmed and glossy eyes. "You actually willing to go head-to-head with me because of some piece of pussy that you haven't even claimed?"

Diesel tightened his hands into fists, but Dallas just kept right on talking.

"Or maybe you have fucked the shit out of that pussy and feel like going another round? I know you aren't all about dipping your dick in sloppy second cunt." Dallas was piss-ass drunk, and when any of the members were that trashed they seemed not to have a filter on their mouths, but that shit was going to get Dallas's ass beat, and that time was right now.

Diesel gripped the edge of the table and turned the thing over in one powerful surge. His reaction was ludicrous, intense, and uncontrolled, but his bear was taking charge right now. Dallas had the fucking balls to still stay seated, and there was no doubt the asshole knew how close to shifting Diesel was. "I'm going to beat your ass."

Dallas stood, finished off his beer, and tossed the bottle. He swayed on his feet, but righted himself and chuckled softly. "All this over some female that grew up around you?" Dallas shook his head.

""D, man, Dallas is clearly drunk," Court said. "He's been in his own world. You know that."

Yeah, Diesel had noticed, but that didn't mean shit right now. "Don't fucking talk about Maggie like she's just another warm hole to stick your cock in." He spoke to Dallas and pointed a finger at where he knew Maggie stood. Diesel had no fucking idea what in the hell had gotten over him. But he didn't question it because he always went with his instincts, always trusted his gut, and right now everything inside of him was roaring out that he needed to do this. Hell, he was just thinking about doing the exact same thing to Maggie as he accused Dallas of doing. He shouldn't give two shits who talked about her, or what they said. But it was like this possessive side of him, the one controlled by his bear, had risen up so swiftly he couldn't comprehend what was happening to him. But he couldn't deny that the moment he had seen her sitting there, looking all womanly and curvy, had this very deep need inside of him coming to the surface. Had it always been there and just now decided to rise up like some kind of damn beast intent on staking some kind of claim? Yeah, it really had.

He felt everyone watching this altercation, and the smart thing to do was to just walk away, and maybe he could have if Dallas hadn't been running his fucking mouth. Drunk or not, Diesel couldn't let it go. His bear wouldn't allow it, and his human side didn't want to forget about the anger.

"Dallas, if you were smart you wouldn't say another damn word," Court said and took a step toward them. "You're drunk and need to sleep it off. Clearly you don't know what in the fuck you're doing right now."

"Damn, D, you're getting soft in your old age, and actually starting to care about shit other than what cunt you're going to stick your dick in—"

Diesel didn't let him run his mouth anymore. Yeah, this started over Dallas taking about Maggie like she was just another female, and although Diesel had never thought of her as anything more than a kid until now, Dallas needed to know he couldn't say shit like that. He needed to show respect, and Diesel was going to show him with his fists. But then he just kept going, and pissing Diesel off even more. Maggie just wasn't some piece of ass, and certainly didn't deserve to be talked about in that way. Her father was tight with the club, and because of that she counted as tight with the MC, too. Even if she wasn't in deep with the club in any other form than that, she was still under club protection. He moved quickly in front of Dallas, intent on slamming his fist into the other male's face, but a hand on his arm had him instantly stopping. The scent of Maggie filled his nose in a rush of saccharine intoxication and something floral. He didn't have to turn around to know it was her, because there was this intense spark of electricity that slammed into him at the point of where she touched him and rushed through his body. His cock had grown soft from his near fight with the other biker, but now it grew hard as steel in seconds flat.

Court stepped up beside Dallas and gripped his arm. "Come on, man. This is not the fucking time or place for this shit."

Dallas glared at Diesel, and it was clear the other male wanted to go a round. Diesel had never had any issues before with the other man, but the fact he hadn't kept his mouth shut meant he was due to get knocked down because of it. Stinger had been at the bar hitting it up with a female, but he was now on the other side of Dallas and pulling him toward the door. Dallas looked like he was about to say something, but Court made a deep sound in his throat.

"Dallas, just shut the fuck up. Can't you see that D is hanging on by a thread? And if I were going to place bets I'd say D has you on this one given the fact it is clear this concerns a female that is important to him, and the fact you can hardly stand up straight."

They stared at each other for another several seconds as Court and Stinger tried to pull him back, and finally Dallas relented, and the three of them went toward the front and walked out of the door. Court's words slammed into Diesel's head. *It concerns a female that is important to him.*

Diesel took a step back, which caused her hand to fall away from his arm. He turned around and looked at her. Even though he towered over most people, Maggie was especially tiny compared to him. At six-foot-four and over two hundred and fifty pounds of muscle, Diesel was used to looking down at people. Because of the fact he was a bear shifter he was bigger, taller, and stronger than humans and many other shifters, but Maggie was small, even for a human. She couldn't be more than five-foot-one, and although she had curves and thickness that went on for miles and had his arousal climbing even higher until he thought he'd suffocate from it, she was so little compared to him. Her eyes were this off slate grey color with a hint of blue mixed in. They were a unique shade, one he had never seen before, and that enthralled him. The scent of her uneasiness mixed with the alcohol in her system made for a potent combination.

Her friend was only a foot behind Maggie, and the sight of her wide eyes had Diesel taking another step back. Fuck, what in the hell had gotten into him? And over some female he didn't even know on a personal level. Over the years he might have said a handful of words to her, but then he had gone all territorial on one of his brothers because they badmouthed her. Diesel scrubbed a hand over his jaw, felt the day old stubble lining his cheek and chin, and breathed out. There were a lot of people staring, mainly the ones that were passing through. The ones that knew better than to gawk at a Grizzly MC member were busy trying to act like nothing had happened.

"Come on, Maggie." Her friend gripped Maggie's arm and pulled her back.

Maggie stumbled backward, but she never took her eyes off of him, and Diesel found himself rooted to the spot. Her friend became a little more persistent, especially when Diesel found himself taking a step toward her. But right now his bear was taking control, moving closer, wanting to be nearer to her. He wanted to run his nose along the arch of her neck, and the images that slammed into his mind over and over again had him drunk with dark need. What would she do if he tied her to his bed, and made her watch as he pushed his dick into her pussy? She'd try to stop him, try to tell him to go slow no doubt, but fuck, Diesel wouldn't do that, couldn't because he'd want her too much. That need would have him gripping her body so hard she cried out in pleasure and his marks were left on her milky flesh. He wanted to see his handprints bruising her flesh, wanted that mark of ownership. A low sound left him, but he couldn't help himself. The thoughts in his mind were making him feral.

He should turn and leave, because that was the smart and safe thing to do, but he couldn't force the human part of himself to do that. He couldn't find the strength to push his bear aside and be stronger than the fucker.

"Maggie, we should leave. Now." Her friend pulled her toward the entrance, and Maggie blinked a few times before shaking her head and picking up her pace.

Diesel didn't move, but he did watch her leave, couldn't have stopped himself from doing that either. When she was out the front door and he couldn't see her any longer, he took in a deep breath and blew it out.

"Holy fucking shit, D. Care to explain what in the hell that was all about?"

Diesel turned and looked at Stinger. He hadn't even noticed the other male had come back into the bar.

"Dallas gone?" He ran his hand over his face once more, finally having the strength to push his bear back now that Maggie wasn't in front of him. He looked at Stinger who was a few feet from him and had this blank look on his face. After the male had got shot up by Trick over a month ago he had been acting reserved. Diesel had a feeling that near death experience might have brought some realization to the other male, because it was like he had done a complete one-eighty on his normal personality. But he didn't talk about it, and the members of the MC knew that pushing for more from Stinger—or any member for that matter—wouldn't do anything but drive them back more. But instead of Stinger looking at life in a new light as what normally happened when someone almost died, he just kept to himself, and did what was asked of him from the club. He was still there for the MC and the crew, but when it concerned himself it was like he was cut off, totally switched to something stoic and blank.

"Yeah, Court took him back to the clubhouse to fuck a club whore and sleep off the liquor." Stinger watched him silently for a second. "He was pretty drunk, D, and I'm sure he meant no harm." Stinger reached inside his cut and grabbed his pack of smokes. He pulled a cigarette out, put it between his teeth, and lit the end with the lighter he fished out of his front pocket.

"I don't want to fucking talk about it, Stinger." Yeah, Diesel had known Dallas was drunk, and that should have been taken into consideration where Diesel's anger was concerned, but it was hard to tell his inner animal that. The beast seemed to think Maggie was already his, and that was bad fucking news all around.

Stinger nodded once and turned to head out of the bar, but he stopped right before he walked out the front door and looked at Diesel. "You want to hit up the barn and get in a fight to let off all of that steam?"

Although Diesel had more control over himself than he had just moments before, he was still clenching and unclenching his hands at his sides, still felt the adrenalin pumping through his veins, and knew that hitting up a fight in the barn the club owned on their private property was probably the best way to let off this anger. It was that or fucking a female good and hard, and the very idea of sticking his dick in a pussy that wasn't Maggie's seemed abhorrent and not at all arousing.

"Yeah, I think the barn is probably a go." Since the club had gotten in business with Sticks, a human male who was deep in the underground fighting world, and Jace, the Lion MC President, they were making some good money being the muscle and partners of the illegal fighting that went down on their property. Of course it wasn't as much as they had made running drugs for a few former associates, but it still brought in the cash flow. Although no Grizzly MC member had participated in the fighting that went down at the barn, he was about to change that tonight.

Chapter Three

Maggie was far too drunk to drive, but Mora had only had a little and was fine. But after what had happened back at the bar Maggie was surprised her friend could even concentrate on the road. Mora was driving under the speed limit and on her way to Maggie's house, but she knew it wasn't because she tried to go under the radar of the local PD, but because she was just as stunned as Maggie at the fact Diesel had almost beat one of his club members' asses over *her*.

"That did just happen back there, right?" Mora asked, but kept her focus on the road. She kept tightening and loosening her hands on the steering wheel. Maggie swallowed, trying to gather enough saliva to make her closed-off and parched throat less painful.

"Yeah, I'm pretty sure it did."

God, why did she have to drink so much? She saw Mora look at her through the corner of her eye. Maggie shifted on the seat so she was staring at her friend. They stared at each other for only a second, and then Mora looked back at the road.

"Diesel almost kicked that guy's ass because of you, but why?" There wasn't any malice in Mora's voice, just clear confusion.

Maggie felt the same way. "I don't know. I mean I know him and the club because of my dad, and have seen him while growing up, but aside from talking to him a few times at the shop he stayed away from me." She rubbed her hands on her thighs and breathed out. "I couldn't hear what they were saying aside from Diesel pointing at me and saying my name in that angry, growly voice of his." They were both quiet for several long seconds.

Mora pulled the car onto Maggie's father's street and parked at the curb. She left the car idling, but neither moved. "What are you going to do about that?" Mora turned and faced her.

"What do you mean? What am I supposed to do about it?" Why were her hands so sweaty, and why was her heart still pounding a mile a minute?

Mora shrugged, turned and then looked out the windshield for a second, and turned her attention back on Maggie. "Shit, I don't know. But you walked up to him, touched him on the arm like he didn't scare the piss out of you like everyone else, and he just stopped." Mora lifted her hand and snapped her finger in front of Maggie's face. "I mean, Maggie, it was like your touch just stopped the fight."

Yeah, Maggie had no clue why she had walked up to him and gotten between them. And when he had faced her and she had seen that his normally blue eyes were swallowed up by the darkness of his pupils, she had known that what she was looking at was more animal than man at that moment.

"I don't know, Mora. Something just came over me, and before I knew it I was standing right next to him and had my hand on his arm." Even now she could feel the tingling in her palm and fingers at where she had touched his hard, hot, bare flesh. She curled her fingers into her palm and set her hand on her thigh. "Maybe it was the fact I drank way too much alcohol and had balls of steel." She glanced at Mora, but her friend had her attention focused in front of her once more.

"I'll tell you this, Maggie, I have never seen a guy look at a woman the way Diesel looked at you."

"What do you mean? He didn't look at me any way." But that was a lie, because there had been this feeling she got when Diesel had looked right at her, and she just couldn't ignore the way this spark had traveled up her arm when she had touched him.

Mora looked at her again. "Like the way a man looks at a woman he wants to possess. Maggie, that biker was staring at you like you were his." Mora licked her lips and leaned back in the seat. "Yeah, that was exactly what it was. Hell, I think he was more bear at that moment than human. He wanted you, no doubt about it. It was like you stopped a derailed train with only a touch."

"That's crazy, Mora." The words came from Maggie in a harsh whisper. Shouldn't she be excited that Mora was saying the man Maggie had wanted for years reciprocated those feelings? Yes and no, because the way Diesel had looked at her was so intense, so powerful, that she had felt it consume her as if a fire was inside of her, intent on drowning her alive in flames.

"Yeah, it really fucking is."

Maggie snapped her head up and looked at her friend, only just realizing that she had been looking at the hand that had touched Diesel's arm.

"But I want to know why you were the one to start the fight—in so many ways—and what exactly you plan on doing about it."

Maggie didn't say anything for several seconds. "I'm not going to do anything about it, Mora."

"Well, I can tell you this, I don't think a man like Diesel is just going to walk away from you."

Maggie's heart pounded fast and fierce at those words.

"That's crazy. The man hasn't said anything to me that didn't have to do with buying parts for Harleys. And you're trying to say he thinks he has some kind of claim on me after he sees me for the first time in five years?" That whole thing sounded ludicrous and ridiculous, and Maggie wasn't about to dwell on it any more. Yeah, she wanted Diesel, but she didn't want crazy. "He was just drunk, just like the other biker. That was all. For all I know they were talking about my dad, my name got thrown in there, and the liquor took care of the rest."

Mora was still staring at her, but hadn't responded. She tightened her hold on the handle of her purse. "Maybe you're right," said Mora.

Maggie breathed out. Yeah, that was all it had been, because anything else didn't make sense. "I hope that you're right, because I don't think anything short of a bullet to the head can stop a guy like Diesel from coming after what he wants."

Maggie nodded, but didn't say anything. She didn't know what to say. The night had gone from her admiring him from across the bar, to her watching as he took on this very scary demeanor, and looked seconds away from kicking that other guy's ass.

"Okay, well, I better get in before my dad wakes up and realize I'm as drunk as I really am."

Mora smiled, but the look on her face told Maggie that her friend was still thinking about what happened back at the bar. Maggie climbed out, leaned down to wave at Mora through the closed window, and turned to head to the front door. When she had the door unlocked and closed behind her, she leaned against it and breathed out roughly. It was surreal the way the night ended, and honestly, if Mora hadn't pulled her out of there she didn't know if she would have left. Honestly, Maggie might still be standing right in front of him, letting him do whatever he wanted to her. That intensity that poured from him as he stood only inches from her had been like a blast from a furnace, and Maggie wanted to feel more of it.

She pushed off the door and went into the kitchen for a glass of water and some ibuprofen. She knew tomorrow was going to be horrible in the hangover department, but for how drunk she was, she was strangely coherent enough to remember every little detail of how Diesel had looked when he had stared at her. But no longer in his presence and breathing in those dark pheromones, the alcohol that had taken a backseat to her stunned arousal and confusion was now back full force, and her stomach turned. She should eat something, preferably loaded with carbs and fat to combat the booze in her, but just thinking about eating anything had nausea settling heavily inside of her.

Instead she sat at the table, rested her head in her hands, and breathed out. This was the most intense experience she had had since living in Steel Corner, and how sad was that?

****

Diesel stood in the center of the circle formed by all the men that had come to watch a dirty fight. There was a good mix of humans and shifter spectators, but Diesel was focused on his opponent. The tiger shifter stood just as nude as he was, but there was nothing sexual about what was about to happen. When they got the all clear they would shift and start this fight. Diesel needed this desperately, needed to burn off the residual rage that he still felt for the shit Dallas had spouted off. He also really needed to get rid of this need to have Maggie that pumped through his veins. She had looked up at him with a hint of fear, and although he was a violent, scary asshole, she had nothing to be afraid of from him.

"We got a special treat tonight. A member of the Grizzly MC is in the fight to face off with a tiger," the announcer said, and there was a loud roar of cheers.

Diesel kept his attention on the male in front of him. He wasn't as tall as Diesel, but he had a stockier build. He was also sporting several bruises and cuts on his body, which told him that he liked to fight. Diesel cracked his knuckles, rolled his head around his neck, and stretched his arms. He was ready to kick some ass, knock this fucker's teeth in, and have the blood coat the dirty floor beneath their feet. There wasn't a bell that started the fight. They just knew when it was time to go after one another, and that time was now.

Both shifted at the same time and went after one another. Diesel's bear rose up to its full ten foot height, and he easily had hundreds of pounds on the tiger, but the other male was smaller, quicker, and could attack before Diesel knew it was coming. But although the tiger might be swift on its feet, Diesel had a lot of anger powering his actions right now. The tiger moved to the side right when Diesel swiped a paw out. He turned and roared out when the tiger sank his claws into Diesel's arm. They moved back and forth for several seconds, and Diesel reached out again and knocked the tiger back a few feet. The spectators moved back to give them more room and to keep out of the violence. Diesel went after the other male before he got back on his feet and opened his jaws wide. He roared out loud enough to make the wood all around them shake, and leaned down to sink his teeth into the tiger's side. He growled and hissed out, and the tiger dragged his claws down his neck hard enough that Diesel felt the flesh open up under his fur. But he loved the pain, revealed in it, and wanted more.

The tiger managed to move enough that Diesel fell forward, but he anticipated the quick movement from the cat. He twisted to the side, wrapped his paws around the feline's neck, and sank his incisors into the tiger's side. He roared out in pain, and the tangy, metallic flavor of the cat's blood filled Diesel's mouth. He tore away from the tiger, took several steps back, and huffed out. He waited for the tiger to come back for more, but the other male lay on the ground panting as blood pooled around. After a couple of seconds Diesel shifted back to his human form. There were a few guys that groaned as they had bet against Diesel, but the rest roared out and started exchanging money. Sticks went around and collected the cash, and walked up to him.

"Good fight, man." Sticks slapped a thick wad of cash in his hand.

Diesel looked down at it. There were a few guys—tiger shifters as well and presumably the friends of the shifter currently bleeding heavily on the floor—that walked up and lifted his body off the ground and hauled his ass out of the barn.

"You should fight more often, D. You could bring home a lot of extra cash for taking down guys like that."

Diesel shook his head. "Nah, this was a night I had to let my bear out to burn off some fierce energy."

Stinger stepped up to him and tossed Diesel a towel. He started wiping the sweat and blood off his body and applied some pressure to his neck. It hurt like a motherfucker, but a little pain made him stronger.

"What about you, Stinger? You want some extra cash and to beat a few guys' skulls in?"

Stinger had a joint between his lips and inhaled before pulling it out and blowing the smoke in Sticks' face. "I'm not into the whole spectator shit. When I fight I want to do it in a back alley where I can crack a skull against a brick wall."

Sticks was human, but he was also a hard-ass and didn't take shit from anyone. Running and being the main organizer or these fights required the man be tough as nails, and he was for a human. But he was also dealing with shifters, and it was smart when Sticks took a step back and nodded.

"Yeah, Stinger. Just thought I'd throw the offer out there." There was a decrease in the volume in the room, but Diesel was busy walking over to the corner where he had stashed his clothes. He started putting them on, and when he shoved his arms through his cut and smoothed the leather across his chest he noticed movement by the double doors toward the front. Stinger was leaning against the wall smoking on his joint, but his attention was at the front as well. Four big fuckers walked through the crowd, and instantly Diesel could tell they were human. But they were huge for humans, easily as big as he and the other members of the Grizzly MC were. They wore cuts as well, and the one at the front wore the patch that stated he was the president. He glanced at Diesel, eyed his cut up and down, and smirked. Diesel let out a low growl, but instead of having the human show fear, it had the bastard smirking bigger.

Everyone started forming a circle for another fight, and the four MC humans turned to watch. Diesel got a look at the back of their cuts. The patch was of a burning phoenix with its wings spread and a motorcycle in the center of that. The top rocker read "Brothers of Menace", and the bottom rocker stated they were of the Colorado-bred variety. The fact they were in Steel Corner and he didn't know about it didn't sit well with Diesel. But calling Jagger would only have his president's voicemail picking up since he was out of town with Sonya until tomorrow.

He looked over at Stinger, who was staring at the humans that had just walked in as well. "Come on." His bear was still pacing inside of him, and it was like he hadn't just fought even though his neck burned from the claw wounds marring it. Stinger pushed off the wall, and they made their way past the biker humans. They slowed marginally when the President looked over his shoulder, grinned, and lifted his chin in acknowledgment, but before Diesel or Stinger could say anything the next fight started, and the cheering and shouts for more blood increased.

They headed out without incident, although Diesel wouldn't have minded doing a little bare knuckle fighting with the human biker that had that smug fucking smirk on his face. They stepped into the night, and there were a few drunks stumbling around, smoking pot, and laughing loudly. They made their way toward their Harleys by the tree line.

"You know them?" Stinger took one more drag from the joint, kept the smoke in for a few seconds, and flicked the roach away. He exhaled, and the sweet scent of marijuana filled the space around them.

"Nah, I've never heard of their MC, but I don't like them, and neither does my bear," Diesel said. There were a lot of MCs in the country, but that didn't mean The Grizzlies knew every single one, even if The Brothers of Menace were from Colorado.

Stinger straddled his bike and put his helmet on. "Me either. They had my hackles rising, though." Diesel grunted at Stinger's word and got on his bike. "You headed back to the clubhouse? Big ass party happening."

Diesel snapped his helmet in place and looked over at the other male.

Stinger made a low noise in his throat. "You good to ride?"

Diesel didn't respond, just stared at Stinger until he nodded again, revved his engine, and pulled away from the barn. Diesel knew the other bear was talking about his anger and the wild, fierce energy still running inside of him. Was he good to ride? He was always good when he was on his bike with the road rushing beneath him, but even that fierce fight didn't stop this strange and ludicrous need to have Maggie.

He started his engine and pulled away from the bar. Once he was on the main road he just rode. He didn't want to go back to the clubhouse, not when it would be filled with females he didn't want, ones willing to spread their thighs at the snap of a member's finger. But his ride ended up taking him to a residential part of Steel Corner, one that was older, with the houses close together and the yards postage stamp sized. Then he found himself pulling next to the curb across from a white house with black shutters and a small flower garden in the front.

"Shit, D, why are you here?"

And now he was fucking talking to himself.

Chapter Four

The sound of a motorcycle had Maggie setting her cup and plate in the sink and moving toward the small kitchen window. She had made something to eat even though it was going on midnight, and she felt much better and less intoxicated. But when she pulled the curtain aside and stared at the dark figure straddling the motorcycle right across from her house, her heart stopped. Although she couldn't see exactly who was on the bike with the shadows around him and the light from the kitchen behind her, Maggie knew that it was Diesel who was sitting out there. She could see that his head was lowered, and against her better judgment she stepped away from window, went into the foyer to grab her jacket, and opened the front door. The sound of his bike was so loud that she quickly shut the door as to not wake her dad. Diesel was still looking down, and she didn't know if he realized she was walking toward him or not. When the only thing that separated them was the small strip of road, she just stood there and stared at him.

He slowly lifted his head and looked at her, but there was no surprise that she was standing just a few feet from him. There was this clear indecision on his face, and he was probably wondering why he was at her house the same as she was. Maggie somehow found the courage to step off of that curb and move toward him. Her heart was thundering so fast in her chest that she felt it at the base of her throat, and her pulse filled her ears. She stopped when she was only a foot from him, and the scent of leather and exhaust filled her nose. The asphalt was rough beneath her bare feet, and a breeze blew by, moving up the thin cotton of her pajama bottoms.

"What are you doing here?" She heard how breathy she sounded, and she cleared her throat, feeling embarrassment and knowing that the steady arousal inside of her was increasing the longer she was this near to him. He didn't answer right away, but she didn't feel uncomfortable around him.

"I don't know, Maggie."

God, his voice was so low and deep that she felt it in every erogenous zone in her body. The way he said her name was like he was having sex with her, and the dirty, explicit images that claimed her were enough to nearly have her knees buckle from the force of them. He shifted so his upper body was more toward her, and she made a small noise when she saw the nasty looking claw marks peeking up over the collar of his cut.

"Oh my God. Did you get that—"

He was shaking her head before she even finished. "No, this wasn't because of the fight that was started with Dallas at the bar." He didn't elaborate, and she didn't delve in with the questions. They stood there another few seconds before he spoke again. "I was just riding, and I found myself in front of your house."

She nodded and swallowed. "I…" She stopped talking because the words failed to come.

"Yeah, Maggie, I know. This whole situation makes no fucking sense."

No, it didn't, and she didn't know where to go from here. One minute she was imagining speaking to Diesel in more than a professional manner at her dad's shop. And in the next everything had turned into the Twilight Zone. Now she was standing in front of the man she had wanted for years, and unless she was totally reading the vibes wrong he acted like he wanted her, too. But she knew the kind of man Diesel was, hell, the kind of men that were involved with the Grizzly MC. They didn't do relationships, and going from woman to woman seemed to be a trending hobby for them.

"You want to go for a ride?"

Her mouth went dry, and she glanced back at the house. Her dad's light was still off, but he was a pretty heavy sleeper. She turned back to look at Diesel, and although this was a crazy thing to do, probably the craziest thing she had ever done, she nodded. "I need to change."

He nodded, and right when she would have turned and headed back inside he reached out and wrapped his hand around her wrist. She looked down at where he held her, and felt the zing of electricity slam into her. He was so attractive in a darkly devilish way. His helmet covered his blond hair, but she could see the short strands tied at the nape of his neck. Even with the darkness she could see how blue his eyes were. He tugged her forward, and she didn't resist.

"This is crazy."

He searched her face with his eyes and nodded. "Yeah, baby, it really fucking is. But it feels pretty damn right, too."

Oh God. Hearing him call her baby had a gush of wetness leaving her, and his nostrils flared. She had to make herself remember that this wasn't just any kind of man, but one that held a dangerous, wild animal inside of him. In a move so fast and powerful she didn't realize what was happening until it was done, he pressed his mouth to hers and pushed his tongue inside. There was nothing left for her to do but to accept his possession, and that was exactly what he was doing. He was marking her as he thrust his tongue in and out of her mouth, and moved his hand along her lower back to pull her even closer. Maggie tilted her head to accept more of his kiss, but before it could go any deeper he was pulling away from her.

"Go get some different clothes on, baby."

She didn't have to be told again. Once she was inside and had a pair of jeans on, a new top, and some shoes, she headed to her dad's room. The door was cracked, and she saw him sleeping in the center of his bed. The deep snores coming from him told her he was out, and although she was an adult and didn't have a curfew, she also didn't want him to worry about her. She'd only be gone for a little bit, she told herself. Just long enough to take a ride with Diesel. That thought had a tingle settling between her thighs, and she left the house and made her way toward him once more. He hadn't moved, and in fact watched her like how she imagined an animal might watch its prey before it struck. His eyes lowered as he looked at her body up and down, and although she had jeans and her jacket on, she felt completely naked in front of him. He had taken off his helmet and handed it to her. Once she had it on her head and strapped in place, he reached out and wrapped a hand around her upper arm. She straddled the back, but before she could get situated he took his other hand and wrapped it around her waist, pulling her toward him. The V of her legs fit perfectly against his body, and she swore she heard a deep rumble leave him over the purr of the bike when her pussy was snug against him. Maggie closed her eyes and fought through the arousal pounding heavily inside of her like a drum. He turned his head to the side.

"You ever been on the back of a bike before?" Maggie shook her head and watched his grin spread. It was cute, but so damn dark and sexy that the inner muscles of her pussy clenched from that simple gesture. "Hang on, baby."

It was still so strange yet arousing to hear him call her that. She wrapped her arms around his lean and hard waist and pressed her chest to his back. The smell of aged leather from his cut filled her nose, and she briefly closed her eyes. This was surreal. In essence they were all but strangers, but being this close to him, touching him, and riding on the back of his bike felt so right on every level. Maggie didn't want to question it, didn't want to try to analyze it. All she wanted to do was let herself experience this one moment and see where it took her. Was she a fool for thinking that she could have more than one night with Diesel? No, but that didn't mean she couldn't hang on for what she knew would be one hell of a ride.

He pulled away from the curb, and the vibrations from the bike speared right to her clit. A tingling that had already been based in her pussy intensified, but she held in her gasp of sudden pleasure and tightened her hold on him. Diesel took a left onto the next street, and she shifted her hands, but he wrapped his big, strong fingers around her wrists and pressed them tightly to his abdomen. The hard ridges of what she knew were his six-pack clenched beneath her touch, and she breathed out roughly.

They hit the main road, but it was late and the streets were deserted. There was a kind of freedom riding on the back of his Harley, and after a while she relaxed against him and let the tension fade away. Maggie even rested her cheek on the center of his back, and watched as the buildings soon became trees as he ventured further out of town and more into the thick wilderness of Colorado. Things looked different on the back of his bike, with the wind blowing across her face and nothing holding her down except her hands around his waist. She didn't know how long they rode, but her face felt like ice. Aside from that the rest of her body was burning up alive. The longer she was pressed against Diesel the more she wanted him, and the harder her resolution to do what she really wanted to do slammed into her. He turned onto a side road, but before he took it he made a U-turn as if he planned on heading back into town. This was her moment as they moved at a crawl right before he got back on the main road.

"Diesel?" Her voice was low, and she didn't know if he could hear her, but when she felt his entire body tense she knew he had. He braced his feet on the ground to steady the bike and looked over his shoulder at her. Strands of his shoulder length blond hair had come undone from his tie and hung around his masculine face. He was not handsome, per se, but his whole persona screamed masculinity. She felt so very feminine around him, and she knew that if she were to give herself up to him, even if for this one moment, it would be the experience of a lifetime. For several seconds all he did was stare at her, but she didn't miss how his pupils dilated. She wondered if he could see the desire written across her face. He was a shifter, and no doubt could smell how wet she was, but there was no embarrassment in that knowledge, and in fact Maggie found it made her hotter.

"What is it, Maggie?" His voice was low, but she still heard it over the roar of his bike.

Parting her lips, she didn't know if she could actually ask him what was on the tip of her tongue.

"You like the ride, baby?"

She felt her face heat from his words, because she thought of riding something that wasn't his bike. Before she lost her nerve, and because this was the opportunity to actually have something she had wanted for a long time, Maggie took the bull by the horns and just asked him. "Diesel?"

"Yeah, baby?"

She glanced at his hands on the handlebars, saw the way he kept clenching and unclenching them, and knew that although his face was stony and emotionless, he was just as affected as she was. "Why don't you show me your place?"

This very low, very animalistic sound left him, and she felt the vibrations leave his chest. He looked down at her lips, and she found herself licking them. When he slowly brought his gaze back up to her eyes, there was so much need reflected back at her that if she hadn't been holding on to him she knew she would have crumbled to the ground.

"Is that what you want, Maggie … to see my place?"

She couldn't form any words, so instead she nodded. He stared at her for another second before facing forward again, revving the engine, and moving back onto the main road. He only drove for about five minutes before turning onto a dirt one. He maneuvered his bike through the twisting and turning narrow road until the sight of a very small cabin became illuminated from his headlight. He pulled the bike to a stop in front of the cabin and cut the engine. Even though the bike was off Maggie could still feel the vibrations from it between her legs, or maybe it was the fact she was so turned over the likelihood she was about to have sex with Diesel.

He dismounted from the bike and turned to help her off. She took off the helmet and handed it to him. Diesel placed it on a handlebar, and for a moment all they did was stare at each other. The sexual tension between them was electric and could have started a forest fire for as hot and wild as it was. At least that was how she felt, knew that she wasn't hiding her lust for him at all, and wondered how this man could be so in control when she felt anything but. He didn't say anything, just grabbed her hand and led her to the front door. He opened it and led her inside and turned on the light. Maggie stepped inside further and looked around. The place was very small with an open floor plan. The only door she saw was the one at the end of the short hallway, and she could see it was the bathroom from the side of the sink peeking just inside of it. The living room was to the right. There was one dark brown leather couch that sat in front of a stone and blackened fireplace. To the left was an equally small kitchen with natural cabinetry and a stone butcher's block in the center. There was rustling to her right, and she looked back to see Diesel removing his cut and placing it on the back of the couch.

What in the hell are you doing, Maggie?

His back was to her, but she could easily make out the lines of muscles through the thin material. She had never thought backs an attractive part on a man, but with Diesel's broad shoulders, the way she could see the strength in his body as if it were living thing, all the way down to his narrow hips, she realized every part of this man was attractive in the most wicked of ways. He turned, and the front view was even more delicious. She could see the buckle of his belt peek just under the edge of his shirt, and his jeans looked like they were especially made for him. They were worn, slightly stained with what looked like grease, but lord, it was the most arousing sight.

"You keep looking at me like that and I won't be able to control myself."

The thought of Diesel going wild on her had a fresh gush of liquid heat leaving her. He growled low in his throat and stalked forward with determined steps. Maggie should have stayed put, let him know that she couldn't be intimidated, but she found herself moving backward until the cold wood of the wall behind her stopped any and all retreat.

Diesel stopped when he was a few inches from her, and the way he looked at her had her toes curling. "You wanted to see my place." He kept looking at her but lifted his arm to the side as if emphasizing his point that this was indeed his place.

"Yeah."

He didn't drop his arm to his side, but instead placed it on the wall beside her head and leaned in. "But you didn't want to come here to look at my shit, did you?"

Oh, she wanted to look, just not at the furniture kind of things. Maggie wanted to see what he was hiding behind the cotton and denim. She wanted to run her hands along the hard expanse of his chest, see how far that ink that covered his entire arm went when he had no clothes on, and she wanted to hear that gruff voice saying all kinds of dirty things to her. But before she could answer he started talking again.

"No, you didn't want to come here to take inventory on my décor." He leaned in another inch until she could smell the clean sweat on him, saw how blue his eyes really were, and could see the wicked looking scratch on his neck up close and personal. "I think you wanted to come here because you wanted me to fuck the hell out of you."

A small sound escaped her, and she clenched her jaw as to not do it again. He didn't crack a smile, didn't say a word. He just continued to stare at her and wait for a reply. Maggie ran her tongue along her bottom lip, and Diesel lowered his gaze so he was watching the act. He moved even closer yet until she felt the stiff, huge outline of his erection pressed snugly against her belly.

"Go on, tell me exactly why you wanted to come to my place if not to have me shove my cock into that sweet little pussy of yours."

The air left her in a whoosh, and she shook her head. He was so damn intense and vulgar that it was almost too much, but she had known he would be like this, and although it was intimidating as hell, she was also more turned on than she had ever been. "Yes." That one word came out a hell of a lot stronger than she felt inside. The low rumble that left him went straight to her clit, and she swore she felt the little bud swell even further.

"Say it again, but say it *all*." His stare was penetrating as he looked directly in her eyes.

Maggie took a deep breath, trying to steady herself. "I have wanted you for a really long time."

He made a deep noise in the back of his throat.

"I saw you tonight, and even though it has been years since we have interacted, this need I have just grew to the point I couldn't handle it." She had to force the words past her lips because her throat felt tight and dry. He lowered just his head until she felt the hot puffs of his breath move along her neck. She closed her eyes because keeping them open was just too hard with him so close. The heat of his body was so hot that beads of perspiration started to dot the area between her breasts.

"Go on."

Those two words had her nipples beading. "But I knew I couldn't ever be with a man like you." This had him moving back marginally, and she forced herself to open her eyes. He didn't say anything, but she could see in the look on his face that he wanted to her elaborate. She must not have spoken fast enough because only seconds later he was speaking in that rough timbre of his.

"A man like me?" He lifted one of his blond eyebrows in question, and although she saw a hint of humor in his face, she also saw his desire was far stronger. "And what kind of man is that, baby?" He lowered his head again to her neck, and ran the tip of his nose up the length of her throat. She heard the deep inhalation that came from him, and the fact he smelled her shouldn't have had her pussy and nipples tingling the way they did. But there was almost something primal in the way he scented her, like he wanted to memorize her.

"The kind of man that knows how to use a woman well." That had him pulling back again, but there was no amusement on his face this time.

"Use? Baby, I don't fucking use women. I fuck them good and hard until they can't walk straight the next day. I send them on their way with a grin on their face and a sore fucking pussy. But I never use them."

She swallowed roughly, glanced down at his lips, and nodded. Hearing him talk about the other women he screwed wasn't particularly attractive, but then again this man was a rough biker that did whatever he wanted, when he wanted.

"Now, what I think you need is something only *I* can give you. And what I need is something only *you* can give me." He captured her lips in a deep, almost painful kiss, and when he pulled back she swore her mouth was bruised. "All you have to do to make that happen is say the words. And if you really just wanted to come to my house to look at how I decorated, then you can tell me what colors I should paint the walls. But, Maggie, you and I both know you coming up here was not because of the latter, baby." No, it wasn't, and he knew that as well as she did.

"Diesel?"

He ran the tip of his nose up and done the side of her throat once more and growled out. "Yeah, Maggie."

She clenched her thighs together, and knew that even though this would be the one and only time she was with Diesel, it would be so worth it. "I want you to fuck me."

THE GRIZZLY MC: VOLUME TWO

Chapter Five

Diesel had known the reason Maggie wanted to come to his place, had smelled her sweet pussy every time a fresh gush of moisture left her. But he still gave her the choice to back out if she wanted to. He wouldn't have had any hard feelings, and would have taken her right home without complaining, but he sure as fuck would have had a case of the blue balls. He took a step back and looked down at her. All he could hear repeating in his head like a broken record was her saying she wanted him to fuck her. His cock throbbed to be buried deep inside of her tight cunt, and all he could picture were these carnal images that had the tip of his dick becoming moist and the zipper of his jeans digging into his shaft. She looked scared of what he might do to her, but it was a good kind of scared, the kind that had anticipation moving between them like a powerful current. He didn't stand there and think about what he was going to do, that all of this was moving pretty quickly, or that she was a hell of a lot younger than he was. Maggie wanted him, wanted him to fuck her, and that was exactly what he was about to do.

Diesel knew they couldn't have more than this one night, because his life was far too dangerous to have an old lady. If Jagger and Brick wanted to have a female, to protect her, watch over her, and make sure no motherfucker messed with them, then more power to them. But Diesel was happy with just random sex, and he knew that this hard need he had for Maggie was the fact his bear wanted her as much as his human side did. There was nothing more to it, and when he finally had her, claimed her harder than he had ever claimed a female before, then this need within him would be purged and his bear would be satisfied.

At least that was what he kept telling himself. The truth was he had never this strong of a desire before, and certainly not one that made him nearly get into fights with other Grizzly members, or have to release the anger in an underground fight. But Diesel didn't want to think too deeply on it. He just wanted it fuck this female in front of him until they were both sweaty, exhausted, and he passed out with her by his side.

He moved toward her, wrapped his hand around her throat, and tightened it just marginally. He didn't want to hurt her, didn't want to cut off her oxygen either, but he also wanted her to know who was in charge tonight, and who would be taking control. "You wanted to come here, want me to fuck you, and that is exactly what I'm going to do." He tilted her head to the side, moved his hand just enough that he could see a swatch of her creamy neck, and leaned in to run his now elongated incisors over the spot. He had always been in control when he had sex, and never let his bear take part in this aspect of his life. But the bastard wanted to taste Maggie, wanted to feel her beneath him, and Diesel knew that if he planned on getting this desire for her out of his system he would need to let his animal take part in this experience, too.

He moved his hand away from her neck and gripped her upper arms. His nails were curving into claws, and he curled them gently into her flesh. He didn't break the skin, but the gasp that came from her told him she knew the threat was there. He started to grind his dick into the softness of her belly. He grunted and groaned against her neck, pressed his erection harder into her, and knew that he wasn't about to do any fucking foreplay. Sliding his hands down to her ass and gripping the big, spongy mounds, he lifted her up easily and turned to stride toward the butcher block. She wrapped her arms around his neck and her legs around his waist. Holding her weight up with one forearm under her ass, he used his other arm to push off the bullshit that was on the block. It wasn't very big, but it was big enough for what he was going to do to her.

Diesel set her ass on the slab of wood, speared his hands through her hair, and tightened his fingers around the strands. He yanked her head back, and she gasped from what he knew was a sliver of pain. But he could see her eyes glossy from her arousal, knew that she liked it a little rough from the blush on her cheeks and her increased heart rate, and he smelled the sweet and musky wetness of her pussy. "You know what I want to do, Maggie?" It was a rhetorical question, and he didn't give her a chance to respond anyway. "I want to get you naked, push you back, spread your legs, and feast on your cunt until you come all over my face." Her eyes were big, her pupils dilated, and he knew that it wouldn't take her much at all to have her getting off. "You'd like that, wouldn't you, Maggie?"

She panted, licked her plump lips, and nodded.

"Yeah, you and I both would like that, but I don't have the willpower to do any foreplay, baby. I need to be balls deep inside of you before I come in my jeans like some kind of fucking teenager." He stared right into her grey eyes and saw her reach for her top. Diesel grabbed her hand, stopping her, and making a low sounding his throat. "We do this my way, Maggie." If she wanted him, then she'd have him the way he wanted her to have him. He was an alpha male all the way, needed that control that only a female could give, and he wanted her to acknowledge that she wanted that, too.

"I want it your way, Diesel." She slipped her hand out from under his and rested both of hers behind her back on the slab of wood. The she just stared at him, kept her body still, and waited for him to devour her, and that was exactly what he was going to do.

In a move that was fast, impatient, and right to the fucking point, he gripped her shirt and pulled it up and over her head. She wasn't wearing a bra, and her huge, natural tits bounced free from his forceful action. Diesel's mouth went dry at the sight of her rose colored nipples hardening right before his eyes. "*Christ*, Maggie." He had to touch them, and so that was exactly what he did. Diesel reached out, grabbed those huge mounds, and curled his fingers around the soft flesh. They spilled out from around his hand. He was used to the club whores and either their big fake tits, or the ones that were rail thin and had nothing in the chest department. But Maggie was all natural, and so were her breasts. His mouth watered, and he leaned in to sample her flesh. She tasted sweet, and he ran his tongue along one hardened nipple. She moaned and thrust her chest forward more. Looking up with only his eyes he saw the look of ecstasy wash over her face. Good, his female was responsive to him.

No, she isn't your anything. She is here so you both can get off, and then you'll go your separate ways.

For the next several seconds Diesel sucked and licked at her nipples, alternating between the two until she kept pressing her thighs together as if to ease an ache. He pulled away, and the wet suction of his mouth on her breast caused a popping sound to fill the space around them. He forced himself to take a step back, because if he didn't he could have sucked on her tits all night long, and what he desperately needed was to bottom out inside of her. He took hold of the bottom of his shirt and pulled it over his head. The way she looked at him, all drugged-up, had his cock jerking against his fly. He went for his belt and quickly removed it. Then he was undoing his button, zipping his fly down, and getting out of the restricting material. Diesel was free balling it tonight, and he grabbed the root of his dick as soon as it sprang forward. Her eyes grew wide at the sight of his size. He wasn't cocky by any means, but he also knew his dick was big, and she'd be feeling the aftereffects of him using it on her tomorrow when she went to sit down.

"Oh, God."

He smirked, but it wasn't filled with amusement. She would be saying a lot harsher things than that by the time he was deep inside of her. She started to quickly get out of her pants and shoes, which took a little effort seeing as she was on the butcher blocker still. With her legs hanging over the edge of the block he could only see the slit of her pussy that disappeared between her legs. The small thatch of trimmed, dark pubic hair was at the top of her mound, and a gritty image of his cum all over that hair slammed into his mind. He started to stroke himself harder, faster.

"Spread your thighs and let me see the cunt that I'm going to be fucking."

Her chest rose and fell. He watched as her belly hollowed out from the force of her breathing. She lifted her legs and placed her feet on the edge of the butcher block, and so slowly he could have roared out in frustration, parted those thick, creamy thighs. When he saw her pussy for the first time, all glossy and pink, swollen and primed for him, a drop of pre-cum beaded at the tip of his dick. His balls pulled up close to his body, and all he could think about was taking her right there. And as much as he wanted to taste her, wanted to have all those juices covering his mouth and sliding down his throat, he needed her too badly. Stepping close to her he got a concentrated scent of her pussy juices. He looked down, saw the way her cunt lips spread open, showing him her inner labia, and a guttural sound left him. But when he slowly drew his eyes up her body, over all those luscious curves she had, along her heaving chest, and back to her face, it was to see this carnal and animalistic need reflected back at him. His bear recognized something in that expression, and it pushed forward, tried to shift and take what was his, but even though he was allowing his bear a small amount of room to experience this, too, Diesel wasn't about to let him have full control.

"I want you. God, Diesel, I want you."

Her words snapped something inside of him, and he reached out and wrapped a hand around her hip, yanked her forward, and claimed her mouth. He fucked her between the lips with his tongue, fantasized that he was doing the same between her legs, and knew it was only a matter of minutes before he really lost fucking control and had her. She had her hands buried in his hair, and she tugged on the strands until the tie at his nape came undone. He didn't think she realized the little mewls she made. He broke away, trailed his lips down her jaw and to her neck, and scraped his incisors over her flesh. A gasp left her, and he knew he hurt her, but she didn't push him away. In fact she wrapped her legs around his waist, pressed her heels into the small of his back, and pulled him closer. She scored his back with her nails until he hissed against her neck, but fucking hell the pain felt good.

"I want you so fucking badly, baby." He moved back up her neck and took possession of her mouth. "Give yourself to me."

"Yes." That one word was murmured against his mouth, and she surprised the hell out of him by reaching between their bodies and stroking his dick from root to tip.

Gritting his teeth through the exquisite pleasure she caused within him, he pulled back and looked down to watch what she was doing. His dick was so close to her pussy, and if he just pushed his hips forward an inch he could easily slide right into her body. Wrapping his arms around her shoulders, he easily lifted her, and although it caused her hand to fall away from his dick it brought her chest right up against his. Diesel turned, but she pressed her mouth to his, momentarily stunning him and having him stumble forward. He slammed into the wall, and the cold of the wood seeped into the bare flesh of his back. Turning around so Maggie was the one now pressed against the wall, he hissed out when she tugged on his hair especially hard.

"I'm the one in fucking control." He growled out the words, but she was too far gone in her lust to fully understand. That much was clear on her face and from the scent his bear picked up from her. She was his, all of her, and there was no stopping this. The sight of her looking so deliciously disheveled and the scent of her cream covering her pussy, had his bear pushing forward that last inch, breaking to the surface, and roaring out in triumph over the fact. He was still in his human form aside from his claws and incisors, but it was his inner animal that was taking control. Without thinking, and just reacting on the need to feel her clench around him, Diesel reached between their bodies, took his dick and lined it up with her hole. She didn't stop him, didn't protest, and instead moaned out for more. She was just as high off of this as he was, but he wasn't a human thinking rationally now. He was an animal needing to fuck this female so thoroughly that there wasn't any part of her that wasn't marked by him.

He thrust forward an inch, felt her pussy opening give way for the thick crown of his dick, and then shoved every single fucking inch of himself into her. He let his head fall back on his neck, closed his eyes, and tensed at the tight, hot, and wet feel of her cunt clenching at him in rhythmic spasms. The sound she made was almost inhuman in nature, and she thrashed her head back and forth. He felt like he was wild inside, like he couldn't get a grasp on what was happening. He pulled back, and as if his body had a mind of its own his hips jerked forward again, and he was shoved all the way back inside of her. He couldn't help himself. He leaned back so he could look down at where his body met hers. Her pussy looked small, felt tight, and was stretched so far around his cock-head that his entire body shook from the sight alone.

"Look at that pussy all stretched around my shit." He had to force the words out. "And that's my pussy taking all of my dick, Maggie." He didn't look at her face, just kept his focus on the small part of his cock that he was currently pushing into her. His voice was guttural and deep from his bear taking control, and he heard the tinge of warning laced in his voice. The warning may not be evident to her, but it was there, telling her without actually saying the words that he was going to do whatever the fuck he wanted, and he had no problem fucking people up to make that known.

"You're so big. God, so big, Diesel."

He wouldn't last long once he started thrusting in and out of her, but he also wasn't a onetime comer. He sure as fuck planned on having her in every way possible tonight until she screamed his name and begged him for more.

Chapter Six

Maggie knew she should be worried about something. It was a prickling in the back of her head, but with every thrust and retreat that Diesel made that uneasiness got pushed deeper and deeper into her mind until she just didn't care. He was so hard, so thick and long that she felt like she would split in two. Every time he pushed back into her that painful pressure increased and then broke into a million different sensations of pleasure. He felt hot inside of her, like she was burning from the inside out. With every pump into her she was forced harder against the natural wood wall. It might have been smooth. But it hurt like a bitch, and that pain mixed with the engrossing pleasure that was slowly climbing until it would combust into one huge explosion, which was quickly approaching. She could barely see clearly from the fog of desire that was a wall around her, but she looked into Diesel's face and saw the intensity in which he stared at her body. It was a look that screamed he was in bear mode, that right now she was letting an animal fuck her even if he was in human form. That realization had her orgasm claiming her so hard she threw her head back and cried out in pleasure. Her skull slammed against the wall, but there was no pain, only the bone shattering ecstasy that started at her toes and moved through every part of her body. Her pussy clenched over and over again around his plunging erection, and then he was gripping her waist so tight she knew there would be bruises. But Maggie wanted Diesel's marks on her, wanted to be able to look at herself in the mirror and know that this moment really did happen.

He buried his face in her neck, and the sound of him inhaling deeply had her mouth parting and another smaller climax cresting inside of her. His shaking body caused hers to do the same, and the root of his cock pressed against her clit every time he pushed forward. But then he was cursing foul, filthy words against her throat and picking up speed.

"God, you're so fucking tight, so wet and hot that I am going to come so damn hard." He slammed into her especially hard, and a low sound of desire left her.

She was so sensitive between her legs, but it felt too good to tell him to stop.

"I'm going to mark you, claim you, fill you with my cum until you smell just like me." He didn't sound human, and the rough growl in his voice, the way his claws dug into her waist, and the feel of his thickening even further inside of her was evident that he was in shifter mode. "Your pussy will be so fucking sore when I'm done with you." He pulled her hips down with his hold at the same time he thrust up. "But I won't stop there. I'm going to spank your ass hard enough that your flesh turns a pretty shade of red, and then I'm going to spread your cheeks and eat out your asshole until you come again and are thrusting back against my mouth for more."

And just like that she came again. Getting off just once during intercourse was hard enough, but this male had accomplished three of them in less than twenty minutes. His groans mixed with hers, and she felt the gush of warm liquid slipping from between her thighs, and knew it wasn't just her arousal. He had come, yet he was still so hard inside of her and still pumping away like he hadn't just gotten off.

She sagged against him, sucking in a great lungful of air, and feeling dizzy from the endorphins rushing through her veins. He turned and started walking, but with her eyes closed and this heavy, pleasurable sedation covering her, she didn't bother opening her eyes and seeing where he was going. But it was only seconds later and he had her on her belly atop his bed. Every part of her body was numb, but in a very good way, and it didn't take her long to realize that Diesel wasn't nearly finished with her yet. He lifted her ass up until she was forced to get on her knees, but with her upper body still flat on the mattress her lower half was popped out obscenely.

"Fucking hell, baby, look at this ass." He took hold of her cheeks and squeezed them until pain lanced through her flesh. Over and over he did this, and then he was slapping her ass cheeks with his open palms. His spanks were intricately placed, never landing in the same spot twice, and causing these little tweaks of heat to spear to her core. "You should see what I see, baby." He spread her cheeks, and the cool air smoothed along her back hole. "You're so fucking open and wet for me." He leaned forward and ran his tongue over her anus.

She snapped her eyes open. Never had a man done anything remotely taboo like this, and gauging by her past sexual experience this was taboo all the way. She opened her mouth to say something, to say anything that could make sense of what was happening, but he started fucking her in the ass with his tongue like he had with his cock in her pussy. But it was when he started rubbing her clit back and forth with his finger while he thrust his tongue in and out of her bottom that she came one more time.

She collapsed on the bed, panting, her stomach cramped, and her head feeling woozy. She was flipped over roughly, her breasts shaking from side to side from the force, and she watched in arousal and surprise as Diesel moved between her thighs and started jerking himself off. He moved his palm over his dick faster and faster until his neck tendons strained, his muscles contracted, and he came all over her lower belly and mound. His hot cum came out in great white arcs, covering her flesh and the small thatch of pubic hair at the top of her pussy. The sight shouldn't have been hot, but it was. When he was done he sagged forward, bracing one hand beside her head and breathing out just as hard as she was. But after the post-euphoric buzz faded and reality set in, she realized they had made a very, very bad mistake. He lifted his head, maybe sensing the change in her, because Maggie sure as hell felt different all of a sudden. Her eyes felt huge, and she shook her head in shock at herself and the very irresponsible thing she had allowed to happen.

"We didn't use a condom." She pushed at his chest, feeling pissed at herself and annoyed that she had let this irrational desire for Diesel cloud her better judgment. She was on the pill to regulate her periods, but that wasn't one hundred percent foolproof either. Scrubbing her hand over her face she couldn't believe she had been so stupid. "I'm on the pill, but having sex without protection—more than just birth control pills— was so stupid, Diesel." She was at least thankful that she still had one more month of her pills left. With losing her job and not having insurance anymore through her employer, birth control pills were not an extra expense she could afford. If they had had sex next week when she would have been done with them, well, that wasn't even something she wanted to think about. He didn't say anything for several seconds, and she glanced over at him. He was staring at the mattress with this hard expression on his face.

"Yeah, it was fucked up to not use a condom." He stood and started pacing, and although she shouldn't be staring at the glory that was his hard naked body, the way his now flaccid cock was still a very impressive size, it was hard not to admire his form. The tattoo that covered one of his hard, defined pecs was the small design of the patch that covered the back of his cut. The sight of the darkened motorcycle over those claw marks, and the way the words "Grizzly" and "Colorado" lined the top and bottom part of that design, was so detailed and intricate that it was frightening as well as beautiful. But a man that wore a tattoo like that, a brand of his affiliations, meant he was dangerous. And she had just let him fuck her.

He paced a few times and stopped to pick up their clothes that were in his kitchen a few feet away. He came back over to toss them on the bed before turning and disappearing down the hallway. He had grown so silent, and the air was pressurized around him. The hairs on her arms stood up when he came back with a wet rag. He looked so unsure for a few seconds as he stood in front of her with the washcloth, but she took it out of his hand and thanked him. She sure as hell wasn't about to clean herself in front of him. She stood and went into the bathroom. Once the door was shut she hurriedly cleaned herself and looked at her reflection in the mirror. The woman that stared back at her looked like she had been thoroughly fucked. Dark hair a hot mess around her head, a blush covering her cheeks, and lips that were red and swollen was her current appearance. She shook her head again and left the bathroom. He sat on the bed with only his jeans on, but they were left unbuttoned. The defined ridges of his six pack and that V of muscle that disappeared beneath the denim were clearly visible. He glanced up at her, and she quickly went to the bed to get dressed. Standing in front of him naked while he was dressed was not an option.

"I'm clean."

She slowed her movements and looked over at him once those words left his mouth. Pulling her shirt on the rest of the way, she sat on the bed now fully dressed and played his words over in her head.

"I always wear a condom, but I also get tested weekly."

Her stomach cramped at that thought. Someone would have to have a lot of sex to need to get tested that frequently.

"I got tested last week and haven't fucked anymore since then. Not until you at least."

She saw the image of that skank all over his lap just earlier tonight, and her thoughts must have shown on her face because Diesel responded.

"Yeah, I may touch those club whores with their clothes on, but I don't fuck every one of them that rubs her shit all over me." Diesel growled out the words, but he didn't sound angry.

She looked away, because even if she knew he slept around a lot, she shouldn't think such vile things about what he did in his sexual life.

"You said you always use a condom."

He nodded.

"But you didn't even consider it with me."

He glanced over at her. "I didn't hear you saying anything about it either." No, she hadn't, and that had heat rising to her face. He sighed heavily. "Listen, what we just did was irresponsible in every way, and I have no excuse except to tell you my bear was in control. That was the first time in my life my animal had ever been so fucking intent on taking part, and my human side wasn't strong enough to keep it back." He ran his hand through his hair and leaned forward to rest his forearms on his thighs. "It's a piss poor excuse, but that's the truth."

"Listen, it isn't just one person's fault. I was just as frenzied as you were." There was a small part of her that felt a bit awkward having this conversation and feeling these things, especially after what they had just experienced together, and to say it was a big bucket of ice water over their once raging wildfire was a pretty accurate description. He didn't say anything, but he was still focused on her.

She stood and searched for her shoes. She had kicked them off in the kitchen, but she couldn't find them now. She gave up momentarily and rested her ass on the back of the couch. "I'm clean, too." God, it was almost shameful for her to be having this conversation. She had been with a total of two guys, both of whom had come within ten minutes of sticking it in her. They certainly weren't as potent or masculine as Diesel, but having to tell someone that she didn't have any STDs was bizarre and humiliating, in a way.

"I know. Maggie?" He must have been waiting until she looked back over at him because he didn't say anything else until she did. "Listen, it is what it is. We can't go back and change anything. You're clean, I'm clean, and you're on the pill. No worries, okay." He didn't phrase that as a question. He stood, and although he was trying to go for this unconcerned persona, she could see that his was angry. Whether it was with himself or with her was left to be determined, but right now all she wanted to do was go home. This experience hadn't been what she thought. Physically it had been so, so much more than she ever expected or dreamt about. But there hadn't been any cuddling, and no pillow talk or soft caresses along her bare flesh. Even if their conversation hadn't gone down this path and they were a hell of a lot more careful, she had known that there wouldn't have been that stuff afterward anyway. But she had at least hoped to sleep beside him and not feel like one of his one-night stands, even though that was exactly what this had been.

She swallowed and nodded. "Yeah," Of course she would. She might trust people to an extent, but this little sexual encounter had earned her a trip to the doctor. "Maybe you could just take me home?" She didn't expect Diesel to ask her to stay, but she also didn't expect him to all but jump up, put his shirt and cut on, and haul ass toward the door. He grabbed the keys to his Harley and opened the door, but stopped and looked over his shoulder.

"I think taking you home is probably a good idea. Tonight was ... nice, Maggie."

She looked away when he said the last part. She would not get even more humiliated.

You knew this was the outcome, knew that this would only be a short experience with him, and if you're disappointed at the outcome it is your own fault.

Maggie nodded and spotted her shoes on the other side of the butcher block. Once on she followed Diesel out of the cabin and to his bike. He had a cigarette between his lips and lit the end. She watched him inhale, and he flicked his eyes toward her. "I don't normally smoke." She didn't respond, because really she didn't care. He didn't smoke, yet he had a pack? Or he only smoked when he was stressed or pissed like some people did? He straddled the bike and handed the helmet over to her without looking at her. Yeah, she just needed to get home, put this behind her as one of those experiences that was good and bad, and move on. She had given herself to Diesel, helped to ease this ache deep inside of her to have him—which hadn't vanished in the slightest—and now knew that maybe playing it safe was the best option. She didn't say anything as she put the helmet on and sat on the bike behind him, but then again neither did he.

He drove her back to her house, and although she knew it wasn't that far of a drive, it felt like an eternity with this weird vibe moving between them. He pulled up to the curb in front of her dad's house, and she climbed off and handed him the helmet back. For a moment all she did was stand there, and she should have said bye and headed inside, but even that felt weird. Maggie had never been in this situation where there was this after sex awkwardness. All of the guys she had slept with before, she had been in a relationship.

"I'll see ya around, Maggie." He was watching her, and she glanced down and watched as he kept curling and uncurling his fingers around the handlebars, but he must have noticed where her focus was because he stopped. She lifted her eyes back to his eyes and felt her mouth go dry. There was heat in the light blue depths, but there was also this almost frightening quality in them. "Take care of yourself." But he didn't wait for her to say anything, just put the helmet on, pulled away from the curb, and headed down the street until he turned the corner and his headlights disappeared.

She stood there for several seconds just staring at the now empty street, breathing out and turning to head into her father's house; she didn't miss the movement from the living room curtains. The porch light flickered on and the front door open, and she groaned internally when her dad stepped out onto the porch. His beefy arms were crossed, and his face set hard, but with his light blue velour bathrobe the whole intimidating appearance was lessened. Of course her night would end like this. It seemed fitting.

She didn't say anything as she moved past her dad and stepped into the house. He followed her inside and shut the door. And the tension in the small foyer intensified. Going to bed and not having to talk to her dad about this would be ideal, but it was also not going to happen. She turned around, just wanting to get this over with.

"I tried calling you, Maggie."

She breathed out. "I'm sorry, Dad. I left my bag here with my phone in it. I didn't mean to worry you."

He didn't move, didn't even respond to what she said until several moments had passed. "Care to tell me what in the hell you were doing out with a Grizzly member?" Her dad was in his early fifties, but for his age he was still in shape. Being in the military for years had him following certain rules when it concerned his life. He could be just as scary as any MC member.

"I was just out for a ride, Dad. It isn't like Diesel is a stranger. I've known him nearly my whole life."

"You've known *of* him nearly your whole life, honey. There is a big difference."

She supposed there was, but she sure as heck knew a lot more about him now. That random thought was totally misplaced, not what she wanted to be thinking about right now while standing in front of her dad, and she felt her whole body flush. Ever since her mother died ten years ago in a car accident it has just been her and her dad. He had been protective before, what with her being an only child and a girl on top of that, but after her mom died it had gotten even worse. But he had had to let her go when she had gone off to college, for the last four years, and then when she got a job right after college and stayed away. But now she was back in her hometown, laid off, kicked out of her home where her piece of shit ex-boyfriend lived, a twenty-three-year-old living with her dad again. He dropped his hands and pinched the bridge of his nose. It was something he did when he was annoyed.

"You're an adult, Maggie, and don't need rules binding you, even if you have moved back in with me."

He let go of his nose and stared at her with eyes the same color as hers. "You'll always be my little girl, and I will always worry about you, but I don't have to tell you that any member of the Grizzly MC is dangerous."

"I know, Dad, but I can handle myself, and as you can see I'm in one piece." She smiled, hoping to soften the fact her dad wasn't pleased with the fact she had been out at this hour with an outlaw biker. "He is really a nice guy, Dad." She didn't really know much about Diesel on a verbal level, and aside from the very dirty things he had said to her, she knew just as much as she did before.

"You going with that guy now?"

Wow, let's take it to the next level of awkwardness.

"Dad, no, I am not going with anyone. I don't need to jump into a relationship right after John." Her dad made a gruff noise, but she could see on his face that he wasn't a fool. He knew what she had been doing this late with Diesel. At least he wasn't calling her out on it.

"I don't like the fact of you hanging out with those bikers."

"You've known them forever."

"I don't care, Maggie. They are dangerous. Being acquaintances and selling them parts for their Harleys doesn't mean I want my daughter getting comfortable with them."

She pushed her hair off her shoulder. "Don't worry. I don't think I'll be seeing Diesel again." On the outside she knew she was doing a good enough job on portraying the fact she was fine. But on the inside saying those words aloud did bother her. Because even if deep down she had known that she wouldn't have had more than a few hours with Diesel, there was this small, very naive side of her that thought maybe he would see something different from the other women he was with.

Yeah, it was stupid and she had known better, but it was an inevitable feeling and one she had pushed deep down inside of her so she could enjoy her time with Diesel. Now that it was over with she just felt like shit, and even worse when she thought about the crap that happened after *that*.

"Okay, honey." But she could hear in his voice that he wasn't all that convinced. He moved past her and kissed her on the head before making his way toward his room. The sound of his door shutting behind him filled the silence.

She went into the bathroom and shut the door behind her. Turning the light on and staring at herself in the mirror showed that she looked like she'd just gotten fucked, and if she could see that then she knew her dad could see it as well. Maggie got undressed and started the shower. She went back to the sink and got her toothbrush, but when she glanced at the mirror again it was to see the marks Diesel had left on her body. She had known there would have been bruises, had felt the pressure and pain from his hold as he slammed into her repeatedly, but now to see the marks of his "affection" toward her had her insides liquefying. She ran a finger along the finger and thumbprint sized bruises on either side of her waist. They were barely formed, and she knew by tomorrow they would be a stark contrast to her pale flesh. Maggie turned her attention away from the sight and headed into the shower. The sooner she put Diesel and what they had done behind her, the better. But it was going to be damn hard with the memories of him, the marks on her body, and the soreness between her thighs.

Chapter Seven

Diesel sat at the club table and listened to Jagger go over usual daily business concerning the bar and underground fighting. The money was lucrative, especially with the hype moving around Steel Corner and the surrounding towns. More guys were training to fight, and more were coming in to place their bets. Stinger and Court chimed in on some of the less favorable things, included a local gang that was trying to butt heads with them on a small part of territory that was just outside of Steel Corner, but still within the city parameter. Diesel had tried calling Jagger last night after he dropped off Maggie, mainly to fill him in on the unknown MC that he had seen at the barn, but also because he had needed to occupy his mind. It had been hard to just drive off, because as much as he knew seeing her again wasn't a good idea, he also knew that fucking her hadn't eased any of his need for her. If anything it made it stronger. But he had seen the way she had looked at him, all freaked out and shit because he hadn't used a condom. He couldn't blame her, that had been stupid as hell, but he hadn't been lying when he said he had no control while he had fucked her. His bear had been the one taking control, and all his human side had been doing was enjoying the ride. And shit had it been one hell of a ride. He should have known he hadn't put a condom on when he felt the intense heat of her cunt all the way around his dick, and the slickness of her arousal coming from her and soaking the area between them.

"Yo, D, my man?"

He looked over at Jagger. All the members were staring at him, and he shifted, realizing that he had been thinking too hard about Maggie and screwing her, and now he was sporting massive wood. He reached under the table and adjusted himself since his dick was digging into his zipper, and cleared his throat.

"D, I said I missed your call, but you didn't leave a message. This have anything to do with that MC you and Stinger saw at the fight last night?"

Diesel looked at Stinger. "Yeah. I didn't want to leave that shit over a burner, and knew I'd see you today, but looks like Stinger got to you first." Stinger grinned and brought the joint he seemed to always be smoking back to his lips and inhaled. "You know anything about the Brothers of Menace MC?" He looked at Jagger and watched as his President leaned back in his chair.

"I know they are originally from Arizona, but heard from McNamara and his gang that they are trying to set up a club in River Run." Diesel nodded. "I just found that shit out this morning. After Stinger let me know about them showing up on our turf and going to the barn I called McNamara to see if he heard anything." McNamara was one of the local thugs that were stationed out of River Run, the next town over. McNamara and his crew ran smaller, illegal operations that had to do with drugs and petty theft. No one could get to Steel Corner without passing through River Run, and no one passed through River Run without McNamara knowing. "When I got that news from him I did a little digging on that MC. Seems like that MC is made up of a bunch of Nomads from different charters of the Brothers of Menace. They got together, patched each other in for Colorado, and are now making River Run their home."

"What the fuck were they doing in our town and hanging at our fight center without letting us know?" Brick said with that hard edged tone he always had. It was common knowledge that if someone was hitting up another MC territory they were to inform that crew of their presence to show respect. Clearly these Brothers of

Menace hadn't put the call in to get in touch with Jagger or the Grizzlies, and that was a major problem. Clearly these human assholes needed a lesson on MC territory etiquette.

"Right now let's just sit on the information. They should have made themselves known instead of just hitting up the barn and coming into Steel Corner like they owned the shit, but I don't want to make an enemy of them … just yet." Jagger looked at each of them. "We don't know what their intentions are in River Run, and they might be a good MC to have in our corner."

"Jagger, man, if they are in River Run there isn't any doubt they heard of us, especially if they are setting up shop there." Brick had calmed down marginally since getting with Darra, but he was still this dark and hardheaded bastard on the best of days. But Diesel had seen the way Brick's whole demeanor softened when he was with Darra. That female had this pretty fucking powerful hold on their Sergeant at Arms, but then again Sonya had the same kind of power over Jagger. Diesel shook his head at the thought, because although he didn't have a female—and frankly didn't think he needed one— that didn't stop him from thinking about Maggie. Staying away was good, really damn good, and he needed to realize that sooner or later, and get it through the thick skull of his bear that spending that one night with her was it. There would be no more of sticking his dick in the female, no matter how much he wanted to.

"Diesel, you good, brother?"

Diesel looked over at Brick. "Yeah. I just got a lot on my mind."

Brick grunted.

"That brings the next issue to order." Diesel looked over at Jagger, who was staring at him, but then looked over at Dallas, too. "You boys want to tell me what the fuck was going on at the bar last night? Why you feel the need to fight each other?" There was a heavy silence across the table. "We have enough people trying to bring us down. We don't need to be trying to do that with each other."

"It is what it is, Jagger." Diesel leaned back in his seat. He might have put the shit that happened with Dallas behind him, but he hadn't forgotten it. He glanced at the other male, and grew pissed when he noticed Dallas watching him.

"And what the fuck is that supposed to mean?"

Diesel looked over at Jagger again. Diesel wasn't about to mince his words, because this shit needed brought to the table regardless. He had planned on taking to Jagger about it privately and seeing what his President said, but since it was brought to the table everyone was going to hear him. "It means Dallas running his mouth when he's piss drunk seems to happen more frequently." The once Nomad had joined their crew a short time ago. Diesel had known the male for years before he got patched in with the Grizzly MC, but all he had ever really heard on his Nomad status was he didn't want to be tied down to any one charter. He didn't drink all the time, but when he did he always managed to get drunk enough to start running his mouth. Well, last night when he started talking about fucking Maggie had been a step over Diesel's line.

"Dude, you flipped the fuck out when I started saying shit about some piece of ass dancing on the floor." Dallas kept his voice even, but his words had Diesel's rage rising swiftly.

"Man, you aren't even drunk and saying shit that you shouldn't."

Stinger shook his head and chuckled. "There is going to be another brawl started, and I'm not going to stop it this time." Court had been there last night, too, but he was smart enough to keep his mouth shut.

"D, this was about some tail last night? What, you wanted a go at her and Dallas was trying to hit her up, too?"

Diesel gritted his teeth and snapped his head toward Jagger. He had known the other male for a long ass time, but he was stick of people talking about Maggie that way.

"She isn't a piece of tail, or a piece of pussy. She is Brian's daughter, Maggie, and when that motherfucker," he pointed at Dallas, "started running his mouth about Maggie, saying the shit he was going to do to her, I thought he needed his ass knocked out because of it." Diesel wasn't about to bust out that he had been thinking the same stuff regarding Maggie, but when he had heard the lust in Dallas's voice, and smelled the need to only fuck her like she was nothing more than a club whore, Diesel had felt protective, possessive, and territorial of her. Thinking that being with her sexually would get rid of this hardcore desire to be with her had been a dumb fucking idea, and it clearly wasn't working since he still had her on his mind. That never happened to Diesel. When he fucked a female he wanted that was the end of it. He didn't think about them, wonder what they were doing, or want to be with them again. But as much as he liked his sex rough, and although he hadn't nearly done all the things he wanted to do to Maggie, he also wanted to go slow with her. He wanted to lick every inch of her body, memorize the curves and dips of her body, and mark her with his canines and his cum.

"Shit, D, what in the hell are you thinking about?" He snapped his eyes at Court and glowered. "You're fucking stinking up the entire room with your arousal, and frankly it ain't doing anything but making all of us miserable."

Diesel looked at all the guys. They all held the same expression: one of annoyance and amusement.

"Fuck you all." They all started laughing, and Diesel shifted in his chair again. "I'm going to make myself perfectly clear." The room grew silent, and all focus was on Diesel. "I don't want anyone saying shit about Maggie. She isn't up for discussion, and if I hear anyone talking about how they want to fuck her or do anything else with her I'll personally take you out back and beat your ass."

No one said anything, but there was clearly a feeling of weirdness that came from each male.

"Everyone is cool with that, D—"

"You placing a claim on her, Diesel?" Jagger's words were cut off when Dallas decided to open his mouth.

Diesel curled his hands into tight fists, but kept them on his thighs.

"Dallas," Jagger growled out. The tension in the room was growing to a volcanic level.

"No, Jagger, I want to know. This conversation started when D decided to tell us all she was off limits, but he can't really make that kind of demand unless he is related to her, has some kind of history with her that doesn't have anything to do with her dad selling bike parts, or if he claimed her as his own." Dallas was either drunk, high, or both to be starting this shit now.

Court and Stinger all shifted in their seats, Brick stared at Dallas with an inscrutable expression on his face, and Jagger wore a scowl.

"Dallas, this is not up for debate." Jagger spoke before Diesel could tell Dallas off.

"I'm not trying to start shit."

Diesel grunted, because that seemed like an outright lie. "What in the fuck is your problem, man?" Diesel didn't hide the growl in his voice. "Since you got patched in you can't seem to stop running your mouth."

Dallas slowly leaned back in his chair. "There isn't a problem. I am simply stating that if I wanted to go after Maggie it shouldn't be a problem since you have not staked your claim."

"The only thing you're interested in is getting between her thighs." Diesel didn't realize he had been about to stand until Jagger put his hand on his forearm.

"Easy, brother." Jagger kept his voice low.

Diesel sat back in his seat and kept his focus on Dallas. There was a moment of silence where no one did anything but look between Diesel and Dallas.

"I mean it. Stay away from her, Dallas. She isn't up for grabs whether I have claimed her or not." Diesel gritted his teeth and forced his bear not to come out, scale this table, and kick Dallas's ass.

"Dallas, I think the smart thing is to just back the fuck off on Maggie. This is a brotherhood, and respecting each other is our code. I don't know what shit you're going through that is making you act like this, but back the fuck off." Court was the one to speak. "If D doesn't want you near her, then that is the end of it."

Dallas didn't respond right away.

"We don't screw with brothers, no matter what shit we are going through," Jagger said, and although he didn't say that they had all noticed a change in Dallas, it was clear from Jagger's voice that they had. "Especially when it concerns a female they are protective of. D might not be sleeping with her, but he has said what he needed to say. This goes for any of the members in this club." Jagger looked at each Grizzly that sat around the table.

"And I think it is safe to say Diesel, as well as all of us, don't want to see Maggie hurt. She isn't just a female, but Brian's daughter, and we respect the hell out of him."

Diesel would have been happy if no one had gotten involved in this. He wanted to make it clear to Dallas that Maggie was not up for discussion, but Jagger was the President, this shit had been brought up at the table, and it was clear this was how it was going to happen.

"There are plenty of chicks for you to fuck, Dallas." Brick chimed in, which surprised the hell out of Diesel. "In fact, go fuck a few of the club whores. They would be more than happy to fuck you until you are comatose."

Dallas still didn't say anything, and the rage inside of Diesel increased.

"Understand?" Diesel made that one word come out on a harsh growl. His bear was right there, just about to come out and do some real fucking damage. "I don't care if she is mine or not. Just back off, man."

Dallas looked down at the table, and there was a lot of emotion passing across the male's face. Diesel didn't know what was going on with Dallas, felt sorry for him since it was clearly eating away at his soul, but he still wouldn't ease up on having him back away from Maggie.

"Yeah." Dallas scrubbed a hand over his face and then finally lifted his head and looked at Diesel.

"If you want to talk, you know we are all here for you," Jagger said to Dallas. "You're one of us, a brother, and you don't need to keep your problems buried inside of you."

Dallas's expression turned dark, and the sound of him grinding his teeth came through like a whip cracking. "I don't need to talk about anything. That is the end of it." He stood with enough force that his chair skidded backward and slammed into the wall. He looked right at Diesel. "Maggie is off-limits. I got it, but if you don't want anyone going after that female, then maybe you should lay your mark on her. As it is I—as well as I know everyone else at this table—can smell the fucking sex on you," Dallas said with a growl. He looked at Jagger. "We done here?"

Jagger normally wasn't one to let anyone talk to him the way Dallas just had, but there was no mistaking that there was pain coming from the other member, pain that he was trying really fucking hard to mask. Because of that, and whatever shit Dallas was going through, Jagger didn't rip him a new asshole.

"Yeah," their President said with a sharpness to his voice. That was all it took for Dallas to get the fuck out of the room.

No one said anything for a while, but there was confusion in the air. The other members were lucky they didn't bring up the fact Dallas had called Diesel out on fucking Maggie, because even if he had showered that morning, there was no getting rid of the scent of her that seemed to cover his skin, the fact he was constantly thinking about her, or that he was so fucking hard from said thoughts that he couldn't sit comfortably.

"Brick, I want you and Diesel to head over to River Run and get any information you can from McNamara on that new MC. He was stingy with the details, but he also isn't all about talking on the phone."

No one gave out a lot of information on the phone. Even if they were on disposable phones it was too risky to talk anything "business" related, seeing as it was usually illegal.

"When you want us to head out?" Brick asked.

"This afternoon. McNamara is expecting you."

Diesel and Brick stood, but before he could leave Jagger spoke again.

"Sit down a minute."

He did, and waited until Brick shut the meeting room door behind him before he started talking again. "What's up?"

Jagger leaned back in his seat. "Want to tell me what's going on with you and Brian's kid?"

"She isn't a kid. She's twenty-three." Everyone in the club knew about her because of their affiliation with Brian, and Diesel knew that was what this was all about. "Besides, nothing is going on."

Jagger cocked a brow. "No?"

Diesel shook his head.

"Then why can I smell the fact you had sex with her?"

Diesel didn't know how to reply.

At Diesel's silence Jagger signed and rubbed his eyes. "D, man, she is Brian's daughter. What were you thinking?"

"I was thinking that I wanted her pretty damn badly." His annoyance grew over the fact first Dallas and now Jagger was giving him shit about it. "If she wasn't Brian's daughter we wouldn't even be having this conversation. She is an adult, and was consenting. Why the fuck does anyone care who I screw?" But it hadn't been just fucking Maggie. It had meant more, and that scared the shit out of him. He rested his elbows on the table and leaned forward. "Jagger, I don't know what is happening to me, but when I was with her my bear took control. I couldn't think rationally, and honestly didn't want to. I just wanted *her*, in every fucking way imaginable. I was so damn possessive of her, too." He never talked about this kind of stuff. Maggie was a clear weakness for him.

"Fuck, dude." Yeah, that about summed it up.

"You going to take her as an old lady?"

He was already shaking his head before Jagger even finished. There was a frown between Jagger's eyes.

"No? Why not if you clearly want her this badly?"

Diesel thought about what he said but didn't have an answer. "I don't know, Jagger. I really fucking don't know. What I do know is I don't want an old lady right now."

"Why?"

Damn him for his quick response.

"Because I don't think bringing in a female into the fucked up life I lead is smart. She's a good girl, and if anything happened to her under my protection..." He clenched his jaw. "I would go off the deep end for sure."

"I would rather be there for my woman than try to fight how I feel and end up missing out on a really fucking special thing. You get my drift?" Jagger didn't wait for Diesel to respond. "Diesel, you make it sound like it is the end of the damn world having an old lady, when it is actually the opposite. Since being with Sonya I feel different. Yeah, I still have all that anger and violence inside of me, but she soothes it with just a touch or the sound of her voice. I won't lie and say that when all that shit went down with Trick I wasn't a fucking mess with worry over her. It's a part of life, and can't be avoided."

Diesel glanced out the window and saw Brick making his way over to Darra. The Sergeant at Arms embraced her, and whatever he said in her ear had her throwing her head back and laughing.

"You will never know the satisfaction you get knowing you have someone to protect, or the feeling of this possessiveness and territorial need to make it known she is yours. My animal revels in it, and I don't fucking fight him."

Diesel didn't know what to say. He had never heard Jagger speak this "deeply" about anything aside from the MC before.

"I love that female, Diesel, and would take a bullet in my head for her. And if what I'm picking up from you is accurate, you might be feeling some pretty deep shit for Maggie as well. Did you ever think you'd see Brick or me settled down, and pining for women?"

No, he hadn't, but then again he didn't think he could have ever imagined any member of the club claiming a female. "This isn't something I want to talk about, Prez."

"No? Well, you may not want to talk about it, but you're going to hear me out regardless. You want to screw chicks, I got no problem with that, but you make damn sure you don't mess around with a female of the club's associates unless you are willing to claim her as yours." There was a threat in Jagger's voice. "Brian's been working with the Grizzlies for years. He's a good man, and Maggie is a good girl. I don't want to see her get hurt. If you want to not have a member go after her, then you need to be the one to treat her right. Understand?" There was this fatherly figure in Jagger, even if he was a mean motherfucker at times. He was protective of everyone and everything he considered family.

Diesel clenched his jaw. "I'm the last person that would ever hurt her, and if anyone tried to fucking touch her I'd kill them."

This smug look crossed over Jagger's face.

"That's what I thought. Why don't you think about that proprietary attitude that just came out of you, and the fact your bear was the one that growled out those words? You don't want an old lady? Seems like you do, and her name is Maggie Drake." Jagger held Diesel's gaze with his own and then turned and left him alone.

"Shit." He rubbed his hand over his face and breathed out. "You are so fucked, D."

THE GRIZZLY MC: VOLUME TWO

Chapter Eight

Maggie put the last box of air filters on the shelf in the back room. The sound of the bell above the front door of her father's supply store dinged with a customer. She wiped her hands on the off white apron tied around her waist and headed back out front. At first she didn't see anyone when she stepped into the main floor, but then Mora popped out from behind one of the shelves with a huge grin on her face.

"Good God, Mora. How about not being creepy as hell this early in the morning?"

Mora stepped up to the front counter and leaned on it.

"This early?" She looked down at her cell in her hand. "Girl, it is noon, and lunchtime." She smiled brightly and popped her gum.

"No, it's early still, and sleep sounds a lot better than food right now." Maggie leaned on the counter and rested her head in her hands. She closed her eyes for a second, and although she wouldn't act like this if there were people in the store, Mora wasn't a customer, and, well, she just didn't care. That was how much she wanted to go back to bed right now.

"Why are you so tired?" Mora pulled at a strand of her hair that had come down from her bun.

Maggie looked up. For a second all she did was stare at her friend, but honestly she was trying to think of how to go about telling Mora exactly what had happened.

Mora's eyes grew wide, and she took a step back. "Oh my God. You got laid." Mora said the last word loudly, and Maggie shushed her even though at the moment no one but the two of them was in the store.

"Keep your voice down, Mora. Lord." Maggie pushed herself up and crossed her arms.

"Well, then tell me, because I know I dropped you off at your dad's house. Did you go out after that, or maybe have someone come in?" Mora wagged her eyebrows, and Maggie couldn't help but laugh, but then she thought about exactly what had happened last night.

"Um, well, it is kind of complicated—"

"No, it's not." Mora was still grinning. "Just lay it out. I know you are kind of on the prude side compared to me."

"Mora, everyone is on the prude side compared to you. Well, maybe not Diesel." Maggie snapped her mouth closed when the latter came out. Oh shit, she had really just said that aloud?

It only took a second for Mora's eyes to get as big as saucers, and then her mouth gaped open. "No. Shit. You slept with Diesel? Like the Grizzly MC Diesel?" The excitement coming from Mora was thick, but she also could tell there was a little uncertainty in there also.

"But, uh, you saw the way he was last night, and you were just as freaked out as I was. Why all the excitement?" Maggie said, and Mora's happiness faded as she grew serious.

"You weren't hurt, clearly, and would have called me if he put some kind of bullshit alpha attitude on you, so aside from the fact he was intense as hell last night, I'm just glad you got your lady bits taken care of."

Lady bits?

Mora's eyes narrowed. "But then again, why are you just now telling me about getting it on with him? I should have gotten a call last night when it was all said and done. I want the details. *Need* the details."

"Do you sound this desperate with the guys you are trying to go after?" Maggie grinned and teased Mora.

"Pfft, honey, they beg *me* for more." Mora winked. "But seriously, I know you wouldn't have gone with him if you didn't trust him. I want to know, was he like, all badass in bed?" She snapped her fingers, and her eyes grew wide once more. "I knew he wasn't going to just give up. Didn't I tell you?"

"Mora, please, stop making this a big deal. It really isn't." It was, of course, but Maggie wasn't going to say that aloud. She needed to wrap her head around what had happened, and how she was going to process her feelings.

Mora looked at her incredulously.

"He came to my house, took me for a ride on his Harley, and I went back to his house to have sex."

Mora opened her mouth again, and a low sound came from her. "You make it sound like it was nothing."

Maggie shrugged. It was something big, at least for her, but it was probably just about a romp between the sheets for Diesel. She didn't want to squeal and giggle with Mora, and look like an idiot over it when nothing more would happen. "I had sex with a man. Of course it was something, but I don't want to talk about it. We did it, he dropped me off, and that is that." She hoped she was hiding herself well enough from Mora, but her friend really was good at reading people.

"So that's it? It wasn't anything extraordinary, and was just as good as having sex with John?"

Just hearing her ex's name had Maggie wrinkling her nose.

"Yeah, that's what I thought." The sound of Mora tapping her foot and glaring at her told Maggie her friend wouldn't just let this go. She may have moved away for the last five years, but she had always kept in contact with Mora. Whenever Maggie had come back to Steel Corner for holidays and breaks during school, they always found time to get together. "You know if you don't give me something to go on I will just keep bugging you. This isn't just some romp between the sheets." No, it wasn't, but she was trying to not think about Diesel—which was impossible of course. There was no point in remembering their night together, even if she had the soreness and marks to prove it, because there wouldn't be another time. But she did want to tell someone, and Mora was her closest friend.

"Okay, come on. I'm not getting into this out here." She led Mora to the backroom. They'd have privacy, and she could still hear if someone came in. Maggie shut the door so there were only a few inches of it left open, and exhaled.

She started from when she saw Diesel come to her house, but also told her friend that she had wanted him for years. She never thought she'd have a chance with him, because the women she had seen him be with were total opposites of her, and they were also ready and eager enough to give it up to the MC members. She told her everything, didn't mince anything, and when she was done she actually took a step back and waited for Mora's response. The fact she was silent was a little unnerving. Mora never was one to bite her tongue.

"Okay, but it was good?"

She nodded, but that was a bland way of putting what she did done with Diesel.

"So good that you two forgot to wear a condom?"

Maggie licked her lips and nodded again.

"Dammit, Maggie, you know how stupid that is?" But Mora kept right on talking. "It doesn't even matter that you're on the pill. Shit like that isn't even one-hundred percent foolproof against pregnancy, and definitely not when it concerns STDs."

"I know that, Mora."

"And who cares if he said he was tested last week. Why would you believe him? You said yourself he's a mega man-whore."

Maggie rubbed her eyes and exhaled deeply. "I know all of that. I can't say anything else than tell you it was a stupid move. There isn't anything I can do about it now." She dropped her arms to her side and stared at Mora. "Since I don't have insurance anymore, and am not paying an arm and a leg for the private insurance, until I can get something else put together it is the Free Clinic in River Run for me."

"Well, that's all right. There isn't anything wrong with that. In fact, where do you think I got my birth control pills when I started having sex? No way was I asking my mom to take me. You know how she is with that shit." Mora started laughing at what she had just said. "She would have flipped if she knew I was having sex with Craig in the back of his pickup at sixteen." Craig had been Mora's boyfriend all through high school but had decided he wanted a more experienced woman. Last Maggie heard he was with some thirty-year-old who had a six-year-old from her previous marriage. "So, when do you go?"

"Well, they are booked for at least two weeks for an initial visit, which is what I have to do since I've never been there before."

Mora nodded. "That's great."

"Great? I wanted to get this shit done and over with."

"I know, but the whole reason I came in here was to see if you wanted to come hang out with me at my parents' cabin in the Springs." Mora pulled her keys out of her pocket and jangled them. "I asked my dad if he'd mind you and me heading up there for the week. I know you've been in the dumps because of the job, John, and moving back in with your dad. Besides, you and I need a little girl time. We didn't have a lot of that when you would come over for the holidays."

Maggie smiled, and was really touched by Mora wanting them to spend some quality time together, but she couldn't just leave. She had just come back. "I can't just leave my dad without someone to help him at the shop for a whole week. And I don't really have extra money for a trip like that."

Mora waved off her concerns. "Girl, I already mentioned this to your dad this morning. In fact, he seemed pretty adamant that you get out of town for a while. Not sure what that was all about, but I'm not complaining since you and I will be spending our days floating in a raft on the lake, and our nights getting fat as we eat junk food and sit in front of the fire."

Maggie knew why her father had been good with her leaving town, especially if he thought there was something happening between her and Diesel. Did he actually think leaving for a week would just make everything go back to normal? Maggie had already learned that once something was set in motion it just couldn't be undone. But going to Mora's family's cabin in Colorado Springs sounded like a dream, and a pretty good way to help get Diesel out of her head.

****

Brick and Diesel pulled their motorcycles up in front of the club owned by Jordyn McNamara, or McNamara as he was known to everyone in River Run, and anyone else that liked filthy and illegal things. The city of River Run was only about a half hour ride from Steel Corner, but bigger population wise, and had more of the raunchy type of businesses as it wasn't leaning toward a "scenic retirement community", which was what the residents of Steel Corner would have liked. Brick and

Diesel dismounted and took their helmets off. There were a few crotch rockets parked in front of the club, but Diesel knew they belonged to McNamara's men. It was only a little after noon, but the place was open. The MC had been to "The Shake" a few times when doing business with McNamara years ago, but now Jordyn and his crew stuck to the local shit. Last Diesel heard they were running a smalltime heroin operation to some of the smaller towns around the area. Drugs had never been what Diesel wanted to get into, but when they started the drug runs it had been a majority vote to try it out with the club. Fortunately, they were now out of that and focusing on the underground fighting.

Brick pulled the front door open, and Diesel followed the other male inside. The room was dark as fuck, but his eyes adjusted instantly and he saw the two bouncers standing on either side of the entrance. There was a stripper on the stage with a red light spotlighted on her, and she danced slowly against the pole. The bar was on the opposite side, and a young man in a wife-beater was drying glasses. Diesel looked at the four men sitting in front of the stage. Their voices were low and barely distinguishable, but he could see McNamara's slicked back platinum colored hair. Brick and Diesel made their way over to the group of men. Those two bouncers looked ready to tear meat from bones, and they were only humans.

The stripper was wearing a blindfold and had clamps on her nipples, but Diesel knew when Jordyn threw these little private shows it was to cater to the men he was doing business with. They stopped in front of the human males, and McNamara looked over. He gave them a chin lift.

"You boys want to sit down and see how flexible Tatiana can be?" He grinned, but Diesel only shook his head.

"No, we need to get this done. I have shit to do." McNamara might have been big in River Run, but that didn't mean anything to Diesel or the Grizzlies. He said something low to the other men still seated. Diesel knew this was a drug business deal, and not because there were lines of coke on the glass table in front of them, but because they reeked of that trade. He didn't have to be a shifter to smell the type of male that made his living off drugs. They were led to a back room, and McNamara went behind his desk and sat down. The little asshole was only in his late twenties, but had already made a pretty big name for himself in the area.

"So, gentlemen, what can I do for you today?" McNamara was a smug little bastard that acted like he was some kind of businessman on Wall Street.

"Don't fuck around. Jagger told you why we were coming up," Brick said in his deep, harsh voice.

"We need you to tell us whatever you know about The Brothers of Menace."

McNamara gestured to the chairs in front of his desk. Once he and Brick were seated he began talking.

"I don't know a whole lot. I heard that they were in different MC charters, or maybe it was Nomads," McNamara shrugged, "I don't know, but the end result was that they formed their own charter, have bought a piece of property out on Sterling Hill for their headquarters, I presume. The President goes by the name of Lucien Silver. Don't know if that's his real name or not, but it sounds fake as fuck if you ask me. They keep to themselves and don't really head into town all that much."

"Do you know how they get their revenue?"

"All I know is they have a few working girls in their clubhouse now, for the time being at least. Not sure if they run a prostitution business or if those women are just for them to play with." McNamara shrugged again and leaned back in his chair. "They haven't been here that long, and I know Jagger just heard about them because they came to your territory, but that's really all I know. If I hear anything else I'll call the club."

Although they wouldn't consider McNamara an associate or friend, they had helped him out a few years back when he was held at gunpoint. If not for the Grizzlies being there at the right time this little shit would be dead. Ever since then Jordyn was very cooperative in anything the club needed from him.

Brick and Diesel stood. "Yeah, give the club a call when you know anything you might think is pertinent." McNamara nodded, but they left before they could be shown out, and once outside they stopped at their bikes.

"You think this MC is going to be trouble?" Brick asked. He slipped his sunglasses on over his eyes and looked at Diesel. Ever since the Sergeant at Arms for the club had gotten an old lady, something had definitely changed in him. He was still this scary bastard that could break an asshole in two, but when with Darra he melted for her. It was so unlike the Brick Diesel had known for years.

"I don't know, but I have a feeling we will find out soon enough."

THE GRIZZLY MC: VOLUME TWO

Chapter Nine

One week later

Maggie sat in the waiting room at the Free Clinic in River Run. She had already filled out her information and handed it back to the receptionist, and now sat in the very uncomfortable chair and looked at the people sitting around her. The majority of the ones waiting to be seen were younger women, even some girls that didn't look older than sixteen. Some were obviously pregnant, and there were a few that appeared to be with their mothers, who looked less than pleased.

Spending the week with Mora at her parents' cabin had made a world of difference in perking Maggie up, but as soon as she had come back to Steel Corner and seen a few of the Grizzly MC members riding through the square of town, the thought of Diesel had slammed in her head. But honestly he hadn't really left her mind, not even when she had been laughing with Mora and soaking in the sun by the lake. The distraction she got from relaxing and having a good time with her friend had helped her in keeping anything Diesel related buried. The side door opened, and an older woman in faded scrubs stepped out holding a cream colored folder.

"Miss Drake?" Her attention was on the folder, but when she called out Maggie's name she looked up and scanned the waiting room.

Maggie stood and walked toward her and into the hallway behind the door. After she was weighed she was showed into the exam room, her vitals were taken, and she was left alone. All of it had seemed to take less than five minutes with the nurse barely saying a few words to her. Maggie rubbed her arms, suddenly grew nervous, and then wiped her clammy hands on her pants. She glanced at the poster that was right across from her. It was the image of a mother holding a newborn, and the words below it listed all the benefits of breastfeeding. There was a knock on the door, and a woman who had to be in her fifties walked in. She had on a white lab coat and held a small laptop.

"Miss Drake?" She smiled, and the gap between her two front teeth was pretty pronounced. "What brings you in today?" Maggie had never understood why they asked patients what brought them in since they always asked why she wanted to be seen when she made the appointment.

Actually saying she needed to be tested for STDs because she had stupidly had a one-night stand without using proper protection was humiliating, even if Maggie was an adult and this was a professional. But she did finally get all of that out. The doctor nodded and smiled warmly. She probably saw and heard these types of things all the time.

"I'll have the nurse get some blood and run some tests. We will also run a pregnancy test since it is pretty standard, given the reason for your visit." Maggie nodded again. "But I'd like to get a Pap smear done since you have never been here before, and according to your history it's been about a year since you had one last."

Maggie nodded.

"It'll take at least a week, maybe ten days to get the results back. We are backlogged, and we send the samples to Denver to be run." The doctor smiled again, handed her one of those paper gowns, and left her alone.

Twenty minutes later, and Maggie was stepping out of the office. It had been gynecological hell and some needle pricks thrown in. Maggie left the office and headed to her car, but stopped when she heard the rumble of motorcycles nearing. She stood there and watched four tricked out Harleys ride past. They stopped at the red light, and she saw that they were called the Brothers of Menace, according to the backs of their cuts. The rider in the front turned his head and looked over at her. She didn't know what it was about this stranger watching her, but her stomach dropped and her pulse increased. He wore dark sunglasses and a skullcap helmet. She could see his dark hair peeking out from under the helmet. But it wasn't his huge frame that made her wary. It was this very strange, almost apprehensive feeling she got when she looked at him and the other members. These men were dangerous, lethal, and she gathered all of that—even with her human senses—with just one look. A chill raced up her spine, and fortunately the light turned green. The guy she took as the leader from the simple confidence that seemed to come from him, and the fact he was the one in front of the others bikers, grinned at her. There was a boom of an engine being revved, and then the bikers were taking a right and disappearing behind the large buildings of River Run. There was something scary and wrong about that man, and her instincts had known it.

Maggie climbed into her car and started the engine. She didn't like River Run, and not because of that biker gang she just saw. The scenery was beautiful, when she was actually out of the industrial part of the city, but she knew a lot of illegal things happened in this town— even more so than what happened in Steel Corner. Drugs, guns, and prostitution were some of the rumors that had circulated to her part of the woods. But here, in this town, there was this nervousness that she felt, one that she couldn't quite understand and didn't want to analyze. Maggie didn't feel this tightening of her skin or uneasiness about the Grizzlies, though. Maybe it was because she had grown up around the MC, and although she knew they weren't priests and did a lot of questionable things, it seemed to flow well with Steel Corner. At home she didn't feel like she should be watching over her shoulder, but she sure did when she was in River Run. Once in her car she headed out of town and back home, but for some reason she found herself continuously glancing in her rearview mirror until she was out of River Run.

****

Diesel sat at the bar, his back to the counter, and his attention on the party commencing in front of him. The clubhouse was popping with loud music, booze, joints, and of course club whores that were already greedily giving themselves to the guys. Court was getting a private lap dance by a scantily clad female, and Drevin and Stinger were sitting at the couch watching a stripper reach for the ground and pop out her ass. Dallas was leaning against the wall, a beer bottle in one hand and a pool stick in the other. But Dallas wasn't focused on the game or the women around them, and instead was staring right at Diesel. He pushed away from the wall, set his pool stick down, and moved in Diesel's direction. He stopped at the bar and asked the tender, a prospect that was nearing his year stint with the club, for a double shot of Crown. Johnny Boy, the prospect, handed the shot to Dallas. He brought it to his mouth and tossed it back. Neither of them said anything, but Diesel didn't have shit to say to the other member. He was still fucking pissed at Dallas running his mouth about Maggie. He had managed to steer clear of the other male, kept his anger and the violent need to punch him in the jaw at bay, but having him this close, and feeling like Dallas was taunting him with his presence, had Diesel clenching his teeth.

Dallas moved a few steps closer until they were only a few feet apart. "D, man, can I have a word with you?"

Diesel could see out of the corner of his eye that Dallas was looking at him, but he wasn't in the mood for this shit. "Dallas, I don't really want to get into this right now." He did, but he didn't because he had been actively thinking about everything Jagger said, and how he felt for Maggie. He wanted to make this real with her, and give a relationship with her a shot.

"I don't want to fight, and I'm not about to badmouth your woman."

That had Diesel looking at him.

"I just think I should probably talk to you and explain some shit."

Diesel faced forward again. "You don't need to explain shit to me, because I don't fucking care." He was done with this conversation and pushed up from the bar, but Dallas reached out and wrapped his big hand around Diesel's bicep. Diesel looked down, tensed all over, and then looked back at Dallas. "I suggest you get your fucking hand off me, Dallas."

He did, and ran his hand through his short blond hair. Dallas's green eyes were red-rimmed, and the stench of pot and liquor surrounded him. "Can you give me a minute? Please."

Diesel stared at the other man, and the fact he had said please with this almost desperate tone had Diesel relaxing and nodding. Dallas seemed to relax as well, and he started heading out the front door. Court and Stinger glanced at them, but when it looked like they were going to stand Diesel shook his head. They sat back down, but he could still sense that they thought shit was going to go down with him and Dallas.

They stepped outside but didn't go very far from the front doors. Dallas moved over to the truck used by the club and leaned against it. He reached inside his cut and grabbed a joint, lit it, and inhaled from the end twice before he finally started talking.

"I don't apologize for a lot of shit I do, but I want to say sorry for talking all that shit about your girl." He brought the joint to his mouth again and looked at Diesel as he inhaled. Once he exhaled he looked down and kicked a rock across the parking lot. "The reason I've been drinking a lot, keeping to myself, and not able to filter my mouth is because I have this dark anger inside of me." A moment of silence passed between them.

"We all do, brother, but we just have to deal with it, and work with each other, not against one another."

Dallas was shaking his head before Diesel even finished. "No, you don't understand. I've been trying to help numb the toxic shit going through me, but as you can see it's only been making it worse, and all I've been doing is taking it out on the people I consider my family."

Diesel didn't say anything because he knew Dallas had more to say. The sun was starting to set, and the sky was this pink/orange color. It was a beautiful setting to what was turning out to be a very dark conversation. For the first time since Diesel had known the male, he saw a deep vulnerability and sorrow in Dallas's green eyes.

"Did you know I was married and had a kid with Meghan?"

Diesel nodded, but even though he did know that, as did every Grizzly member, there was a lot of shit members kept to themselves. With broken and battered pasts and violent, animalistic natures, it was common for a lot of shady information to be kept hidden. Not saying this was particularly "shady", but some guys just didn't feel like sharing. Dallas nodded and took another hit from the joint. He held it out for Diesel, but he shook his head. He had plans later this evening, and he wanted to be clear headed and sober when he dealt with them.

"Yeah, I got married to Meghan right out of high school. We were together for five years after that, even had a little boy together during that time. But she couldn't handle the MC life." Dallas looked up at the sky and breathed out. "I wasn't always a Nomad, was even patched in with the Texas charter for a long fucking time, but..." He looked back at Diesel, "A few weeks back I got word that Meghan had gotten into a car accident. Some motherfucker ran a stop sign, T-Boned her car, and she died, as did my son who was in the passenger's seat." Dallas finished off his joint in several rapid intakes after he spoke. The air was thick with a lot of emotions, but all Diesel could do was stand there.

"Man, I am so sorry." He took a step forward.

Dallas shook his head, held out his hand to stop his advance, and looked up at the sky. "Yeah, me, too. She divorced me when Maddix was little, and I haven't seen her in years, man. I was sending money to her for the kid, but visits with him had been few and far between. Shit." He flicked the roach away and rubbed his eyes, and although he didn't cry, the scent of his sorrow was thick. "She was actually taking Maddix to college." Dallas smiled, but that faded and this painful look crossed his face. "My kid was smart as hell, D, even got a scholarship to CSU." He lowered his head so he was staring at Diesel again.

"You must be really proud. I know I would be." Diesel was trying to go along with the conversation, but this was downright heartbreaking. Dallas was a hard male, strong and didn't take shit from anyone. Some people thought being patched in was a harder life than being a Nomad, but there was different roads people took, and different hardships on those roads. Seeing Dallas like that had a lot of empathy filling Diesel, and he wasn't used to that. He was out of his element here.

"Yeah, I was." He pushed off the truck. "I didn't mean to get all emotional on you, but I wanted to let you know that since I got the news my head hasn't been in the right place. And to make matters worse Meghan's folks always hated me. The only reason I found out about their deaths was because a female we both went to high school with that still talked to Meghan reached out to me. I didn't want to upset anyone and make the situation worse by showing up at the funeral, so I stayed back and had to watch from my bike as they lowered them into the ground." Dallas clenched his jaw and turned away, and seconds later the scent of his tears filled the air. Diesel moved toward him, but Dallas held up a hand to stop him. "I'm good."

"I'm really sorry, Dallas." And he was, from the bottom of his heart, because he couldn't even imagine losing a female you cared about and had a life with once, and your child all at the same time.

"Thanks, man. I didn't tell anyone because I didn't want to bring it up." He breathed out and then cleared his throat. "It hurts like a motherfucker thinking about it, and saying this shit out loud feels like a fucking hot poker in my heart." He scrubbed a hand over his face. "But then I realized that adding misery to others' lives because of how I felt wasn't right." Dallas kept his back to Diesel. "I wish I would have done a lot of shit differently, man. I wish I would have stayed in contact with Meghan, because even if we didn't love each other and were through relationship wise, we still had a kid together and should have been there for him." There was a hard moment where neither said anything, and the scent of Dallas's rain-scented tears surrounded them. "So, yeah, that was that, and I think I need to sleep off this buzz."

He switched the conversation so rapidly that all Diesel could do was stand there and watch as he turned and walked away. Diesel stood there for a moment and reflected on what Jagger had told him last week, and now what Dallas had said. He had already planned on going to talk to Maggie, but hearing what had happened to one of his brothers cemented the fact that he didn't want to wait any longer to be with her. He had been stubborn and hardheaded his entire life, but after feeling Dallas's sadness as if it were his own, it now seemed very frivolous.

He went over to his bike and got on. Maggie's dad's house was only a ten minute ride from the clubhouse, but that seemed like a long fucking ways off. The parts store would already be closed, but he'd swing by there just in case and see if she was there. What he needed to do was talk to Brian first, because if he couldn't make the man understand how he felt for his daughter that would be one big fucking obstacle.

****

Diesel sat on his Harley in front of Brian's house. He saw the other man's truck in the driveway, but for some reason Diesel still hadn't gotten off his bike. There was a lot of shit going on, and the MC life was anything but glamorous. It was violent, volatile, and filled with a lot of dangerous and illegal things. But he didn't want to be in Dallas's situation where all that filled him was regret and heartache. If things didn't work out then that was the way it was meant to happen. That didn't mean he couldn't try, show her what she did to him, and see what could become between them. But Maggie wasn't just any female that he had fucked. There was something different about her, something that made his bear alert, feeling protective, and wanted her as badly as it wanted to take control of his human side. He had sat on Jagger's words and how he felt for a week, and talking to Dallas had made everything clear. And although that wasn't a very long time, it had felt like an eternity, especially when she had been on his mind every second of the day. It wasn't just that his body craved hers, and all he could picture was her curvy, naked form as he pounded into her. He also liked the way she spoke to him, liked the sound of her voice, and really fucking liked the way she touched him and made him feel.

He was so lost in thought that he didn't realize Brian was striding toward him until the human was standing a few feet from the curb. He had his arms crossed, and this really fucking pissed off look on his face. "What are you doing here, Diesel?" The way Brian sounded solidified the fact his rage was targeted right at Diesel, but he couldn't blame the other man.

"You know why I'm here." Brian didn't move, and Diesel didn't think he even breathed. Diesel took off his helmet and dismounted his bike. If he was going to have this talk out in the front lawn, then he was going to be eyelevel with Maggie's father.

"This better be about you wanting some parts ordered, and have nothing to do with Maggie." There was a stilted moment of uncomfortable silence.

"Brian, I didn't come here to piss you off."

"I'm already pissed off, Diesel. I've known the Grizzlies for nearly as long as Maggie has been alive. I care about all of you guys, and would help you out if you needed anything. I want you to put yourself in my shoes for a moment. I want you to imagine seeing your little girl get off the back of the bike of an outlaw MC member, one that I know for a fact deals in illegal bullshit, and sleeps with more women than probably live in this town."

Diesel gritted his teeth. No one dared to talk to him this way without getting their asses kicked. But of course he did see Brian's point of view, and couldn't fault the guy or resort to violence for the way he was being talked to. Maggie was his little girl, even if she was a grown woman.

"I know, Brian—"

"No, Diesel, I don't think you do. I don't think you've ever seen your daughter come home, smelling the sex on her, seeing it on her face, and having to look in her eyes and seeing this dreamy expression because she thinks there will be more than one night with a biker." Brian shook his head and dropped his arms. There was the scent of resignation, anger, and also fatherly love coming from Brian. Diesel couldn't say it wasn't awkward as fuck at having this conversation, and knowing that Brian was well aware that he had been with Maggie, but in the end it didn't matter, and no one and nothing could dissuade him for moving forward.

He stayed silent for a second. "But maybe you haven't been in my position either." Diesel clenched his jaw and heard the way Brian ground his teeth. "No, I have never had to look into anyone's eyes and see that. I have never felt the way you felt, but you don't understand why I am here."

"You're right, I don't understand why you're here. Why don't you enlighten me, because as it is, Diesel, I am pretty fucking pissed that you would go after Maggie when there are a lot of women that are more than willing to give themselves to you." Brian looked down at the ground.

"Brian, man, I am here because I want Maggie as my old lady." That had Brian shutting his mouth shut with an audible snap. "She isn't just a one-night thing for me. I care about her, my bear cares about her, and I came here to let you know that I plan on talking to her about it. I want her, Brian, and even though she is an adult and will decide what she wants for herself, I wanted to be a man and talk to you about this." Diesel clenched his hands at his thighs. "You know what it means to have an old lady, Brian, and that is what I want with Maggie."

Brian was now looking at him, but hadn't said anything for several seconds. He then exhaled, looked up at the sky for a moment, and then stared back into Diesel's face. "Why her? I mean I know my daughter is beautiful and intelligent. I'm not talking about all that. I'm talking about why *her*?" It was a hard question, yet it wasn't. Brian was asking him on a fatherly level. Diesel didn't know how he was feeling, but he hoped that one day he would, because the protective instinct of a dad was a powerful one. "The life you lead is too much for her, Diesel, too hard. She is all I have left. You want to take her away from me, take her into a life that could kill her without even a thought, and then where the fuck will I be?"

"I'm not taking her way from you. I'm not doing anything than offering her a life with me. You know that we protect our own, that I wouldn't let anything happen to her. I'd just as soon die than have her get hurt." And Diesel meant that with everything inside of him. It had been hard to get to that point even though he had felt it down to his blackened soul, but it had finally hit him in the damn head. He didn't want to be without Maggie by his side. Brian didn't respond for several moments, but before he could have the sound of a car approaching had them both turning. Even before Diesel saw Maggie pull into the driveway and beside Brian's truck, he had known it was her. There was a tightening of his skin, and the hairs on his arms had stood up. His bear had also come alert, moved out from deep inside of him, and made low, demanding sounds. It had been only seven days since he had dropped her off at her house, had been seven long-ass days since he had smelled the sweet scent of her, and touched her soft skin. But his self-doubt, uncertainty, and stubbornness all faded away when he watched her climb out of her car and look between the two of them. There was confusion and worry on her face, but even with both of those things taking the front stage he could scent her instant arousal at the sight of him, hear the increase of her pulse, and see the way her breath hitched. Yeah, his female wanted him just as much as he wanted her, and that was a really good fucking thing.

THE GRIZZLY MC: VOLUME TWO

Chapter Ten

Maggie stood by her car for several seconds, just clutching her bag over and over again. Diesel was here and clearly talking to her dad, who didn't look very happy. What had they been talking about? Was Diesel telling her father what they had done, like it was some kind of obligation since Brian was close with the club? Her heart was beating a mile a minute, and she seemed frozen to the spot, but then her dad turned away from Diesel and strode toward her. He stopped in front of her, and she tried to calm her sudden nerves. Her dad stared at her for a moment, and for the first time since her mother died he didn't try to act strong or try to hide his emotions. He was worried about her, and that had her shoulders sagging and her heart swelling. She glanced over at Diesel, who was leaning against his bike. He wasn't watching them, but she knew he was very aware of what was going on.

Swallowing the lump in her throat, she moved closer to her dad. "I'll be fine." She knew he wanted to be here, to make sure Diesel didn't hurt her, but she also knew, even if her father didn't, that Diesel wouldn't intentionally do anything like that. "Really, everything will be okay. Let me just talk to him in private. Please." She didn't know if she was trying to convince him or herself, but after a second he nodded—if a bit reluctantly—and cast one more glance at Diesel. She didn't know what they had been talking about before, but there was clear tension between them. She didn't have to be a shifter to feel it either. Her dad faced her and leaned down to kiss her on the forehead, and then he was turning and striding toward the front door. Only when they were alone did she look at Diesel again. He still leaned against his bike, but he watched her now. Finding the strength to go to the man she had been intimate with shouldn't have been that hard. He had seen every part of her, had *come* inside of her, and touched her like he owned her. This wasn't about letting loose and enjoying the carnal need that had thrummed through both of them. This was going to be a situation where she had to hear what he said, and a part of her knew it wasn't going to be good. But why would he come out here just to give her bad news? It didn't make sense, but then again a lot of things didn't.

Maggie forced herself to move closer toward him. When only a foot separated them she waited to see if he would be the first to speak. But all he did was watch her with this strange expression on his face, and then to further surprise the hell out of her he reached out, wrapped his arm around her waist, and pulled her toward his body. For a moment all she could do was stand there, tense and unsure of what she was supposed to do. This was certainly the last thing she expected to happen when she saw him sitting at the curb.

"Maggie, usually when someone hugs you it is customary to hug them back."

She pulled back enough to look in his face, saw the amusement in his expression, and tried not to be so tense.

He rubbed his hand up and down her back and stared into her eyes. "All I'm asking for right now is a hug." His voice was soft, and that was so unlike the Diesel she was used to.

But she leaned in, wrapped her arms around his broad shoulders, and rested her head on his chest. "I don't know what brought this on, but I can't say I don't like it." Pinching her lips together because she so hadn't meant to say that out loud, she heard and felt his deep chuckle. "I didn't mean to say that."

I know, baby." He continued to stroke her back, and then moved his hand over the back of her head to cup it. He just held her for a long minute, but it was so damn nice. Maggie didn't know how long they stayed like that, but she wasn't concerned if people were watching out their windows. This felt right on every level.

"Not that I'm complaining, but maybe you can let me know what is going on."

He chuckled again, but grabbed her upper arms and gently pulled her back so they were looking at each other again. "I want you to be my old lady, Maggie." He cupped one of her cheeks in his hand and stared into her eyes. His hand was so big he nearly engulfed one side of her head. She thought about his words hard. Having a member want an old lady wasn't something small. This was big, and Diesel wanted *her* to be his. "Your silence isn't too comforting, baby." He stroked his thumb along her cheek, and she blinked several times.

"That's big." Those two words were softly muttered, but he didn't smile or laugh.

"Yeah, baby, it's really fucking big, and I mean every single damn word."

"But I don't understand." She wanted to say more, but couldn't find the words to explain that this was a one-eighty and a scene from the Twilight Zone. "I just don't understand."

He shook his head. "Me either, Maggie, but this past week I have tried to convince myself that not being with you for more than that one time was the right thing." He continued to stroke her cheek, and moved his thumb along her bottom lip. "It took some very wise words and a broken male to show me that I shouldn't fight what feels so incredibly right." The way he stared at her was consuming.

Her breath hitched, and she felt as though this was the most surreal moment in her life. Diesel spoke so softly, so gently, that he didn't appear like the hardened, angry biker she was so used to seeing. How bizarre that it was only a week's time that she had been with him, and already she felt like it had been a lifetime. Maggie may have known him nearly her whole life, had wanted so much more from him when she realized what that meant, but she knew that time didn't really mean anything. She felt *something* with Diesel, something that she had felt the moment she had seen him at the age of seventeen and realized that it was lust that churned within her. And then the sex with him had been incredible, but it was so much more than that.

"That's what I really want, Maggie, if you want that, too."

"I…" She looked down, at a loss for words, because even though this was going very fast, it also felt as though it had taken a lifetime to get to this moment. "Yeah, Diesel, I want that, too."

He pulled her toward his chest again, speared his hands in her hair, and tilted her head to take her mouth in a kiss that couldn't be called anything but proprietary. When he pulled away from her the possessive and territorial light in his eyes had her heart palpating.

"Do you know what it means to be my old lady, Maggie?"

She licked her lips, but Diesel's stare was unwavering. "Yes, Diesel."

He slowly shook his head. "No, baby, I don't think you do." He leaned in close so there were only centimeters that separated them. "It means you're mine. It means no other male will touch you, look at you in sexual way, or even think about being with you." His words were in a growl, a crass statement. He wrapped his hand around her hair and leaned in so their lips were touching. "It means that if any male tries anything on you I'll fucking kill them." There was promise in his words. She should be frightened, should turn and head back inside, and never look back. But this was his animal talking, *his* animal making the demands. The flash of black that covered his blue irises told her as much. "I won't smother you, won't keep you a prisoner, but I also won't share, and I am a pretty territorial bastard, Maggie."

Her mouth was dry, and her throat closed up. "I like that you don't want to share, because I only want to be yours. But I also don't share."

He grinned and then took her mouth again. She melted into the hardness of his body. The smell of his leather cut had sparks of remembrance from over the years slamming into her head, and she knew this was only the beginning of what she hoped was a new chapter in her life.

****

"So, what, you guys are like an item now?" Mora grabbed one of the chips out of the red plastic basket in the center of the table and dipped it in salsa. She shoved it in her mouth, and the crunch and Mora's voice were so loud Maggie looked around to see if anyone had heard. It had been a week since she and Diesel had decided to give this relationship a go—if that was the right title for it— and everything was still fresh and intense. Even now she tingled between her legs at the remembrance of Diesel taking her roughly on his bike in the middle of the woods last night. It had been exhilarating and exciting, and each time she was with him only seemed to make her feelings for him grow deeper.

"Can you keep your voice down?" she said in a hushed whisper.

Mora stopped chewing, but reached across the table for another chip. "Would you quit diverting and just answer?"

Maggie leaned back in her seat and stared at her friend. Was Maggie upset she really didn't have a lot of people she considered close, that she hung out with, or felt comfortable enough to talk about this stuff with? No, because for every handful of fake friends she could have, there was still that one that she would always turn to, and that was Mora.

She breathed out and reached for a chip herself. She ate it, but she was just stalling because she knew Mora was going to scold her for jumping into this … whatever *this* was that she was doing with Diesel. Were they together, yeah, they were, but they didn't have a label aside from her being his old lady. She knew of the MC, but certainly wasn't an expert. But what she did know was that what she was to him was more than just being his girlfriend. "He wants me to be his old lady."

Mora stopped crunching again, but seemed to catch herself and swallowed her food. "Old lady? As in his biker bitch?"

Maggie coughed on the piece of chip in her throat and reached for her water. "Um, I guess, but I kind of prefer the term old lady." Maggie started laughing, because although she certainly wouldn't consider the term "biker bitch" derogatory, not when it concerned the Grizzly MC, and she was Diesel's old lady.

Mora started laughing, too. "Okay, well I have to admit I think I like the idea of you being a biker bitch. It has this bad-ass feeling to it."

Maggie rolled her eyes, but she was smiling.

"But really, is this thing serious with him? I mean I assume it is because I don't often hear of the Grizzly members getting serious with a woman. Although I've seen women on the backs of Jagger's and Brick's bikes, ones that wear those 'Property of' leather jackets. Those two members are some of the least likely ones I would have thought would settle down."

"I mean it is pretty serious. He came over and talked to my dad."

"I guess it must be pretty serious for Diesel if he was the one that came over and talked to you about it."

Maggie had asked Mora out for lunch because she desperately needed to talk to someone. Her father was out of the question since half the time he grumped around the house, growling about dirty bikers taking away his little girl, but she knew that even if he was upset about it now, he would support her in whatever she decided to do in the end. He had been uncomfortable when she left for school and had never liked John, but he had dealt with it, and he'd do the same with this. If this turned out to be a big mistake, well, it was her mistake to make.

"Yeah, I suppose." Maggie couldn't help the smile that curved her lips.

"Oh, God. Did he go all 'Mine' on your ass?" Mora shoved another chip in her mouth, but her expression was filled with eagerness. But she didn't let Maggie answer. "The look on your face tells me he did." She leaned back in the seat and breathed out in almost euphoria. "I need to find a guy like that."

"Like what?"

Mora rolled her eyes. "Don't be coy. I need to find a guy that will kick guys' asses if another dude looks at me." She tossed her hair over her shoulder and gave this almost wistful sigh. "You know the douche-bags I've been dating. I mean look at that asshole Craig. Oh, and let's not forget that little blip in the romantic department I had with Keith." The waiter came by with some fresh drinks, and Mora took that opportunity to flirt with him.

He was cute, but couldn't be more than nineteen, maybe twenty at the most. Maggie watched as Mora really put on the charm and had the young man blushing. The sound of her phone going off in her bag had her turning away from the current entertainment to get it. She had programmed the Free Clinic's number into her phone, and when she saw those digits flash across the screen her heart pounded hard.

"I'll be right back," she said to Mora.

"Everything okay?"

She held up the phone, but didn't need to say anything, because Mora understood well enough. Maggie headed out of the front of the restraint and away from a small group of kids. "Hello?"

"Is this Miss Drake?"

"Yes." Maggie walked back and forth. She trusted Diesel, had to if she was going to give their relationship a go, and even if she had known him all her life, the truth was still right in her face.

"I have the results of your lab work."

Maggie listened for the next few minutes as the woman went over the tests. She also scheduled her first appointment. Once she disconnected the phone she stood there a moment. She could hear children laughing, cars passing by, and a dog barking, but nothing could fully penetrate the news she had just gotten. She forced herself to walk, to go back into that restaurant, and sit back down at the table. The waiter was gone, and after a minute of Maggie not saying anything she saw Mora's eyes grow large.

"What is it? What did they say?" Mora leaned forward, the concern coming from her fast and hard, and the worry clear on her face. "Maggie, talk to me. You're starting to freak me out. You are far too quiet and have this 'Oh fuck' look on your face."

Maggie loosened the hold she had on the napkin, not even realizing that she had grabbed it. "I'm pregnant."

For what seemed like forever Mora didn't move, didn't speak, and just stared at her like she had grown another head. But then she blinked rapidly and leaned back in her chair. "Well holy motherfucking shit." Mora gestured for the waiter, but this time ordered herself a big-ass margarita. "But aside from that everything else is okay?"

Maggie nodded. She had tested negative on the STD screening, but all she could focus on right now was the fact she was pregnant with Diesel's baby. "Mora, what am I going to do? I can't even support myself right now. How am I going to support a baby, too?"

Mora reached across the table and took her hand. "Maggie, I'm here for you, and your dad is here for you." She rubbed her fingers back and forth over her hands. "And if Diesel is this serious about you and him being together, then he'll be supportive of this, too."

"Mora, I'm pregnant." Maybe she was in some kind of shock, because she felt numb, almost as if she wasn't fully connected with her body. Mora smiled at her sympathetically. "I'm scared."

"Of course you're scared. That's some scary shit right there, but that doesn't make it bad. You have people that care a lot about you, so there isn't anything to be scared about." Maggie pulled her hands away and looked down at her lap.

"How am I supposed to deal with this?" Maggie looked up again. "How am I supposed to tell my dad? God, how am I supposed to tell Diesel? We just slept together two weeks ago, have just started seeing each other, and now I have to drop this freaking bomb."

"Just calm down, Maggie." Mora didn't looked freaked out anymore, didn't even look like this was shocking anymore. She appeared in control, something that Maggie felt nothing like. "One thing at a time, okay?"

"How am I supposed to calm down when I just found this out? Not that I thought I'd be married first before I had kids, but Mora, I don't even have a place of my own, let alone a job." She covered her eyes with her hands and breathed out. "And working for my dad isn't something I see myself doing long term." Suddenly her head her, her stomach was in knots, and she felt like crying.

"Maggie, this isn't the end of the world."

"Easy for you to say." Maggie's words were muffled with her hands covering her face.

"Come on, you'll get through this like you get through everything else." Maggie dropped her hands and looked at her friend. "You don't give yourself enough credit for your strength. Look at how tough you have been after everything that has happened in the few months since you've been back in Steel Corner?" Mora smiled. "Did you ever see yourself getting with Diesel?" Mora shook her head, answering her own question. "No, but look at you now. I don't know much about the guy other than what I see around town and hear through the rumor mill, but I do know that the Grizzly MC is loyal, strong, and protect what's theirs. And you're Diesel's, Maggie. That baby growing inside of you is his. Do you actually think he would just walk away from that?"

Maggie didn't know what to say, because for how smart mouthed and easygoing Mora had always been, right now she spoke with determination in her voice.

"Of course this will be a shock to him and your dad, but everything will work out, honey."

They sat there for another twenty minutes, but they didn't really say much else. Maggie's food tasted bland, she felt hot and nauseous, and all she could think about was sitting her dad and Diesel down—of course not at the same time because that was just a war waiting to happen—and actually telling them. She wanted to believe Mora's words, that everything would be okay, and maybe there was a part of her that did know that. But there was also a part of her that couldn't help but worry that she would have to deal with this on her own, because sometimes life just didn't work out the way people wanted.

THE GRIZZLY MC: VOLUME TWO

Chapter Eleven

Diesel wiped the grease from his hands on an equally filthy rag. The sun was beating down above his head, and parts of the bike he was trying to restore were around him. This was definitely a work in progress seeing as the engine needed to be totally rebuilt as did the entire frame, but this was a passion of his and any other Grizzly MC member. It helped take his mind off the less pleasant things that happened in his life, and also helped to steer his thoughts away from Maggie. Not that he didn't want to think about her, but every time he did he got harder than a fucking steel pipe, and shit was that uncomfortable when he didn't have her around to help ease him.

He grabbed a wrench and started loosening some bolts. Drevin and Stinger were looking under the hood of the Dodge, and Court, Jagger, and Dallas were inside. The sound of Harleys in the near distance had him stopping what he was doing and rising. He heard at least four coming toward the clubhouse, but there shouldn't be any since the only member missing was Brick and that was because he was spending time with his old lady. Instantly his bear rose to the surface, and he sensed the other club members' animals rising, too. The clubhouse was more toward the edge of town with the thick evergreens on three sides of them, and the growth of the town in front of them. They had erected a fence around the perimeter of the building, but the front part was left open for everyone to come and go. Four Harleys pulled up to the gate, and a couple prospects looked over to the patched in members for permission to let them enter. Diesel looked at the patched in members behind him, and once they gave their nod of approval he did the same to the prospects. The gates were open, and the bikers drove up the driveway and parked when they were only a few feet from the entrance. As it was the actual clubhouse was like a damn fortress made of cement and wood on the outside. It kept everyone safe, for the most part because they did have that incident with Trick, the President of the Wolverines, busting in. But they had reinforced everything, patched up their weaknesses to make them stronger, and were now ready for anything that was thrown their way.

All four bikers dismounted and removed their helmets before making their way over to Diesel and the other members now standing behind him. Diesel recognized the man that led the other three bikes as the same one he had seen at the fight a few weeks back—The Brothers of Menace. The President, whom Diesel now knew was named Lucien, led his little pack toward Diesel and the other Grizzlies. He stopped a few feet away from Diesel, and the sound of the clubhouse front doors opening and closing told him that Jagger and the other members were heading their way.

"Who the hell are you, and what the fuck are doing in our town and at our clubhouse without giving us a heads-up?" Jagger stepped forward and stood toe-to-toe with Lucien.

"You know who I am," Lucien said, but Jagger didn't respond. "You and I both know you had some of your boys in River Run asking about us, checking up on what we have been doing and why we are here."

Again, Jagger didn't say anything.

"And yet you have the balls to ask us what we are doing in your town without letting *you* know?" Lucien chuckled, but it wasn't filled with humor, but instead had this almost sick satisfaction in the sound.

"I'm going to ask you again, and if you don't fucking tell me why you and your damn crew are in my town, and standing in front of my clubhouse, I'm going to unleash my bear on your ass." There was a collective shifting behind Diesel as the other members grew excited over the prospect of letting their animals out. These men were humans—huge for their fucking species—but they were still humans and no match for a shifter when in their animal mode.

"Listen, we didn't come here to start shit."

Jagger crossed his arms over his chest. Diesel took a step forward and eyed the bastard.

Lucien grinned at Diesel. "You were at that fight, right?"

"Just answer the fucking question before we take out all four of you and hide your bodies in the woods behind the clubhouse." That should have scared the shit out of these assholes, but instead there was absolutely no emotion that came from them. The scent of fear was absent. Yeah, these guys were cold motherfuckers.

"Well, you already know who I am, but I'll properly introduce myself as gentlemen do."

Diesel growled out. "I didn't see any fucking introductions when you showed up at one of our fights."

Lucien grinned, but didn't respond to what Diesel said. "I'm Lucien Silver." He pointed to his President patch like they were fucking morons. "And this is a small part of The Brothers of Menace." He grinned and started naming off the three members behind him. "Kink, Malice, and Tuck." Two of the patches on their cuts read Sergeant at Arms and V. President. The other guys looked like damn linebackers for how damn big they were. "I have a proposition for you and your crew, one that I can promise will make you a nice wad of cash."

Diesel looked over at Jagger.

"And all you have to do is help a fellow MC out."
He grinned, but it looked far more wolfish than
welcoming.

"We already have our hands full as it is, and
taking on anything else isn't that appealing."

Lucien didn't move or respond right away. He
looked between Jagger and Diesel. "What if I told you
that your club doesn't have to do anything aside from
allowing me and my crew to use the main road that runs
through Steel Corner?"

"All you want is the main road?" Jagger sounded
suspicious, but then again they weren't so stupid as to
think what this MC was transporting wasn't illegal.
Lucien nodded in response. "What are you hauling?"

Lucien turned around and looked at his guys. He
turned back around to face the Grizzlies. "We have some
precious cargo that we need to get into our town. All the
access roads that go into River Run are intersecting with
the highway, which is monitored by the Highway Patrol a
little too heavily for our taste. But there is a back road
that runs through three smaller towns, avoiding the
highway altogether, and eventually moves through your
town and into ours."

"You still didn't answer what you're hauling."

"You afraid of being associated with a little illegal
activity." It wasn't phrased as a question, because of
course he knew that they did illegal shit. If he didn't
know that then he wouldn't have been at the barn. Lucien
laughed, and it was filled with amusement this time. "But
we all know that our clubs thrive off the illegal shit."

"We don't associate with trafficking humans."

Lucien slowly sobered. "Neither do we."

Jagger looked over at Diesel before turning his
focus back on the bikers in front of them. "When you talk
about precious cargo I doubt you mean drugs or guns. So

the only other thing that comes to mind is you're in the sex trade business, and the Grizzlies don't mess with that shit either."

Lucien grinned again and tipped his chin in acknowledgment.

"No, we aren't in the guns and drug business, but we also don't deal with human trafficking." Lucien looked behind him, but they were far enough away from the main road that no one could hear. "Our girls are with us willingly, but we have a piece of property in Bainsworth that we take the girls to so they can meet up with high paying clients."

"What kind of men are these high paying clients?" Dallas jumped in, but it was a question they would have got to eventually.

"Senators, judges, cops. High profile professions. You name it, they come to us. But they are ones that don't want to be seen in River Run or associated with the club." Bainsworth was two towns over from Steel Corner, but it was an older town that had turned down having a turnoff to the highway. With that being the case it was more on the outskirts, so it was a smart move building their little "establishment" there.

"So you pimp these girls, and need our road to transport them to your little whorehouse?" Diesel asked.

Lucien turned his attention to him and nodded, but there was a spark of humor in his eyes. "Yes, if you want to put it crudely."

Diesel grunted. "Why sugarcoat what the fuck you're doing?" A dark mask covered Lucien's face, and Diesel grinned. Now they saw the real Brothers of Menace President.

"You just got out of coke hauling, right?" He didn't wait for an answer. "We haul willing pussy instead of drugs. Our girls are treated like gold, they are protected, and no one fucks with them, or they answer to us." There was a growl in the human's voice, reminiscent of the animals the Grizzlies harbored inside.

"What percentage are you offering?" Jagger diverted the clear anger that was brewing inside of Lucien. The human turned and looked at Jagger, but his annoyance was still visible.

"We do a run every Friday night. That is when the majority of the high rolling clientele come in. Your cut for just keeping out of our fucking way on those nights will be ten grand for the month." Stinger whistled behind them. That was a lot of fucking money to just turn the other way and not bust their balls for using their road. "You'll get paid on the first of every month. There might be a few times we might need to make special trips during the week, but these are usually done in the middle of the night." No one said anything for several seconds. "For those special circumstances I don't have much time to give you a heads-up, but you don't need to know about that anyway, right?" Lucien smirked. "You'll get two grand for those times, but that also is for all the girls that are taken back and forth on that night. Sometimes it is only one, and sometimes it is ten different trips. Your town won't be bothered, and won't even realize that we are passing through. We just need the asphalt and space to get our shit done."

"It isn't my call to make. We have to take a vote, you know that."

Lucien nodded slowly. "Yeah." He reached into his cut, took out a pen and a small slip of paper, and wrote his number on it. "I have my girls settling in over the next two weeks, so you have until then to decide."

"And what if the club votes it down?" Diesel asked. "You do know you'll be fucked or have to use the highway."

Lucien stared at him for a long fucking time, but he didn't say anything, just tilted his damn chin again, turned with the rest of his boys, and got on their bikes. No one moved as they watched them start their bikes and leave the clubhouse property, but when the sound of their engines faded in the distance Jagger turned and eyed all of them.

"Well, I guess we should vote on this shit since everyone is up to speed, everyone aside from Brick, but I'll give him a call and have him head up." Jagger didn't wait for anyone to respond, just turned and headed into the clubhouse. There was a moment when each of them looked at one another, and then everyone followed suit.

Twenty minutes later they all sat around the meeting table, Brick included.

"You all heard what The Brothers of Menace MC was offering, and Brick, you've been brought up to date."

Brick nodded.

"They want nothing but clear passage for their whores." Jagger looked at each of them. "Do you want to let them travel Steel Corner to get to Bainsworth, or tell them to fuck off?"

Brick sat there silently, Court ran his finger over the table, Stinger and Dallas had their attention on Jagger, and Drevin was lighting a cigarette.

"Well, let's hear it, brothers." Jagger leaned back in his chair.

One by one they said their vote, and when it got to Diesel all eyes were on him. "Yeah, let's go for it." The vote was unanimous, but no one showed their excitement in gaining a shit-ton of money for doing nothing. Even though this seemed easy enough, Diesel knew that nothing ever came for free. At some time he knew shit would hit the fan, and when it did it would be one big clusterfuck.

THE GRIZZLY MC: VOLUME TWO

Chapter Twelve

Maggie kept glancing at Diesel through the kitchen window of his cabin. He was grilling steaks for them, and she was a nervous wreck. It had only been a few days since she had found out she was pregnant, and this was the first time they had spent any time together since then. Diesel had been deep in club business—business that she was not privy to. But then, she didn't want to know any more about the Grizzly MC than what was on the surface. Call her ignorant, but she was a strong believer in if it wasn't broke don't attempt to fix it, and what was going on with them wasn't broke … at least not yet. She had yet to tell him about what would be gracing their lives in nine short months. Although she had gotten used to the fact she was pregnant, somewhat, it still wasn't nearly enough time for her to grasp all the little details that came along with being a mother. She worried a lot, and knew that would never stop, not even after the baby came, but what she feared most was having to do this alone. Sure she'd have her dad and Mora, but she didn't want her son or daughter having to grow up without a father, or an absentee one at that.

She had gotten the nerve to tell her dad the day after she found out, and that had been so damn hard. He hadn't yelled, hadn't lectured her on how she had ruined her life and how Diesel wouldn't stick around. All he had done was stay silent, shake his head, and tell her she was in for a very hard road. Did she believe him? Because he was her father there was a part of her that did, but she also knew that things had a way of looking up even when it was a very unsure time in someone's life. Diesel brought the steaks in and set them on the table. He looked up at her, and she watched as his eyes roamed up and down her body. She swallowed when she saw his expression turn to lust.

He walked around the table to where she was standing, wrapped his arms around her middle, and buried his face in her neck. "You have no idea how much I want you right now." He dragged his teeth up the side of her neck. "It has been a long time since I have felt you underneath me."

Maggie's nerves evaporated as she melted into the hardness of his body. He was wearing a plain t-shirt and a pair of worn jeans. He was barefoot, and she had glanced at his feet several times, never one for that part of a man's anatomy, but thinking that even his toes were sexy as sin. Even though he was fresh from a shower she could still smell the faint aroma of the leather that always seemed to cling to him, and the tangy scent of grease. The combination had her wet and needy, and all of her nerves seemed to evaporate, too. But she needed to talk to him, needed him to know everything.

"Diesel, it's only been a few days." She smiled, but that amusement left her and she sighed when he ran his tongue along her throat. A shiver of desire worked through her veins.

"Baby, that is a few days too long to be with you. It was torture. Pure fucking torture."

She couldn't help it. She laughed at the pained note in his voice.

"You wouldn't be laughing if you knew the pain I have endured." He squeezed his hands on her sides, and slowly moved them up until he was cupping her breasts through the material of her dress. She was wearing a cotton bra, which her nipples felt like they were stabbing through, and her matching panties felt soaked through already. He kneaded her flesh, teased her neck, and had her putty in his hands in seconds. "How about we go to the bed and we eat later?"

"The food will be cold by then, Diesel." She breathed out and let her head fall back against the wall.

He pressed his erection into her belly and ground the hardness into her softness. A small gasp left her, and she felt him grin against her skin.

"How about we bring dinner to bed and I can eat it off of your body?" He growled those words out at the same time he moved his hand to her dress strap and slowly slid it down. She was slowly losing her mind the longer he touched her. It was going to come down to the fact she wouldn't be able to think let alone talk by the time he got her to that bed, and that was most likely going to happen in the next several minutes.

"Diesel?"

He slipped off her other dress strap, pushed the top of her bodice down, and cupped her breasts through her bra. He moved them back toward the wall and ground his dick into her harder this time. "I want to be inside of you so fucking badly, Maggie." He pushed the cups of her bra down until her breasts popped free and he was touching her nude flesh. "I want to lick your pussy until you come all over my face, and then I'm going to kiss you, make you taste yourself all over my mouth."

She shivered and gripped onto his thick biceps.

"And then I'm going to slip my hand between your legs, pull your sweet, wet pussy lips apart, and guide my dick into your body."

"Oh God, Diesel. You can't say things like that." *Because I am about three seconds away from forgetting my name, let alone what I really need to say.*

"I want to hear you screaming those three words, baby." He went to lift the bottom of her dress up, but she needed to do this now before she got lost in the haze of arousal.

"Diesel, I'm pregnant."

He stilled instantly, and for a second only held her. Slowly he pulled away and looked down at her with this inscrutable expression.

She swallowed, her lust instantly being buried as her wariness and nervousness came forward. She nodded and repeated herself. "I'm pregnant. I just found out a few days ago. It was when I went to the clinic and got tested…" God, this conversation was getting uncomfortable, and she wished it wasn't. She knew it would be a hard thing to bring up, maybe even a very hard thing for Diesel to accept, but she didn't expect for him to just stand there and stare at her. She couldn't even gauge his reaction because he had this stoic mask covering his face. He didn't move, didn't drop his hands away from her, and she supposed that was either a good thing or this big, bad biker was in shock. "Diesel?" She licked her lips and swallowed through the lump that was lodged in her throat.

"You're pregnant." He didn't phrase it like a question, but she nodded anyway. "And you found this out a few days ago." Again, not a question.

"It's your baby." Maggie didn't know why she said that, but she supposed there was a part of her that worried maybe he would deny that it was his since she had clearly gotten pregnant on what she thought was a one-night stand. And then because he wasn't saying anything she felt her damn tears start to form. But before even one could spill he had her in his arms and was leading them toward the bed. It took only a matter of seconds for them to reach it, and even less time for him to get her undressed. Maggie was so stunned by what was happening that all she could do was stand there and let him gently touch her like he thought she would break. There she stood, now completely naked and in front of Diesel who was still fully clothed, and the only thing she could hear was the sound of her beating heart. But he didn't lay her on the bed and cover her body with his like she thought he might. Instead he surprised her to the point that she swore her heart stopped right in her chest.

He dropped to his knees in front of her, placed both of his hands on her belly, and leaned in. For several moments all she felt was the warm puffs of his breath on her bare skin, and could only hear the sound of him inhaling and exhaling. Although neither said anything, this was a powerful moment, and no words were needed.

"My baby." He kissed her stomach only once at first, but then kissed her over and over again, making sure to cover every inch of her flesh.

She felt her knees grow weak and had to sit on the bed before she collapsed. So much emotion was going through her that she couldn't even control the tears that fell down her cheeks. Diesel looked up at her.

"Maggie, why are you crying?" He leaned in and kissed her cheeks, and then ran his tongue along the trails they had made in a slow, very gentle caress.

She tasted the saltiness of those tears on his tongue. "I don't know. I just feel so—"

"Moved?" He kissed her a few more times.

She nodded.

"Yeah, me, too, but also so much more." He trailed kisses along her jaw and down her neck. "I want to hold you, Maggie, just hold you, baby."

She nodded, because that was what she wanted, too, so very much. He moved away only long enough to shed his clothes, and then he was moving onto the bed beside her. His naked body was a hard machine that could do some serious damage, but when he used it with her it only brought pleasure. They lay back on the bed, and he kissed her long and slow, but also moved his hand to her belly and rubbed it. "My baby is in there." To say it was a bit strange to hear and see this softer side of Diesel was an understatement.

She loved the badass biker she was falling for, but she melted at this gentle side of him, too. "This isn't the reaction I thought I would get from you."

He didn't respond, but instead gripped her waist and pulled her so she was forced to straddle him. With one leg on either side of his waist, and his long, thick cock hard between them, pushing against her pussy and making her even wetter and having her arousal climb once more, Maggie knew she wanted him right now.

"Be with me, Diesel." He had his hands on her hips and lifted her easily from him enough that she could take hold of his cock and adjust him so the tip was at her entrance.

"You're mine, Maggie."

She started to press down on him, felt her lips part around his girth, and closed her eyes as pleasure and pain mixed as one. She felt full, so very full, that it was hard getting all of him inside of her even though she was soaking wet.

"You were mine before I found out you carried my baby, but now there is no going back, Maggie."

She pressed all the way down until their bodies met, and he groaned at the same time she sighed in pleasure.

"I won't let you go, won't let anyone else have you."

She shook her head, not because she disagreed with him, but because he chose that moment to thrust his hips up. It felt so good, so unbelievable euphoric that she knew she would come within minutes.

"No male will have you but me, Maggie." He thrust up again, and she bounced slightly. "Say it. Tell me you are mine irrevocably."

She rose up and then pushed down. "I'm yours. *God*, I am yours." Over and over she did this, and gradually went faster and faster. But before she could explode Diesel rolled them over so she was on her back, her thighs open wide to accommodate his large frame, and now he was the one fucking her.

"Yes, Maggie, you are mine."

She came long and hard, and Diesel picked up speed, thrusting in and out of her like a madman. He cursed something low and unintelligible, and then he was coming long and hard, too. She felt the hard jets of his cum fill her, heard the wet sounds of his groin slapping against hers, and then he was collapsing on top of her as his climax ended. They lay there panting, with him over her, their bodies still fused together, and their hearts beating the same frantic tempo.

"I think I've fallen madly in love with you, Maggie." His words were muffled against her hair, but she had heard him as clear as day. He leaned back and looked in her eyes, brushed her hair away from her face, and smiled. "Yeah, I've fallen pretty fucking hard for you, baby."

She stayed quiet for a few seconds, and then let her smile cover her face as relief filled her. "I'm glad I'm not the only one."

He burst out laughing, and she knitted her brows in confusion.

"Baby, that is not what a male wants to hear when he lays his heart out for his female."

She couldn't help but smile. "I'm falling in love with you, too, Diesel. Pretty damn hard actually."

He chuckled again and leaned down to kiss her. "Well, I hope you're in for one hell of a ride, because I think that is what we are in for." He rolled off of her and pulled her close to him so their bodies were still touching. "You're my old lady, and there isn't anyone, or anything that is going to change that."

The End

DEDICATION

To the readers. You guys are amazing, and without your support I wouldn't be able to continue with my dream of writing. Thank you!

THE GRIZZLY MC: VOLUME TWO

NOTHIN' BUT TROUBLE

The Grizzly MC, 4

Jenika Snow

Copyright © 2014

Chapter One

Lilly Winters had always heard that Court Devlin was "nothin' but trouble." Of course he was trouble. He was a classic bad boy bear shifter, didn't give a shit what anyone thought, and did whatever the hell he wanted to. But that didn't stop Lilly from wanting him with a fierceness that rivaled anything else. Of course wanting and actually getting were two very different things.

The music was loud, and Lynard Skynard belted out "Free Bird" through the speakers someone had placed beside the lake. Lilly sat on the back of Court's motor oil smelling and rusted-out pickup truck, her feet dangling off the tailgate, and the big muscular bear shifter right beside her. This had been a bad idea coming to this party. She was only eighteen, and if her older brother Roan found out she was here, let alone hanging out with his best friend, he'd probably shit bricks. But Lilly didn't care. Court Devlin might have been a constant presence in her life for as long as she could remember, and he might even be ten years older than she was, but she had wanted him to be her first, had always wanted him to be her first. Shit, she had wanted him to be her everything. But Court wasn't the type of guy that did relationships, and she had found that out when she really understood what her feelings for the huge, muscular bear shifter were.

She looked over at him, and although it was dark and the only light that there was came from the huge bonfire across from them, she could see him perfectly. His big hands were stained with grease, as were his faded and worn blue jeans. His blond hair was on the longer side, just brushing the tops of his ears, as if he hadn't gotten it cut in a while, but didn't give a shit regardless. That was one of the things she liked about Court so much. He just didn't care what others thought.

When she had seen him at the party flirting with one of the girls she had gone to high school with, the jealousy she had felt had been so damn annoying. Of course Lilly knew she had no claim on him, but dammit, she hated seeing him with Alana. That girl was a slut with a capital whore. She watched as Court brought his bottle of whisky to his mouth and took a long swallow. He glanced over at her, and even with the shadows covering his face she saw how glossy his eyes looked, despite the redness that surrounded them from drinking all night. He was drunk, obviously. He handed her the bottle, and she was so surprised that she actually reached out and took it.

"Roan would hand me my ass on a platter if he knew I was letting his baby sister drink."

Lilly tipped the bottle back, and as soon as the alcohol slid down her throat she coughed and gagged.

Court chuckled beside her and snatched the bottle away. "That'll put hair on your chest for sure."

She wiped her mouth with the back of her hand. "The only thing going on in my chest is that I just swallowed gasoline."

He was grinning at her, but brought the bottle to his mouth again and took another sip.

"I think I'll stick with beer." She grabbed her cheap can of beer from beside her and held it up. "I like not having hair on my chest, by the way." She glanced in front of her at the fire, but felt his eyes on her. When she looked back at him it was to see Court staring at her chest. The shirt she wore was a plaid, tight button up, and she had left the top half of the buttons undone since she wore a camisole underneath. Instantly her nipples tightened at the fact he was staring at her chest. There was no freaking doubt about that.

He seemed to catch himself, shook his head, and looked away. "Yeah, your brother is going to kick my ass for sure." His words were heavily slurred, and she saw his attention move back to where Alana was giggling with a bunch of her other equally slutty friends. Lilly didn't know what made her do it, but she placed her hand on his thigh. He snapped his head in her direction and looked down at where her hand was. "What are you doing, Lilly?" He was holding the neck of the bottle so tight she could see the skin of his knuckles stretched taut.

She looked down at his crotch, saw that he was most definitely hard, and swallowed the sudden lump she had in her throat. Lilly couldn't even claim to be drunk and that that was why she was going to do what she planned on doing. Aside from that one swallow of fire-water she had just consumed, she had been nursing the same beer, now lukewarm, for the last hour. No, she was sober as all get-out, and suddenly had a set of steel balls.

"Lilly?" There was a hitch in Court's deep voice, but she didn't let it stop her from doing what she had wanted to do since she was a little girl. Leaning forward, she rested her other hand on the tailgate, lifted up slightly, and had her lips on his before he could stop her. She pulled back after a second, ran her tongue along her bottom lip, and tasted the alcohol that had been on his lips. Her heart jumped behind her ribs. The kiss probably could have been construed as *almost* innocent, but there was this very heated look in his eyes that had a small sound escaping her. The sound of the bottle he held hitting the ground with a *thump* preceded Court's next move.

He speared his hand in her hair, gripped the strands in a fierce hold, and pulled her forward. Mouth now on hers once more, he speared his tongue past the seam of her lips and pressed it against hers. Lilly was so shocked that he was the one that initiated this kiss, and that he hadn't just gotten the hell out of there after she made a move on him, that she was frozen in place for several seconds. But Court continued to kiss her, licked at her lips, sucked on her tongue, and had her becoming so damn wet that her panties were soaked clean through. He went to pull away, but she gripped his broad, massive shoulders, curled her nails into his flesh, and pulled him closer. At that moment she didn't think about all the people around them, possibly watching what they were doing, didn't think about how pissed her brother would be if he knew she was doing anything remotely sexual with Court. She just let herself feel something incredible.

Her nipples were hard, stabbed through the layers of her clothing, and rubbed painfully against the material. He groaned against her mouth and cupped both sides of her face, tilting her head so he could deepen the kiss. Their breaths mingled together, heated, humid, and so frantic that she couldn't decipher who was panting more harshly.

He broke the kiss and murmured, "We shouldn't be doing this, Lilly." Court trailed his lips along her cheek, down her jawline, and started running his teeth over her pulse, which was beating fast and hard beneath her ear.

"No, I really think we should."

He groaned against her neck, and she let her head fall back as he slid his hands from her face, onto her shoulders, and continued a downward path until he was covering both breasts with his big hands. A moan slipped from between her lips, and she held onto his shoulders tighter. It felt so good. *He* felt so good. Endorphins were pounding through her bloodstream, and she felt high from them, euphoric, and courageous enough to go further. Sliding her hands over his chest, she felt his hard muscles jump beneath her palms. There was so much definition beneath his worn t-shirt that all she wanted to do was rip it off and memorize every inch of his chest.

"If you knew what I want to do to you right now, you'd knee me in the balls and run far and fast." He bit the side of her throat and a gasp of pain left her, but on the heels of that was this incredible spark of pleasure that slammed right between her legs. Her clit pounded with every beat of her heart, and her pussy was so wet she couldn't stand it any longer.

"I am so wet for you, Court."

That had him stilling and slowly moving back to look in her face. He looked really damn drunk, but that didn't stop her from leaning in that small inch and kissing him as deeply as he had kissed her. Maybe she should feel shameful for pushing this. He was intoxicated, after all, but she couldn't find it in herself to stop it. Was she taking advantage of him? She didn't know because he was on her as much as she was on him. *He would stop if he really wanted to, right? God, stop thinking and just enjoy this moment.*

"You have no idea what hearing you say that does to me." Oh, she had a pretty good idea. He broke their kiss and looked at the bed of his truck. There were blankets strewn across the back, thick looking ones that had her thinking of all the really sexual things they could be doing on them. "This isn't right." He said that but had his eyes lowered so he could look at her chest. Could he see how hard she was? She looked down as well, but it was at his lap where she could see the *very* impressive bulge that looked almost uncomfortable.

"It feels right."

He looked back at her face and a low, animalistic sound left him. There was no doubt that this guy was all bear. He may look human, but he was built like a tank, taller than the majority of the guys she had ever been around, and stronger than an entire football team. To say he was masculine was the understatement of the century.

So, knowing that what she was about to say was more than she had ever had the courage to utter … to any guy, she took a deep breath and just went for it. "I want you to fuck me." The sound that came from him this time was so raw, so low, that she felt the vibrations right down to her clit. She grew even more moist, swollen, and ready for him.

He wrapped his arm around her waist, hauled her up and onto his lap, and took her mouth in a brutal kiss that had their lips pressing together and their teeth clashing. And before she knew what was happening she was on her back in the bed of the truck, the blankets indeed thick, and Court's huge body covering hers. The way his truck was parked at an angle would make it impossible for anyone to actually see what they were doing since they were lying down, but Lilly wouldn't have cared anyway.

Court used one of his knees to kick her legs open. He was forceful with the action, and with his kissing, and Lilly felt highly feminine. She might only be eighteen, but she had never wanted anything more than to be dominated by this big, burly bear shifter. He positioned himself between her now splayed thighs, and her jean shorts rode up her legs. The seam right in the middle was pressed hard against the cleft of her pussy as he ground his denim-clad cock against her. Over and over, he thrust against her, pumped his hips like he was really fucking her, and having her perilously close to coming. He hadn't even penetrated her, or touched her below the waist, and she was ready to have an orgasm from dry humping alone.

"Are you sure about this, Lilly?" he said against the base of her throat.

"God, yes." Would she regret this in the morning? Hell no, but there was a little voice in the back of her head that said this could ruin everything.

"At least one of us is." He had said the words low, and they were muffled against her throat, but she had heard him. He had been speaking to himself, there was no doubt about that. Pushing at his shoulders was really hard, physically and mentally on her part, but she wanted to make sure that he at least was conscious of who he was sleeping with. He stared down at her with glossy eyes that were half-lidded.

"I'm not forcing you to do anything."

He closed his eyes and hung his head, and for several seconds stayed that way. But when he lifted his head once more and looked at her, she was shocked to see that his normally green eyes were now black, and that had nothing to do with the shadows that surrounded them.

"No, you're not forcing me, but once we do this there is no going back." His chest rose and fell, and she swore she was talking to his animal right now. His voice was deep, slightly distorted, and very harsh.

"Just fuck me." Maybe not the most eloquent way to put it, but she was so aroused she couldn't think straight, and had been this way for far too long. It was all because of this guy.

"You got a fucking mouth on you, girl. I think you been hanging around your brother and me—"

She rose up and braced her upper body on her elbows, and cut him off with a kiss. No way in hell was she talking about Roan at a time like this. Besides, Court would think on that and decide that this really was a bad idea, because if her brother did find out he'd go Rambo on both of their asses. Bracing her body on just one elbow now, she lifted her hand and gripped the back of his neck. She adjusted her body so she could move her other hand between their bodies and undo the button of her shorts. He broke away, moved back so he was on his knees, and was undoing his own jeans, too. Lilly lifted her ass and slid her panties and shorts down. And then when she had one of her legs free from them, she lay down on her back once more and watched with heat rising to the surface of her skin as Court pushed his jeans down only past his hips, grabbed his cock and stroked himself from root to tip.

Being a virgin Lilly wasn't an expert on dicks up close and personal, had done the whole Sex-Ed thing in school, and watched some pornos with her friends, but nothing could have prepared her for what Court had been packing between his thighs. His dick was thick and long, with the tip round and wider than his shaft. And his balls, holy shit, were his balls big, but then again everything else on the man's body was colossal.

"If you keep looking at me like that I won't be able to go slow with you, Lilly." He reached behind him, grabbed his wallet from his back pocket, and took a condom out. Watching him roll that latex on his erection should not have been as arousing as it was. He moved back between her legs, but he didn't push into her right away. He placed his hand on her pussy, and a moan left her at the feel of the heat that came from his fingers. "You're so fucking wet for me." He started moving those digits up and down, faster and harder until she licked her lips, gripped onto the blankets beside her, and bit her lip to hold off from moaning. She couldn't speak, but she nodded at his statement. "*Christ,* you're so ready for my cock, aren't you, baby?"

"Yeah." She said that word so low that she didn't even know if he heard her, but he closed his eyes and groaned, and she knew he had. For several seconds all he did was move two fingers up and down her cleft, rub her clit back and forth when he got to the little nub, and then move back down. Then when she was about to scream for him to shove his cock inside of her he lifted his hand between them, and to her utter shock brought those digits to his mouth and sucked every last drop of her wetness from them.

Lilly could do nothing but stare at him with what she knew were wide eyes. God, he was making her wetter. He finally stopped, and she found herself sighing in relief. If he had kept that up a minute longer she would have come before he even slid inside of her. He then leaned down and kissed her, speared his tongue into her mouth so she could taste herself on him, and grunted when she nipped his lip. Pulling back from her, he gripped himself and placed the head of his shaft at her entrance. Lilly couldn't breathe as she looked into his face, one that had this hard mask covering it, and this wild quality to it. His eyes were so very dark, and she swore she could see his muscles grow thicker right before her eyes. This wasn't just the man she had wanted for so long, but his bear, too. And while he held her gaze with his own he started to push inside of her.

A gasp left her at the feel of him pushing that huge and thick length into her. She wasn't going to be one of those girls that looked at a dick and said it wouldn't fit, because obviously she knew it would, but she was one of those girls that *would* say he was big enough that he would have to work his cock into her body, and it sure as hell would be a tight fit.

He was stretching her to the point that the pain and pleasure mingled as one, and this burning sensation encompassed her entire body until she felt like she would suffocate from the intensity of it. Sweat beaded along his brow, and the low grunts he made were so arousing that she lifted her ass, trying to take more of him. But he placed a hand on her hip, hard enough that it was uncomfortable, but still felt so good. He was hardly inside of her, but having him just stay there, barely lodged in her pussy, was torture.

"You can't do shit like that or I'll come before I bottom out inside of your cunt." Lord, his filthy and crass words should not have made her wetter, but they did. She hadn't told him this was her first time, but didn't intend on mentioning it either. To some guys that was an instant turn-off, and they had already gone too far for to stop this because he didn't want to be her first. So, before he continued with this slow shit, she reached up and grabbed a chunk of his hair, pulled him down to her mouth, and kissed him to make sure he knew that she wanted this more than anything else. He groaned against her lips, and in one hard, quick thrust, buried himself fully inside of her. A gasp left her, but it wasn't from the pleasure she had felt up until this point, but because when he broke through her hymen that shit hurt.

He pulled back and looked down at her with knitted brows. Could he tell she had been a virgin? She assumed guys could, but it wasn't like she had firsthand experience with it, well, up until now. So, before he started saying anything, she wrapped her legs around his lean hips, causing him to slide in another inch, and the way his expression morphed into ecstasy she knew she had him where she wanted him. God, Lilly almost felt bad for doing this, because clearly he had second thoughts about this, and then she hadn't told him she was a virgin. But he was hard, had kissed her back, and what was the point of stopping it when they had gone this far? Him stopping now would only have her burying her head in the sand and waiting for the ground to open up and swallow her.

"Lilly—"

She shook her head, stopping him from continuing. "Please, Court, just kiss me." His chest rose and fell, and she slipped her hands under his t-shirt and felt the hard, smoothness of his chest. She could feel the ridges of his six-pack, and when she moved her hands up she felt the definition of his pecs. He closed his eyes and groaned, and then started moving in and out of her. When he opened his eyes he stared at her for several long seconds, but each time he thrust deep into her his bear shifted across his face. The stretch and burn of having something so large inside of her gave way to this euphoric sensation that claimed every inch of her. Sweat started to dot his brow, and she felt perspiration slide between her breasts. He covered her body with his and buried his face in the crock of her neck. His breathing was hard, and the humidity from it made her hotter, but not in an uncomfortable way. The discomfort and pain of him being inside of her and taking her virginity waned, and the pleasure started to take control. The hard pants of his warm, humid breath along her throat had her turning her head to the side, needing his mouth. He didn't deny her, and they kissed hard and fast, swirled their tongues together, and moaned into each other's mouths.

Court was pounding into her frantically now, and the truck rocked back and forth. She heard a few male catcalls come from the distance, and although they might not be able to see what they were doing, the rocking of the truck was a pretty good sign as to what was going on. But Lilly didn't care, because she was caught up in this moment, and it was better than she could have ever imagined. Court was making hard groaning noises, and the low, almost inaudible filthy things he said echoed in her ear. There was a tightness that started at the base of her spine, and it grew to the point that she knew this explosion would happen inside of her and she knew it wouldn't take much more to get her off.

"You're so fucking tight and hot, Lilly." He groaned against her when she clenched her inner muscles around his cock. "God, I have never felt anything like this before." With every inward thrust the root of his shaft rubbed her clit, sending her closer and closer to exploding.

Lights danced behind her closed lids, and she curled her nails into his back. The hiss that came from him had her loosening her hold and murmuring her apologies through her breathless sighs.

"No, dig your nails into me, and make it hurt so fucking good."

A gasp left her when he slammed into her especially hard, and at his words. Her orgasm was climbing higher and higher, and as if something opened inside of her, or more aptly a dam had just broken and drowned her in pleasure, she bit her lip and cried out because it felt so good. Neck arched, throat bared, and moaning out as she climaxed, Lilly couldn't grasp reality. Court made this rough noise, and she felt him grab one of her breasts, curve his hand around the mound, and then bite her neck. The sting of pain from him digging his teeth into the side of her throat seemed to set off another chain of smaller orgasms, and she tried to stifle the cry that bubbled up.

"Fuck, Lilly. *Christ*, I'm going to come." Her neck was wet from him licking and sucking at her, and her pussy was so juicy that not even the loud music or the sound of all the people around them could drown out the noise of them fucking. He grunted and groaned against her, and picked up his speed. He pumped into her once, twice, and on the third time slammed his dick hard inside of her and came on a gruff sound. His big body was so tense above her, and his muscles constricted and relaxed repeatedly. Lilly swore she could feel his cock swell even further. He sagged on top of her, and for several seconds they lay there, neither speaking, but both trying to gasp for air.

Court pulled out of her body and lay beside her. Soon their breathing returned to normal, but all the silence made her feel uncomfortable. She turned to look at him, but he sat up, adjusted himself so the condom was now off and his pants were on, and moved to sit on the tailgate. With his back now to her, Lilly had expected things to change between them, but shit, she really didn't think it would have been as soon as he pulled his dick out of her. She lifted her hips and pulled up her panties and shorts, and then hesitantly moved to sit beside him. He reached down and grabbed two beers, and handed one to her.

The sound of Court popping the top of his beer off seemed overly loud, and there was this uncomfortableness that surrounded them. She glanced at him and said, "Court, are you upset?"

He didn't say anything at first, just brought his beer bottle to his mouth and tipped it back. He drank half of it in one swallow. When he rested the bottle on his thigh and stared in front of him at the bonfire. "I'm not upset, Lilly." He said it low, and this chill worked over her body.

"Then why are you acting like this all of the sudden?"

He drank the rest of his beer and tossed it in the back of the truck, right where he had fucked her. He turned and looked at her, and the stoic expression on his face had her clamping her jaw. "Because I didn't just fuck my best friend's little sister, I also popped her cherry."

Her stomach cramped at the hard way he said those words.

"I am drunk, Lilly. I don't really want to think about this right now." Court scrubbed a hand over his jaw.

"Yo, Court. We got a fat ass blunt over here." A group of older guys called for Court, and to her embarrassment and shame—as if she really meant nothing—he hopped off the truck and stalked over to them. Before he moved too far away he stopped and looked over at her.

"You good to get yourself home?"

Okay, so she hadn't expected him to profess his love to her or anything afterward, but she certainly hadn't thought he would act like this. She nodded because she couldn't find the strength or courage to actually say anything. He tipped his chin in acknowledgment, and she swore for just a split second he looked like he hesitated, and like he might come back to her.

"Come on, man." But then his friends called for him again, and he turned and left her sitting there on the back of his truck. She felt the wetness between thighs from her own arousal, and no doubt the blood that was spilled from giving him her virginity. But she couldn't get mad at Court, not really. She had known things would most definitely be different, knew that he was drunk, and knew that sleeping with him wasn't the best idea. But her hormones and her feelings for him had clouded everything else until the only thing that mattered was giving herself to him.

For a few minutes she stared at him with his group of friends as they passed the joint around. She could hear them talking, but they were a good distance away, so she couldn't understand what they said. But Court never looked back at her, and that was okay, because right now she was feeling pretty damn stupid.

Lilly hopped off the back of the truck, made sure her clothes were good to go and it didn't just look liked she got screwed, and walked away from the party. Her house was a good ten minute drive from the lake, but she would just walk it. Steel Corner was a quiet, relatively safe town anyway, and besides, she didn't feel like being around anyone.

Yeah, she really screwed up, but did she regret it, even after the way Court had grown cold and distant? No, she didn't. It was just going to be one of those memories that she locked up tight, and remembered herself in the moment, and not all the shit that happened afterward,

Chapter Two

Five years later

Court sat at the club table, one leg outstretched in front of him, and an arm on the smooth wood. Jagger was talking about The Brothers of Menace, the MC that had moved into the next town over.

"Lucien called and said tonight will be the first run for them. They need the street cleared out, and for us to stick to our end of the deal and look the other way." It had been a few weeks since The Grizzly MC had made the deal with The Brothers of Menace to allow them to use the main road that ran through Steel Corner—Grizzly territory. The payback was a hefty sum, and all they had to do was to turn their heads when Lucien and his guys chauffeured their girls to a house they had in a smaller town to fuck some higher-ups.

"He gave us the first cut, so on our end we are good to go," Stinger said around his joint.

"They are going to use the road, but for the first few runs they make I want some of our guys watching it and making sure all they are doing is passing through."

Court nodded, as did the rest of the club members.

Since Lucien, the President of The Brothers of Menace, had made the deal with them they had been on good terms. Essentially that meant Lucien and his men— all humans— stayed in their town, and the only time they would pass through Grizzly territory was when they were making these pussy calls.

"I'll keep an eye out," Court offered, and Jagger nodded.

"I want Stinger with you. Be at the center of town at two in the morning. Lucien said that's when they are making the pass through." There was a collective grunt of acknowledgment.

"You want us to follow them out to their fuck pad?" Stinger asked and blew out a mouthful of smoke.

Jagger shook his head. "No, I don't want shit going downhill before it even starts. I just want to make sure that things run smoothly. We have only known this MC for a few weeks, and although we did the digging on them and know they are a bunch of Nomads starting their own charter, I still don't want to stir shit or give them a lot of slack." Jagger tapped his fingers on the table and looked at each of them. "Just keep your eyes open." They all nodded in agreement, and everyone got up to leave.

"Man, you want to hit up the titty bar?"

Court looked over at Stinger. The other bear shifter had gotten a haircut, and the normally long dark hair now brushed his collar. He was out of the sling for his gunshot wound, and although he wasn't handling the club money much anymore since that job had been handed to Darra, Stinger was still the expert when it came to money and numbers. When Court didn't answer right away Stinger spoke again. "Come on, man. I'm sick of the club pussy, Court. I want to hit up the titty bar and find a little pussy that hasn't been passed around the club a hundred times."

Court scrubbed his hand over his jaw, felt the three-day stubble coat his skin, and nodded. "Yeah man, I could go for something a little different too." Especially since he had seen Lilly Winters up close and personal in town the other day, and all of his emotions for her had come back full force. She hadn't seen him, he had made damn sure about that. He couldn't look in her blue eyes without wanting her. Time had been really fucking good to her. She was all curves, big tits, and a lush mouth. He could even remember what she tasted like, and what her tight pussy had felt like when he fucked the virgin right out of her. He was a sick bastard for still wanting a piece of her, and a piece of shit friend for letting it get as far as it had all those years ago. He had stayed away, become a prospect for The Grizzly MC for a year, and then patched in. This was his family now, the club, and the members within it.

That was the best thing he could have done for himself, Lilly, and Roan. Because there was no fucking way he could look in his best friend's face, knowing he had slept with his baby sister—fucked her in the back of his grungy truck at a field party—and not feel like shit. But he had tried to talk to Roan, albeit the conversation had been awkward and distant. When he had found out their mother, Diera, had become sick he had gone to see her. She had been like a mother to him while growing up when his own had been shitty and absent.

He wished he could have been a better friend to Roan, and a better person to their family. Shit, the past had a good way of holding onto a person that was for sure. But still, that didn't help him with how he felt now. He was a bastard in the worst kind of way.

He followed Stinger out of the clubhouse, and they got on their bikes.

"Where you guys headed?" Dallas was leaning against the side of the building lighting up a cigarette. Ever since that shit had gone down with him and Diesel there had been a lot of tension, but then one day it was like things just worked themselves out. There was still this darkness that clearly came from the other bear, but Dallas kept to himself, and when anyone had asked him what the problem was he had dismissed it; but they didn't pry. If Dallas wanted to talk, they were there, and if not, well, they still got their shit done.

"Titty bar for some fresh pussy," Stinger called out as he put his helmet on. Court wouldn't have considered the titty bar the best place to get "fresh pussy", but he knew what the other male was saying. "You want to hit it up with us?"

Dallas took a few puffs from his cigarette and snubbed it out. "Might as well. I think I've had the females in the club ten times over."

Stinger grunted, as if he knew exactly what Dallas was saying. Shit, they all felt that way at some point. But pussy was pussy, and it served its purpose for a few pleasurable, mindless hours. The club whores knew what they were getting into when they came to be a Grizzly girl. And if they didn't like it they were more than welcome to get the fuck out. Which none of them ever did.

Dallas walked over and straddled his bike, and the three of them cranked the engines. Court let the purr of the bike underneath soothe him- it always did, and he knew it always would. They pulled away from the clubhouse and headed to Summer's for some ass shaking and some pussy grinding.

****

Exhausting, heartbreaking, and sad.

All of those things summed up Lilly's life pretty well.

She sat at her mother's rusted and fading table, watched as her mom divided her pills for the week in one of those daily medication holders, and suddenly felt really damn tired. At the age of twenty-three she had done absolutely nothing in her life. Aside from the few classes she took at the River Run Career Center in the next town over, she lived a pretty boring, if not exhausting life. But she couldn't complain too much because most of her time was spent taking care of her mom. Diera Winters was a good person, had done a lot for the church in town when she had been in better health, and was still volunteering for things even though she tired easily. With her older brother working ridiculous hours just to help pay his and their mom's bills, he had a lot on his plate, too. Her mother may have cancer, but she certainly didn't let that stop her from doing the things she loved or taking handouts, and there had been plenty of those since her health had gone downhill. Even now, as Lilly looked at her mom, she could see the vibrant life that had once been inside of Diera. But the medication and treatment that she was currently under made her look older and just plain tired.

"What's wrong?" Her mother asked.

Lilly looked at her mom.

"You are thinking pretty hard." She smiled at Lilly and popped the last pill into the medication container.

Lilly took a sip of her tea and set the cup down, smiling. "Yeah, but it was just random stuff."

Her mom didn't like talking about her sickness. It wasn't a secret, obviously, but Diera thought it best to think positively, speak about happy things, and live life to the fullest. It was hard to think positively when Lilly could see the effect this life was having on her mom. She had lost all of her hair, but wore a beautiful wig that was the same dark brown as her hair had been. Although Diera hadn't wanted it at first when Lilly brought it home, she had seen the smile on her lips when she held it. It wasn't about trying to look "normal" but about just feeling better.

"You do realize that I am your mom and know when you're full of shit."

Lilly started laughing and nodded. "Yeah, I know."

Diera reached across the table and patted her hand. Today was a good day. Her mom could actually get out of bed, wasn't throwing up, and was even smiling.

"I'm feeling good today, and called Roan to see if he wanted to come over for dinner." She pushed the pill box away, and her smile widened.

"What?" Lilly asked, suddenly very interested in what her mom was going to say.

"He said he is seeing someone new."

Lilly rolled her eyes and leaned back in her seat.

"I know, I know, but he acted really excited about bringing her over tonight."

Roan Winters, her older brother, and the other person she leaned on for strength, was a good man, but he was also a slut. "Mom, how many girlfriends has he had?" Although Lilly knew her mother knew the answer, Diera didn't answer, which had Lilly laughing. "Yeah, a lot but he never seems to keep them around for more than, I don't know, like a week it seems."

"Oh, Lilly, go easy on him. He's just one of those guys who attracts a lot of female attention. He looks so much like your dad when he was that age that it isn't a wonder."

There was this silly smile on her mom's face, and she always got it when she brought up Davis Winters, their father and her husband. He had died in a car accident when Lilly was really little, and she didn't have a lot of memories of their time together. But her mom had told her story after story about her dad, so many in fact that Lilly could close her eyes and imagine that she had been right there experiencing it too.

"Well, I hope you don't get your hopes up when it comes to him settling down. I think I heard him say a hundred times that he had no intention of ever going down that road." Lilly started laughing and stood. She grabbed her cup of tea and her mom's coffee cup, and took them to the sink.

"I thought it might be nice if I reached out to Court and saw if he wanted to come to dinner, too."

Lilly stilled and looked over at her mom. "What? Why?" Lilly's hands shook, but she forced herself to relax.

Her mom shrugged, but smiled. "I don't know. I have been thinking about him lately, and it's been forever since the three of us have been at the same table." Her mom moved up behind her and set her medicine on the counter.

"Mom, it's been a long time, and you know he and Roan don't really talk anymore." Lilly's nerves were working overtime in her. She hadn't told anyone that she had slept with Court, not even her best friend at the time. The fear that Alexandria would have opened her mouth by accident, or when she was trashed, had Lilly too fearful that it would get back to Roan and Court. Her brother would have gotten pissed. By that time Court had already distanced himself, and she hadn't wanted to make it any worse.

"Honey, if it'll make you uncomfortable then I won't. It was just a thought."

Lilly wiped her suddenly now sweaty hands on jeans and shook her head. "What do you mean? I'm fine. Invite whoever you want."

"Lilly, you're starting to sweat. Are you sure everything is okay?"

"Mom, I'm fine. Just nervous because we have a clinical tonight, and they are having a bunch of volunteers come in to be our human pincushions."

Her mother was watching her very intently, and Lilly knew that she didn't believe her, but she didn't press her.

"Well, it was just a thought. But it is short notice, so maybe I'll ask him another time." Diera put a piece of hair behind Lilly's ear and smiled. "You'll be home by six tonight?"

"I'm not sure." Lilly took a deep breath and felt herself calm. She didn't know why she had freaked out so bad at the thought of Court eating dinner with them. He had practically been a fourth family member while they had been growing up together. "I hope, but it depends on how slow everyone is with their blood draws, and if anyone passes out." She attempted some humor to ease her frantic emotions inside of her, but she just sounded like a high-pitched freak. Her mom wrinkled her nose in disgust. "I asked Roan to be my human pincushion, but he is a pussy."

"Lilly, I don't want to hear you say things like that." Her mom was smiling though, so although she tried to sound stern, it didn't quite reach the mark. Her mom rubbed her back and leaned in to kiss her on the cheek. "Okay, well call me when you know. If you can't make it maybe we will reschedule."

Lilly turned to face her mom. "No, don't cancel, especially if Roan actually wants to bring a girl here. I'll try and make it, okay?"

Diera nodded and smiled.

"You look tired."

"I am, honey."

She took her mom's hand and led her into the living room.

"Lilly, I can manage myself."

"Mom, just let me help you. Here." She gently pushed her on the couch and turned the TV on to one of those sappy love stories about the guy falling in love with the geeky girl.

"You're such a good girl, Lilly."

She gave her mom one of the throws and looked down at her. Today might be a good day, but it was definitely taking its toll on her mom. The bags under her eyes seemed overly dark against her pale skin, and her blue eyes looked big and sunken in.

"Well, I have some errands to run, and then I have to head right to class, but I'll call you before I go in, okay?" She leaned down and kissed her mom before heading to her room and grabbing her bag. On her way out the front door she took her cell out of her bag and sent a quick text to Roan.

Mom's excited for you to bring the new grl to dinner ;)

His reply text was almost instant.

Roan: *She's just a friend*

Lily didn't return the text, but she did grin. Roan never had girls that were just "friends", so that meant this one was pretty special to him. The sound of engines roaring had Lilly's heart instantly pounding fast and hard. Their house wasn't too far from the center of town, so although she could still hear the motorcycles she couldn't see them. But she didn't need to see them to know that amongst all those Harleys would be Court.

Court.

That damn beautiful male that she still compared all other guys to. In the last five years he had changed considerably. He no longer worked at the salvage yard, had joined The Grizzly MC—those bad, mean, and tough bikers—and was a hell of a lot colder and bigger than she ever remembered. She didn't know if something had happened in the time they hadn't spoken, or the fact that he was now in a biker gang, but the few times they had locked gazes she hadn't seen the guy she had known her whole life. It was strange, surreal even, but she still harbored these feelings for him. Feelings that weren't just of a sexual nature, but of a closeness that spoke of years of friendship. One night had ruined all that, and ruined the relationship her brother had with Court.

They hardly talked, and although life and priorities, and the fact they were all grown adults now were a good enough cause for the fact that distance had come between them; but Lilly knew what it really was about. Court probably felt guilt and anger for sleeping with his best friend's sister, and she had all but pushed him to that conclusion.

She sighed. This had been the longest five years of her life. With the combination of her mom's health declining over the years, the stress of life in general, and losing a guy that had been just as much a part of their family as if he were blood related, Lilly just wanted to climb in bed and sleep until everything was back to the way it was. She had known sleeping with him would change things, but she had never thought it would have changed it to the point they didn't even speak anymore, and their extent of communication was stilted looks and awkward run-ins. Not that they had had that much communication before, seeing as she was so much younger than Court and Roan, but still, it just sucked now. But after their little romp at the party, well, she felt like she had never really been in Court's life at all. And of course it had all been her fault because she thought sleeping with Court had been a really good idea.

Well, lesson learned for sure.

Chapter Three

Lilly pushed open the door of River Run Career Center and waved at a few of her classmates. It was going on eight, longer than she thought she would still be at class, but they had a surge of volunteers come in to get their blood drawn. The phlebotomist course she was taking was nearing its end and although she had never seen herself going into the medical field, after her mom's diagnoses, going through remission, and then the cancer coming back, Lilly decided she wanted to help more people. Sure, drawing blood wasn't surgery or anything, but it was still a step. Besides, she didn't have a lot of extra time and if she wanted to take a nursing course she wouldn't be able to spend as much time with her mother as she liked; and that wasn't what she wanted to do right now.

She had called her mom on a break and told her she wouldn't be able to make it for dinner, which was a shame as Lilly wanted to meet Roan's friend that just happened to be a girl. The sun had already set, and she made her way away from the front doors of the center and to the parking lot. There were lights that illuminated the lot, but they were a muted yellow and spaced out too much for Lilly's comfort. But the sound of her classmates behind her as they, too, made their way to their cars eased her uneasiness. She unlocked the door and climbed in, and once in\ the driver's seat she tossed her bag beside her and locked the door. Her car was an older model, and although it got her to where she needed to go, Lilly knew the bitch would just one day not start. But, thank God, when she put the key in the ignition and cranked the engine it flared to life.

Although River Run wasn't a horrible town or overly dangerous, she did know from hearing Roan and

Court talk years ago that there were a lot of girls that sold themselves behind the one and only strip club in town. Not that women prostituting themselves was what had Lilly scared, but the shady guys that came in from other parts of the state tended to freak her out, and also made her feel like River Run wasn't safe at all.

Her phone buzzed with an incoming text. The reception was spotty at best out here, but was better inside. Getting her phone out, she saw it was from her mom telling her to drive safe, but of course she couldn't reply since all of her bars for her coverage decided to disappear. Headlights flashed in front of her, and she squinted her eyes from the glare. Car after car left until she was the only one still in the parking lot.

She pulled out of the parking lot and onto the main road that ran through River Run. The side of town she was on was quieter and away from the square, which was where the bars and strip club were located. That suited Lilly fine but she rarely stayed at class late enough that it was dark, and being out in the middle of nowhere did tend to unnerve her. She headed toward the main part of town which was a necessary evil in order to get back to Steel Corner. A clicking sound had her turning the radio off and leaning forward to listen to where it was coming from.

"Shit." The clicking was coming from her engine, and she knew from hanging around Roan and Court that a sound like that was most definitely not a good thing. She pulled over and cut the engine. It was dark, she was out in the middle of nowhere, and the creepiness of her surroundings sure as shit wasn't comforting. Lilly looked in her review mirror, just barely saw the career center, and cursed. No way in hell was she going to walk that in the dark. She made sure her doors were locked and grabbed her phone again.

And still no bars. "You bastard piece of shit phone." Of course she had to be the last car that left the parking lot. But she knew the instructors stayed later than the students, and it looked like she would be waiting until she saw possibly one of them driving down the road. Problem was she didn't know how long that would be. Lilly rested her head on the back of the seat and cursed her shitty luck. She was tired, her feet hurt, and she just wanted to get home. But of course nothing ever worked out the way it was supposed to.

It had been thirty minutes, half a damn hour that she had been sitting on the side of the damn road, and although normally that wouldn't have been any time at all, it felt like a lifetime. She had constantly checked her phone for a signal, and a few times those bars had flashed, but they had disappeared just as quickly. Before she got comfortable again headlights flashed in front of her, and she lifted her arm to shield her eyes. Her hazards were on, and fortunately the car slowed and pulled up in front of her. The headlights from the vehicle in front of her made it impossible for her to see who was driving, but she could see that it was a truck.

Lilly stayed in the car with the doors locked, but rolled down her window a crack. She was glad to see someone, but she wasn't stupid. The sound of a car door opening and then slamming shut, and then of boots crunching on the gravel suddenly had her heart racing. But when a big burly man with a trimmed beard and wearing a ball cap pulled low over his forehead, stepped beside her driver's side door and leaned down, the instinct to flee was strong inside of her.

"You need a tow?" His voice was pitched low, and with him wearing that hat and the shadows around them, it made seeing his face all the harder. "Your car just up and die?"

"Um, yeah. I think it's my engine. I heard a clicking."

He nodded and straightened, and even though he wore a loose fitting flannel shirt and she could only see his upper body, she could tell he was powerfully built. But her heart was still beating fast, and her throat had gone dry. She didn't know why she was having this reaction, aside from the fact her surroundings creeped her out. He was three times as big as she was, but it wasn't the situation. It was him.

"Pop the hood, and I'll check out what's going on."

She did as he asked, and waited for several minutes as he did whatever he was doing under her hood. Finally he closed the lid, produced a rag from his back pocket, and cleaned his hands off.

"Without any tools I can't say for sure, but I got a pretty good guess that your engine is toast."

She nodded, because she had figured as much. "Yeah, that's what my boyfriend said, too." Lilly knew that she had to act strong, because a predator could smell weakness like spilled blood. Telling him she had a boyfriend would, she hoped, make him back off—if he had any intentions of starting anything. Of course he might be a nice guy, and it was just her own nervousness that was getting the better of her. But even as she thought that she knew it wasn't just her nerves. The guy just stared at her for several seconds after she said that, and she curled her hands around the steering wheel tighter to stop them from suddenly shaking.

"Your boyfriend, huh?" She nodded and licked her lips. "He a mechanic? I've never seen you around before."

"Yeah, I actually called him a while ago, and he should be here any minute. Thanks for looking at the engine though." She smiled, but he showed no emotion.

"You have reception out here?" His question chilled her, and she felt a cold sweat start to move along her spine. He placed a hand on the door of her car. "Because no one ever gets reception on this road." He grinned, and something inside of her screamed that this was a very, very bad situation that she was in.

"Yeah, I made the call a long time ago. Seriously, he should be here any minute." Her voice was shaky, and she kept looking in her rearview mirror and praying a set of headlight would make an appearance.

"I can take you into town and you can have your boyfriend meet you there? You can call him on the way from your phone." He stared right into her eyes, not showing a grin or any other kind of expression. It was freaky as hell. "In fact, I almost insist on taking you into town. It isn't safe for a young woman to be out here all alone in the middle of the night."

It was hardly the middle of the night, and she saw the way he kept glancing up and down the road, as if he were expecting a car to pass by.

"No, no, that's okay. He really will be here soon." She was grasping for straws now, praying that he would just leave. He stood and wrapped the rag he had used to clean his hands on around his knuckles.

"No one really uses this back road much. Shame that career center decided to build so far out from town." He looked down the road again, and her heart started hurting from how hard it was pounding. "Come on out and I'll take you into town. We can talk and get to know each other." He leaned down again and rested his wrapped hand on the doorframe. "I don't get much personal time with pretty, decent girls like you. Only ones that hang around town that will give it up without complaint are the whores working out of the strip club."

"N-No, thank you. My boyfriend will get worried if he comes here and I'm gone." She heard him sigh heavily, and then he lowered his head and shook it a few times.

"No one is coming for you, and you don't have a boyfriend, at least not one that is on his way." She didn't respond, didn't move, and didn't even breathe. "Now, you can come with me the easy way, we can have ourselves a good time, or you can fight me and I can take what I want. If you choose option two it won't feel very good."

She didn't care if her damn engine blew up. She cranked the engine, but nothing happened. Lilly tried over and over again, but the low, deep chuckle had her heart pounding hard. She looked over at him, and he held up a sparkplug. He tossed it aside, and before she could even scream, he rammed his wrapped hand through the glass of her driver's side window with so much force she felt the shards tear through the skin on the side of her face.

Lilly cried out and frantically tried to unstrap her belt, but her hands shook uncontrollably, her palms were sweaty, and her sudden torrent of tears made her vision blurry. The click of her seatbelt coming undone had her trying to move quickly to the other side of the car, but the man reached out and grabbed her neck, slamming her back against the seat. Lilly clawed at his hand as he tightened it and kept her stationary as he reached inside with his other hand and unlocked the door. And then everything after that was like a blur.

He wrenched her out of the seat and tossed her on the ground. The gravel beneath her dug into her palms as she braced herself, and she felt the burning sensation of her skin being torn off. Kicking her legs out, she was about to haul ass into the woods since that was right in front of her, but he wrapped a hand in her hair and yanked her backward. Stars danced in front of her vision as his forceful motions caused her head to connect with the pavement. A groan left her, and she clutched at her head.

"Little girl, we could have had a good time if you would have." He yanked her up by the hair and she screamed out, but she was spun around so fast, and slammed into the side of her car so hard, that her scream became garbled from the grunt of her impact.

"Why are you doing this?" Her vision was still blurry, but she saw him lift his hand. Trying to brace herself for the hit that was inevitable was easier said than done. Lilly kicked her legs out, but connected with his shin when he anticipated the move and blocked her. He brought his fist across her temple, and pain slammed into her with so much force nausea swirled inside of her, and bile rose up in her throat. She threw up, not able to stop herself as the pain controlled every part of her. Rolling onto her back cause a cry of pain to leave her, and her head throbbed like someone was taking a jackhammer to it.

"Come on." He reached for her again, but she brought up all of her strength and lifted her leg right for his crotch. A spark of pleasure left her when she connected with his dick and a grunt of pain came from him. But she didn't wait to watch him fall to his knees. Lilly tried to stand, but her head hurt so badly and she started to feel her eyes swelling shut. Crawling on her hands and knees toward the road, she swore she heard something rumble, but the sound of her pulse filled her ears and it was hard to tell if it was real or in her head. "You fucking cunt." He grabbed her leg, and she kicked out again, felt her foot connect with his head, but the satisfaction was short-lived because he yanked her back, flipped her on her back, and started going for his belt.

"No. Please, don't." Every part of her screamed out in agony, but the sound of the rumbling intensified, and then she heard the man on top of her curse and stand quickly. He tried to lift her up, but ended up ripping her scrub top in the process. The cool air brushed along her exposed chest, and even though she wore a bra she tried to lift her hand to cover herself. It seemed her brain didn't want to give the commands, because her arm felt like it was made of lead. Exhaustion started weighing down on her, and she couldn't see out of her left eye any longer. But that rumbling sound was most definitely not in her head, and the closer it got the more she realized what it was.

Lilly managed to stumble forward, drag herself off the ground despite her pounding head, and moved toward the road, but she didn't get far because he wrapped a thick arm around her middle and hauled her against his chest. He was striding quickly toward his truck, but Lilly got a renewed sense of strength and started fighting harder than she had before.

"What the fuck." The deep, rage-filled voice could be heard clearly through the massive rumbling of the Harleys that had come to a stop in front of them, but with Lilly's swollen eye, and their headlights shining right on them, she couldn't see much.

"Not your concern. Just ride on," the man holding her said in a low, harsh voice. He started moving toward the truck again, and she screamed.

"Help. God, please help me." It was only seconds after she had called out that someone had her out of the other man's hands and pressed against his chest. She smelled leather and a spicy cologne, and all she could think about at that time was Court. It was such a random thing because it had been so long since they had seen each other, but his image slammed into her head and she started to cry.

"You motherfucker," someone gritted out, and then she heard the sound of flesh meeting flesh, of a male grunting in pain, and then of a body hitting the ground. Despite the sound of motorcycles still rumbling close by, it seemed so deathly quiet.

"Hey, you're okay," the man holding her said and rubbed her back. "Can you tell me your name and who we can call?" She pulled back, but winced and moaned as her head pounded hard.

She shook her head, but licked her chapped lips and spoke through her tears. "Lilly Winters." She rattled off Roan's number, didn't know if anyone had written it down, but she was feeling even sicker the longer she stood on her feet.

"Man, I think she needs to see a doctor. She can't even stand up without you holding onto her," another man said from behind her. Lilly didn't know these men, but she didn't feel the dread and need to escape like she had with the asshole that had attacked her.

"We can't take her to a hospital, especially not when we need to take that fucker back to the clubhouse. Kink, call Doc Mason, and get a hold of her family," the man holding her said. Lilly looked into his face, but with the swelling and her tears all she saw was this blurry vision. Dizziness assaulted her and she swayed, but he held onto her tighter, and then she was in his arms and resting her head on his hard chest. "I'm Lucien Silver, and ain't no one gonna fuck with you anymore." He tightened his arms around her, and she tried to breathe through the pain. But darkness was slowly starting to consume her, and she knew she wouldn't be able to hold on for much longer. "Malice, call Ruin and have him get his ass out here to take my bike back to the clubhouse. I'll take that piece of shit's truck."

Clubhouse? So they were bikers.

"You want me to toss this dick in the back of the truck?" a guy behind her asked.

"Yeah, throw his soon to be dead ass with the rest of the trash he has back there."

But that was the last thing she heard because she gave up the fight and finally allowed herself to be swallowed up by the darkness that tempted her.

Chapter Four

Court grabbed his bottle of beer, the one he had been nursing for the last hour, and took a sip of the lukewarm shit. The stripper on stage was currently in the process of slipping her G-string down her thighs. They had been at Summer's for a few hours, but Court would have left sooner if Stinger hadn't gotten trashed and needed a babysitter. Dallas was at least sober, but he had been getting lap dances of his own and wasn't paying any mind to Stinger. The thing with Dallas was he was in his own world recently. He did what needed to do to keep the club going, was there for the rest of the members, but there was this void look in his eyes. Whatever the fuck he was going through it was some heavy shit.

Normally they could take care of themselves, whether they were drunk or not, but Stinger was getting lap dance after lap dance, and a few times the bouncers had to tell him to keep his hands on his lap. The bouncers and owner at Summer's knew not to mess with The Grizzly MC, but that didn't mean they still didn't have to look out for the girls working the pole or the guys. No hard feelings on that account, and after the second time of Stinger being clearly too drunk to give a fuck, Court had stepped in and told him to cut the fucking shit.

He brought the beer to his mouth and finished the nasty thing off and felt his cell vibrate in his front pocket. Once he had it out and saw it was the club he brought it to his ear and covered his other one with a hand. "Yeah?"

"Hey, some guy named Roan called looking for you. Said it was an emergency and wanted you to call him ASAP."

Hearing that had Court sitting straighter.

"What's the number?" Court didn't bother asking if Roan had said anything else, because no way could it be good if he was reaching out to him at this hour and after so long.

He ended the call when he got the number and stood. He grabbed Stinger by the back of the cut, gestured for Dallas to come with him, and started hauling ass out of the strip club.

"What the fuck, man?" Stinger slurred, and then swayed on his feet. They were already outside, and Stinger had to brace a hand on the brick wall to steady himself. Court ignored him and dialed Roan's number. It only rang once before someone answered.

"Court?"

"Yeah." The music from inside was muted, and a couple of the guys that had been smoking outside had gone back in when they had stepped through the doors.

"Christ." Roan sounded out of breath, and there was this frantic quality to it.

"What's wrong?" He didn't bother asking how Roan got the number, because right now his bear rose to the surface, needing to know what the fuck was wrong. Court's heart was beating so fast that he felt it in his throat and heard it in his ears.

"It's Lilly, man."

"What the fuck is wrong?" Court couldn't help the way his voice rose, or the fact his bear was starting to take control at the thought of sweet Lilly hurt. A low growl left him, and Stinger was suddenly alert beside him, but kept his mouth shut.

"Shit, Court, someone attacked the fuck out of her."

It took all of his power not to shift right then and there. "You at your house?" Court was already striding toward his bike, but then he remembered Stinger and Dallas and stopped.

"No, I'm at some biker club in River Run."

Court's blood rushed through his veins. There was only one MC in River Run—The Brothers of Menace. Before Court could say anything Roan was talking again.

"The President, Lucien, called me and said someone attacked Lilly. They got the fucker here with them, and some doctor is checking her out, but shit, Court, she looks bad and is passed out."

The growl that came from him was deep, low, and filled with warning. His entire body shook with his rage. Someone had hurt Lilly—*his* Lilly—and Court was about to break a motherfucker's neck.

"I didn't know who else to call in a situation like this. Fuck, I didn't even tell my mom what happened because she doesn't need this shit. Dammit, I don't know what else to do but kill the asshole that did this to her."

But Court calmed himself enough that he could talk. "Where is the fucker now?" He swallowed, took a deep breath, and clenched his hand at his side into a fist.

"He's out cold, and some of Lucien's guys are watching him. I'd go after him now, but I want the motherfucker awake when I beat his ass."

Oh, Court planned on doing a hell of a lot more to the guy that hurt Lilly than just kicking his ass. "I'm on my way." After he hung up he turned and looked at Dallas and Stinger. "My girl got hurt."

Shit, did he just say that? It didn't matter, because he had been trying to push how he felt for Lilly away this whole time, and it hadn't done any good. He was going to watch over her and protect her so this never happened again. And he was going to make that bastard that harmed her pay with blood, broken bones, and eventually, when he was done fucking him up, let him take his last breath as he ripped his throat out.

"You got a girl? Since when did you get an old lady?" He knew Stinger was loose with his tongue because of the alcohol. If he was sober he would have seen how close to shifting Court was at this moment, and that questioning him about an old lady was not smart to do right now.

"Stinger, shut the fuck up right now." Dallas pushed Stinger over to the building again so he could brace himself against it, and turned to look at Court. "What do you need from me?"

"Can you call the club and have one of the guys come by for his drunk ass?"

Dallas nodded.

"Make sure whoever comes brings a prospect so Stinger's bike doesn't sit here all night."

"Court, you need back-up?" Dallas asked.

"Yeah, man. You need us to fuck someone up?" Stinger asked, too, but his words were slurred. As much as Court wanted to do this alone, he thought about it and knew that wouldn't be smart.

"Shit." He scrubbed a hand over his head. "Yeah, I probably will need to take someone with me, but not you." He pointed at Stinger. "You need to get to the clubhouse and sleep the alcohol off."

Stinger shook his head. "Nah, you're in trouble, and brothers stick together."

This was why Court loved the MC. Whether it was someone that he needed to drink with, to bullshit with, or to help kick a fucker's ass, any one of the Grizzlies rose to the occasion, no matter what.

"Thanks, Stinger, but you wouldn't be much use to me if things went south and you can't even stand up on your own." Stinger flipped him off in good nature, but Court was far from a teasing mood. "Dallas, make the call, and meet me at The Brothers of Menace clubhouse." The air shifted to frigid.

"That MC did something?"

Court shook his head. "No, but I don't know much, and what I do know I don't want to talk about right now."

Dallas nodded.

"Just make the call and meet me there." He didn't wait for a response, just went to his bike, got on, and started it. He knew Dallas would let Jagger know, and he also knew that it most likely wouldn't just be Dallas that met him at The Brothers' clubhouse. All of that was well and good, but all he could focus on was Lilly and exactly how badly she was hurt.

****

Lilly sat on the edge of a bed that smelled like someone had just fucked in it, and rested her sore head in her hand. She had just woken up, but she wasn't in any pain from whatever this Doctor Mason guy had given her. In fact, she was feeling pretty good. But it was the smell of old sweat, cologne, and spilled alcohol that filled her head and made her stomach twist painfully even more.

"You're going to be sore, but the swelling should go down within the next forty-eight to seventy-two hours. The bruising, however, will get worse before it gets better."

She dropped her hands to her lap and looked at the young and very attractive doctor sitting on a chair in front of her. He reached down to where his medical bag sat and pulled out an unlabeled bottle.

"Here are some pain pills. You can take up to two pills every four hours."

She nodded, but she couldn't quite focus. He smiled and looked over his shoulder at Roan. Her brother was by the far wall, and although he had a very worried expression on his face, she could see how angry he was by the way he kept clenching and unclenching his hands at his sides. He looked so tense and had a red tint to his cheeks that told her he was furious and barely holding on. The doctor told Roan that same thing he had just said to her, and her brother nodded once. There were a few biker guys in the room, too, but she hadn't been able to see very well from the swelling. She heard their low, gruff whispers, and knew that the one that wore the President patch on his cut was called Lucien Silver, and he was the one that had carried her to the truck, and then into their clubhouse.

"We'll give you two a few minutes. The Grizzlies should be here soon," Lucien looked over at her. "If I had known you were associated with them I could have called them right away."

"I'm not associated with them," she said, and Lucien looked over at Roan, who just closed his eyes and shook his head.

"That fucker still out?" Roan asked Lucien from between gritted teeth.

The President nodded. "Yeah, one of my guys knocked his ass out cold."

Roan grunted, but she knew he was pleased with that, as was she. Lucien tipped his chin and he and the rest of the men left the room. Once the door was shut Roan sighed heavily and ran his hand over his short dark hair.

"Fucking hell, Lilly." He lowered his arms so they fell to his sides and walked over to her. When he was on his knees in front of her he lifted his hand, as if he meant to touch her, but curled his fingers into his palm at the last moment. "What the hell happened?" He searched her face with his gaze, and for how bad it felt, and the way he grimaced, she knew she looked like she got the shit beaten out of her—which she obviously had.

"My car started making a clicking noise, and I remembered when you and Court…"God, he was coming here for sure, and that brought up a lot of feelings inside of her. "I remembered when you guys were working on your Mustang and were talking about that and having something to do with the engine." The drugs the doctor had given her made her head feel lightheaded, and she had to lie back as the room started to spin. Roan helped her, and once everything righted itself in front of her vision she turned her head to look at him. "Do I look as shitty as I feel?" She was trying to tease, to somehow ease the tension that was suffocating her. This, of course, was so not a joking matter or situation, but she hated seeing Roan look so upset.

He shook his head, but looked anything but amused. "No joking or making light of this, Lilly. He didn't…" Roan swallowed, and his expression went harder. He didn't have to finish his sentence for her to know what he was going to ask.

"No, but if those bikers hadn't shown up—"

He held up his hand and shook his head. "Let's not talk about it, because I am barely holding on as it is." He opened his eyes and smiled, but it was clearly forced. "Now, tell me what happened, okay?" His voice was gentler this time, and she took a deep breath and told him what had happened.

For several minutes she relayed everything she could remember. It was horrible, though, because it felt like she was experiencing it all over again. When she said the last word and brushed the tears away, the silence descended. "I didn't even know him, and can't understand why he did what he did. God, Roan, what if he has done this before?" She had needed to say something because the silence was too much. Roan looked at the ground for several seconds, and she could see the way his jaw clenched and unclenched.

"Lilly, sometimes there are just bad people that do bad things." He looked at her then, and she saw the raw pain on his face. "But I can guarantee that this will *never* happen again." She loved that he was protective, but she didn't tell him that he couldn't make a promise like that, because he couldn't be there all the time. They had their mom to worry about. *Oh, God, my mom.*

"What about Mom? Did you tell her what happened and then just left?" She went to sit up, but Roan gently pushed her back down.

"I didn't tell her anything besides your car broke down and I was going to go look at it. She's going to have to know about this eventually, but I didn't' want to tell her and then leave her at the house to worry."

Lilly nodded. That was the best thing to do, because worrying and getting upset over this was something her mom didn't need right now. Before either could say anything else the sound of loud male voices on the other side of the wall had her pushing herself up and Roan standing to place himself between her and the door. And then there was the sound of footsteps pounding down the hallway, and of the door being slammed open and hitting the wall. She looked around Roan's body to see who it was, but she already knew.

Court stood in the doorway looking pissed and powerful, and so very animalistic. She had seen him around town, but right now, he looked like a totally different male. His body seemed bigger, his biceps flexing so hard that his muscles popped out, and his chest rose and fell as he breathed in and out.

"Lilly." Court said her name harshly, and she could see the bear flicker across his face.

She turned away, not wanting him to see her like this. "Thanks for coming, Court." Roan spoke just as harshly, but her brother's voice lacked the fierce edge that only a shifter had. Lilly glanced to her side and watched as Court stepped inside. Two other Grizzly MC members moved in behind him. She knew them by name seeing as she had lived in Steel Corner her whole life, but she only knew of them by reputation. They kept to themselves, but were scary enough that people stayed away from them. Her brother and Court slapped each other on the back, and it was like all those years they had been distant had just vanished.

Court didn't respond, just moved away from Roan and closer to her. And then, as if she wasn't surprised enough to see him he dropped to his knees in front of her, all six foot four inches of him, and reached out as if to touch her. He was gentle as he wrapped his hand around her shoulder and leaned in to hug her. The scent of grease and beer filled her nose, but it was the wild smell that she remembered from their time together that rose up stronger than the earlier scents.

"Christ, baby." And then there he went and surprised her again with the endearment. He had said it too low for anyone but her to hear it, but he had said it nonetheless.

Lilly looked over Court's shoulder at her brother, and he appeared just as stunned as she felt. They might have grown up around each other, but the age difference had made it so they never ran in the same circles. She was just the little sister of Roan. But now, as he held her, she felt like something more, like how she had felt when he held her and kissed her in the back of his truck five years ago. He pulled away and put a strand of hair behind her ear. The soft look he had given her vanished as he became angrier the longer he stared into her face.

"What the fuck did he do to you?"

"I'll fill you in. She just got done telling me, and I don't want her having to go through it all over again," Roan said to Court, but he still stared at her.

"Yeah." Court watched her for a couple more seconds and then turned and took a step back from her. "You'll be okay for a few minutes, baby?"

She swallowed and nodded.

"Dallas, watch over her until I get back, okay?"

The one she assumed was Dallas took a step closer.

"Lilly, I'm going to talk to Court, and get everything taken care of. Then I'll take you home." Her brother came over to her and kissed her on the forehead, but she didn't miss how he darted a confused look at Court. She could only imagine what her brother was thinking about, and the connections he was making at Court's strange behavior. They left her alone in the room, shut the door behind them, and she glanced over at the big ass biker named Dallas.

"Don't you worry. No one is going to fuck with you anymore," Dallas deadpanned and crossed his arms over his chest. "Didn't know Court had an old lady, but it's clear you're something' special to him." Dallas leaned against the wall, and she was about to correct him on how she wasn't anyone's "old lady", but he started talking again. "When you have something that changes you in here," he placed his fist on his chest, right over his heart, "you don't let it fucking slip through your fingers."

Chapter Five

Court paced back and forth and felt the eyes of The Grizzlies and The Brothers of Menace on him. But he didn't give a fuck, because the female that he shouldn't have walked away from all those years ago had gotten the shit beat out of her and had nearly been raped. He didn't even want to think about all the heinous shit that motherfucker currently tied up like a hog in the garage behind the clubhouse would have done to her if Lucien and his boys hadn't shown up.

He looked at Roan and felt his blood rise violently to the surface of his body once more. He wasn't pissed at his once best friend, but at what Roan had just got done telling Court. Just thinking of Lilly all alone out there, scared to death and getting hurt, had Court's grizzly bear pacing back and forth, ready to hurt something, *someone*.

"You need to relax." He looked over at Jagger. The Grizzly President had insisted on coming with Dallas, but Court was thankful he had the support and backup. Still, no way in hell could he fucking calm down.

"Did you not see what happened to her?" He pointed to the room down the hallway where Lilly currently was. "Did you not fucking see her face, or hear what that asshole would have done to her if The Brothers hadn't shown up when they did?" Court gritted out the last part and had to close his eyes and grapple for control with his animal. He cracked his knuckles and rolled his head around on his neck. "You tell me if you could calm down if that was Darra in there. Lilly is my female, and now way in hell can I fucking calm down right now." Everyone glanced at each other, and Court realized he had called Lilly his female, but she *was* his, whether she knew it or not. It was a fucking shame that it had taken him this long to realize what a coward he had been

THE GRIZZLY MC: VOLUME TWO

staying away like he had. But he had thought it had been the right thing to do, and that all the shit he had felt for her could be buried deep down inside of him. How wrong he had been. All it had accomplished was hiding from Roan, being a shitty friend, and not thinking being with Lilly could ever be anything more than that one night. It could have been so much more if he had just allowed his fears and stubborn ass to accept what was right in front of him. The past was just that, the past, but he could make up for all the time that had passed. He needed to man up and be the male that she needed now and the friend that Roan deserved.

Court scrubbed both of his hands over his face. He was pissed, feral, and wanted blood on his hands and chest as he fucked that bastard up. But he had to remind himself that he needed to control himself around Lilly. He had done a damn fine job when he was in the room with her, but he had barely been holding on, especially when he had hugged her and felt the light tremor go through her body.

"Take me to him." Court looked at the ground and clamped his jaw.

"I want a go at that fucker, too," Roan said with barely repressed anger himself.

Court looked up at Lilly's brother. Roan had every right to go after the man that hurt her—more right than even Court since he really had no claim on her—but that didn't mean he wasn't going to get a round in. Besides, even if he had fucked up by walking away, he cared about Lilly, and that had been brought violently to the surface when he had seen her just minutes before. His crew and Roan might not know that he wanted her, and had all but claimed her if he was being honest, but he was done being a pussy on how he felt.

"Come on, let's deal with this." Court nodded to Roan and Lucien. The Brothers of Menace President didn't say anything, but he didn't have to, because Court wasn't hiding his emotions. They were volatile, rage-filled, and he wanted blood covering his body as the man that hurt his female paid for what he did with his life.

Lucien lifted his head toward the back of the clubhouse, indicating without saying anything that the motherfucker Court and Roan wanted was back there. Lucian then turned, and Court and Roan followed him. Jagger stepped up behind then, too, and the four of them made their way to the back of the clubhouse, headed outside, and continued to where a large garage was. The Brothers of Menace clubhouse was on Sterling Hill, with thick forest surrounding them, and privacy from the populated part of River Run. It was also clear they had renovated the place that, as far as Court was aware of, used to be a lumber distribution center. But thoughts of anything that didn't pertain to violence and bloodshed faded the closer he got to the garage. Court started to get itchy and felt his bear pace inside of him. The wild animal wanted a taste of the man that had hurt his female, too. The bay doors were shut, but Lucien led them to a side door and opened it. Once inside Court took note that there were two of Lucien's club members leaning against a workstation. A few broken down Harleys were in the center of the garage, and numerous toolboxes were lined up along the walls, as well as other items that were needed to work on bikes. But Court's focus turned to the big motherfucker currently restrained to a chair with a nasty, grease-stained rag shoved in his mouth.

"He's awake. Good." Court felt adrenaline and endorphins pump through his body and had to push his bear down, because although he wanted to let his inner animal out and tear this man to shreds, his human side

wanted at him even more. He looked over at Roan, saw
the other man was just as juiced up to do some damage to
this guy as he was, and took a step back. "You want at
him first?" For a human Roan was a big guy, always had
been. Hell, he rivaled a lot of shifters in the height and
muscle department, Court included. The years had only
seemed to harden him, but Court knew he was working
overtime at Horrison Construction, and putting in some
long hours. Being a Grizzly member meant you knew
what everyone in town did. It was the only way to make
sure Steel Corner stayed safe and ran smoothly. He
looked at Roan again. That manual labor showed, and
Court knew the human needed to get all that aggression
out.

Roan glanced at him. "I'm going to fuck him up."

Court grinned, but it was one of sadistic
satisfaction. "Good, but leave some for me."

Roan stared at him for a few seconds and then
nodded. "We'll talk later."

Court didn't need to ask what he meant, because
he knew damn well Roan was talking about the shit he
had said about Lilly being his girl, and the way he had
gone all possessive and territorial when he saw her. Court
nodded once, and tipped his chin toward the bound
human.

"Let's get this fucking thing going." As much as
Court wanted to hurt this guy, he wanted to get back to
Lilly even more. He removed his cut, handed it to Jagger,
and then took his t-shirt off. This was about to get messy,
but he was fucking looking forward to that. Looking at
Roan, he saw him clenching and unclenching his fists,
and then cracking his knuckles as if he were impatient.
They had a lot to talk about, he had a lot of explaining,
and eventually the truth that Court had slept with Lilly,
and that was the reason he had acted like such a fucking

douche-bag, would need to be brought up. Hell, Roan might not even care about what he and Lilly had done, and it would have meant Court feeling guilty over it had all been for nothing. No, that wasn't right either, because he still would have felt like a piece of shit friend that had done something he knew was forbidden. And it had been so damn wrong, yet had felt so fucking right.

Stop thinking about the past right now, Court. Right now think about this piece of shit getting so fucked up he won't survive the night.

Roan turned and looked at Court, grinned the same sadistic smile Court had just been wearing, and faced the bound man again. You know that girl in there?" The guy was bound and gagged and couldn't answer, but it hadn't been something Roan wanted a reply to, that much was clear by the tone of his voice and the way he stalked forward menacingly. "That's my baby sister in there, and the last person you should have fucked with." Roan was right in front of the guy a second later.

Court moved closer, needing to smell the fear that came off of the human about to get his ass kicked by first Roan, and then Court.

Roan grabbed the guy's head, yanked it back with a chunk of his hair wrapped tightly around Roan's fist, and bared his teeth. "I'm going to make it so you can't walk, let alone hurt another innocent woman." Roan slammed his fist into the side of his face repeatedly.

The guy's eyes had already been swollen from when Lucien's men worked him over, and blood and gravel coated one side of his face. He was the worse for wear, but by the time they were finished with him there wouldn't be anything left. He watched as Roan beat the living shit out of the human, so much that the guy started throwing up blood and stomach contents. But the rag was in his mouth, and he was choking on the vile shit. Roan reached out and pulled it out.

"No way you're going out like that." Roan was breathing heavily, and his knuckles were covered in a mixture of his own, as well as the fucker's blood. "Besides, I'm not the only one that is going to have some time with you." He slammed his fist into the guy's head once more, so hard this time that the chair tipped over and took the guy to the ground with it. He groaned and grunted, but he didn't beg and plead for his life like Court might have thought, and there wasn't any fear that came from him. *Huh.* This guy was either insane, or didn't know who in the fuck he had gotten involved with when it came to The Grizzlies or The Brothers. But then, like he was psychotic, the fucker started laughing.

"You're lucky these biker fuckers came when they did, because I was about to tear that pretty young thing up until she was crying and bleeding and begging me to end her pain."

Court growled low, but Jagger placed a hand on his shoulder. The only reason he didn't turn around and tear the male holding him back from killing that human prick was that it was his brother and his President that restrained him.

"Breathe. You'll finish it before you get to enjoy it."

Court knew what Jagger meant. The President wasn't stopping him, but making sure he got the pleasure of killing his female's abuser. Court had been about to shift without his human side enjoying the bloodshed. He took a deep breath and nodded. Jagger let go of him, and Court rolled his head around his neck once more.

"You must not know who we are." Court said the words low, deadly. The human laughed again, and then turned his head and spit out a mouthful of blood.

"Ain't from here, but I don't give a fuck who you are. The lot of you can suck my fucking dick and choke on that shit." He started laughing again. "That's what I was going to do to that pretty little thing until our party gotten broken up."

Hearing the bastard continuing to defile Lilly with his words had Court snapping, and no amount of self-control could stop him. He couldn't control himself, or his bear, and felt the shift move through him so powerfully he didn't even try to stop it this time. His bear broke free. His skin tore apart, bones broke, and muscles swelled as his animal moved through him, about to do some serious damage. He swung his massive head in Roan's direction. There was no fear or shock that came from the man when Court inhaled deeply. He stood before them all in his grizzly form, breathing heavily, his claws scraping on the concrete floor, and his incisors itching to tear into flesh. Roan stepped back to give him free rein, and that sadistic smile once again covered Lilly's brother's face. Moving closer to the asshole on the floor, Court bared his teeth at him. He would have grinned if he could have at the scent of the fear that finally came from the human. He had wanted to prolong this fucker's pain and then inevitable death, to draw out the agony, but he couldn't after hearing the sickness that had come out of this man's mouth.

He attacked without thinking any further. His human side watched the act from deep within him, but it was his bear doing the violence, protecting their female, and making sure no one else ever got hurt by this human again. Dragging his claws into the human's side had the ropes that bound him breaking away. He scrambled on the ground now that he was free, but Court wanted the chase. There was no more arrogance that came from him. He knew he was fucked. Court let the fucker get a few feet before he charged forward, reached out, and dug his nails into his back. The man howled out in pain and fell forward. The scent of his blood filled Court's nose and made him crave more. Court saw red and lashed out repeatedly with his claws and teeth until the human lay on the ground. His body was torn the fuck up, and a pool of blood spread out from his lifeless body, staining the grey concrete beneath him in a grisly red. Court breathed heavily, but he was too amped up to shift back to his human form.

"Fuck." He swung his head and looked at Lucien. The human biker was staring at the now dead human on the floor. He had a smirk and leaned against the wall. "You fucked him up." He looked over at the two other members of his MC. "Can you call Slicks to clean this shit up? Not sure if anyone will be looking, but I don't want anything left of this POS that can be identified." The two men nodded at what their President had just said, and like this wasn't anything they had never heard, and turned to leave the garage. Lucien looked back at him again. "You're gonna need a pair of pants, since I assume you want to see your old lady." Lucien didn't wait for a response, just tipped his chin toward the door. "You need me to step out to give you a minute?"

Court made a gruff sound. He could understand Lucien just fine, but right now he was more animal than human, and the wild nature inside of him didn't want to sit and bullshit, and wasn't nearly as sated in his bloodlust as he should have been. Lucien nodded again without waiting for him to shift back or for Roan to say anything, and headed out of the garage.

Court looked at Jagger, and then Roan. Lilly's brother had an expressionless face. "I hope you get yourself under control because we need to go back and see Lilly."

Court made a low warning sound in his throat. Roan might have been his best friend nearly his whole life, but right now he was on the edge and he could see that Roan realized that. Lucien came back in a few minutes later and tossed a pair of jeans onto one of the toolboxes.

"These should fit you." And then he looked over at Jagger. "You need anything? Need me to call my guys to get her car towed back to Steel Corner?"

Jagger shook his head. "Thanks, but no need. I was about to call one of my guys to get it."

Lucien nodded. "No problem." Lucien turned, looked once more at Court, and then turned and left the three of them alone.

"You good, Court? You need to run off the steam?"

He shook his head after Jagger spoke, well, as well as he could seeing as he was in his bear form. He just needed to get back to Lilly, and he wasn't about to do that looking like this.

He closed his eyes and concentrated on lowering his blood pressure and calming his erratic heart. Slowly, after several minutes, he was able to do that, and soon shift back to a human. When he was no longer a bear he walked over to the utility sink and washed the blood off his body as best he could. Roan walked over and did the same, and once Court was dressed once more they headed back to the clubhouse and to Lilly, the woman that he wanted to claim as his old lady. But the problem he faced was whether he could mend turning his back on not just Lilly, but Roan, too.

Once he was cleaned up as well as he was going to get, he got dressed and headed out of the garage. He closed his eyes and took a deep breath. Court was still ramped up and felt the adrenaline of killing that fucker pump through his veins. But he wasn't nearly sated from taking that fucker's life, and in fact felt even wilder. His bear was greedier for more bloodshed, and he wished he would have taken it slow when ending that piece of shit's life. He sensed Roan and Jagger behind him, but they kept their distance and didn't try to calm him down. Court was too far gone as it was. He paced the length of the gravel driveway, and clenched and unclenched his hands. His knuckles cracked, and he thought for sure his skin would split open from how tightly he was straining. He had never felt this out of control before. Although he did have a wild animal housed inside of him, and the bastard was a beast and tried to exert his supremacy on more than one occasion, at this moment in time Court felt like he could go on a fucking murdering spree for how unstable he felt.

"You need to go hit up a fight at the barn?" Jagger was a few feet away still, but Court heard him nonetheless.

He scrubbed a hand over his face then ran it over the back of his head. Grabbing a chunk of hair that was damp from when he had done a quick clean in the sink, he tugged on it. He probably could use a fight, but first he needed to see Lilly and make sure she got home okay. Court walked over to the treeline and braced a hand on the thick trunk of an evergreen. He closed his eyes again, feeling like he had this whiplash effect going on inside of him. He curled his hands into the tree, felt his nails lengthen into claws as his bear came forth, and heard the pieces of bark fall to his feet. Feeling his blood boil as he saw in his head the images of Lilly hurt, he reared his hand back and slammed his fist into the trunk over and over again, and with enough force that the trunk crumbled beneath his fist. Instantly he felt his skin break open and scented his blood mix with the wood that his hand was currently embedded in, but at least he felt a small semblance of relief. The pain felt good. When he pulled his hand away and looked at the trunk, Court saw the destruction he had done. He heard footsteps move up behind him, scented Jagger, and then saw the rag his President held out. Court grabbed it, and wrapped the cloth around his knuckles. "Thanks."

"Better?"

"A little." Court turned and looked at his President. "I need to see Lilly." He didn't wait for Jagger to say anything, and didn't stop to say anything to Roan. He wanted his woman, needed to see her and smell her in order to further calm himself. He made his way inside and to the girl that he cared about more than anything else.

****

Roan pulled his car to a stop in front of their mom's house and cut the engine. Lilly could hear the sound of Court's Harley right behind them, and she looked at her brother. He didn't say anything, but the look on his face spoke enough. He was still angry over the situation, and still pained over what had happened to her.

They had stayed at the clubhouse for another hour once Court and Roan had come back to where she was. Right away she had known the guy that had hurt her was dead. There was blood that Roan hadn't managed to clean completely from his hands and some blood on Court's neck.

"Let's wait until morning to tell Mom about all of this, please." Roan looked over at the house, and all of the lights were off except the kitchen. "I just don't think she needs to hear this, or see your face when it's so late." He sighed, closed his eyes for a second, and when he opened them and looked at her there was so much pain she swore it was a living entity.

"Roan, you know she hasn't gone to bed, especially not when we weren't home yet."

He leaned his head back on the seat and closed his eyes once more. She reached her hand out and placed it on his forearm. He didn't move, but he did sigh heavily, and finally, after several long seconds, turn to look at her.

"I know, but I just hoped she would be asleep. You know how this is going to make her feel. She's going to freak—and rightly so—but she doesn't need this shit. Fuck, Lilly, you didn't need this shit."

Her face felt sore and swollen, but she knew if she wasn't on the pain meds the doctor had given her it would be a lot worse.

The sound of Court cutting his engine had her looking behind her and out the back window. He was on the phone, and his deep voice was clear, but his words were muffled.

"I know something happened between you two."

She looked over at him, but wasn't surprised. The way Court had acted had been way out of character. Roan might not know about the whole sex in the back of his truck, but she was sure he had wondered how far it had gone. Before she could say something he shook his head.

"Listen, I don't care one way or another."

That surprised her.

"I don't want to know details, but the way he acted when he saw you, and the way he spoke about you, made it pretty clear there were unresolved feelings between the two of you."

Lilly really didn't know what to say, because honestly she had never thought Court saw her as anything more than a mistake he had made with his best friend's little sister.

The silence of Court no longer talking had her looking behind her shoulder again. He climbed off his bike and took his helmet off. She definitely had feelings for him, strong ones like how she had all those years ago, but she honestly didn't think how he had acted today meant anything other than a girl he had known forever had gotten hurt. Of course she wanted to think otherwise, but she was trying to be realistic, because she didn't think her heart could take another cold shoulder turned her way by Court She also didn't know what Roan meant when he had told her that he knew something happened between them because of what Court had said about her. What had he said that would make Roan think that?

A tap on her window had her glancing to her side and seeing Court standing there. He looked so damn good in his t-shirt and cut, but she shouldn't be thinking anything was attractive in her condition. It wasn't just a sexual feeling toward him, but this spark of memories she had shared with him when she was younger. They may not have meant anything to Court, and he probably didn't really remember, but to her they were locked away in her mind forever.

"We'll talk about this later, Lilly." Roan reached over and clasped her hand. There was no anger in his voice, and for that she was thankful. There were too many other things that took precedence right now. She nodded and opened her door. Court was right there, his hands on her waist and helping her out.

"I'm fine, really." She smiled up at him. She really was okay, but then again she wasn't. The image of the guy on that deserted stretch of road, over her, his heavy weight suffocating her, played through her mind like a broken record. She kept seeing that guy reaching for his belt to undo it, and feeling his hot breath on her. She didn't even want to think about what would have happened if the bikers hadn't shown up. It was one of those situations where she would have never thought it would happen to her.

"You're not, but everything will be okay now, baby." He shut the door once she was fully standing.

Lilly looked up at him. "Why do you keep calling me things like that?" Now was not the time to really get into this, but then again she didn't want to act like Court's behavior was normal. She hadn't spoken to him in a long time, and then this happened, and it was like he had put some kind of claim on her.

"I have."

She knitted her brows, well, as well as she could with the swelling. His words confused her. "What?"

"I have claimed you, Lilly, and I shouldn't have walked away all those years ago."

He said that too low for anyone else but her to hear, and she was rocked to the core with shock by his words. Was he serious right now? It had been five years, and because she was hurt something had changed in him and he felt like she was *his*? Lilly was too tired to really analyze it, but it seemed surreal, and she really couldn't wrap her head around it. Before she could say anything Court was leading her toward the front of the house. Strangely enough Roan didn't say anything about the way Court had his arm wrapped around her waist, and had her pressed tightly to the side of his body.

They walked up the front step, but the door was opened before they reached it. Her mom stood in the doorway with her robe wrapped around her body tight enough that it looked uncomfortable.

"I tried calling Roan, several times, but no one answered." She was staring at Roan, but when she looked at Court there was a moment of surprise on her face. "Court?" But that surprise was short-lived when she turned her attention to Lilly. Her mouth opened, her eyes widened, and tears immediately formed. "Oh my God." Diera had her arms wrapped around Lilly seconds later and was leading her into the house, silently crying. When the door shut and everyone was in the living room, her mother finally spoke again. "What happened?" She went to touch Lilly's face, but just like her brother had done she curled her fingers into her palm and stopped right before she made contact.

Lilly didn't have the strength or energy to retell the story, but fortunately Roan was already speaking and going over it with their mother, though his version was condensed considerably. Lilly knew it was to spare her mother the nightmarish details. The drugs that she was on were slowly starting to wear off, and the throbbing in her face intensified. Her palms were cut up, but the doctor had bandaged those up, as well as her ribs. Fortunately, they were only bruised and not broken.

"I think I want to go to bed." She interrupted her mother's crying, feeling horrible that she had to go through this as well as everything else in her life, but right now Lilly just couldn't think straight. Too much had happened in the last several hours, enough to make her head spin.

It was like her words had made everyone move into action, because all three of them went to help her stand. As much as their affection and love to help her was appreciated, she didn't want to have them flock toward her like she was this broken person.

"I can do it. Please, stop fussing." They all took a step back, and she left them in the living room. A shower would have been nice, but she was just too tired and in too much pain. Once in her room with the door shut she sat on the edge of her bed and set her purse down beside her. Reaching inside for the bottle of pain pills, she popped some in her mouth and went for the bottle of water she kept on her nightstand. And then she lay back without removing her shoes or anything else, and let sleep take her away.

Chapter Six

Court sat in the truck with Stinger. They were in the center of town and were waiting for Lucien and his men to make the pass through Steel Corner to their whorehouse. It had been two days since he had killed the man that had hurt Lilly, and forty-eight fucking hours since he had seen the woman that he couldn't stop thinking about. He wanted to go see Lilly, but he had to watch to make sure Lucien, or whoever was transporting the women that were paid to fuck high-profile men, got through town without incident. But after everything that had gone down he trusted The Brothers of Menace, and knew that Jagger and the other Grizzlies did, too. But tonight wasn't about making sure the MC didn't fuck with their town. It was to make sure no one fucked with *them*. It had just taken that one incident to bring the two MCs together. The Brothers had looked out for Lilly and Roan, hadn't fucked around when it came to the bastard responsible for fucking her up, and to the Grizzlies that went a long way in assuring they were as tight as two allies could be. When another MC looked out for the people associated with another club, took care of them until they got there, and made sure to help exact vengeance for the ones that were hurt, that meant they were good fucking men, and respected by The Grizzly MC.

"Your girl doing good?"

Court looked over at Stinger and thought about his question. "I guess she's as good as can be expected given the situation." Stinger may not have been there because he had been drunker than shit, but every member of the club knew what had gone down, and that Lilly was his. The meeting they had earlier that day had cemented that in stone, and what he had gotten from the members of the club was support and brotherly love. He still hadn't really talked to her about why he had gone all possessive and proprietary on her, but she was a smart girl. He had also told her that he had claimed her when she had spoken aloud. Whether she knew what that really meant was still left to be seen. It was like a switch had gone off in his body, his bear had taken control, and he had gotten his head out of his ass and realized what was important to him.

"How many times you been to the barn to fight?"

Court looked over at Stinger again, and on instinct touched the cut under his eye that he had gotten just that night. Yeah, it had been two days since he had seen Lilly and killed that fucker that had hurt her, but he had been on this rampage for violence. Since leaving her house he had been to the barn three different times and taken out three different shifters. He felt a lot calmer now that he had a lot of his aggression out, but leave it to his thoughts of Lilly hurt to have him thinking about kicking someone's ass again. "Enough to help ease my bear and fuck people up." He looked out the windshield once more. His knuckles were also beat to shit, but he liked the pain, especially when he was in this kind of foul mood.

"I didn't even know you were serious about anyone. I mean you've been fucking club pussy for a long ass time."

Court looked forward again. "Well, we haven't really talked in a few years, but we have a history."

Stinger didn't say anything, but the sound of an approaching car had them sitting up straighter in the truck and had their senses going on alert. They watched the blacked out van pass through the center of town, and then pulled out behind it. They weren't trying to be stealthy in following them, because Lucien knew that they were doing it to make sure shit went okay on both ends. Once the van left Steel Corner Court turned the truck around and headed back to the clubhouse. What he wanted to do was see Lilly, but it was late, and the last two times he had tried and gone to see her Roan had said she was sleeping. How much could one person sleep? But he knew she had been hurt pretty badly, was on pain meds, and that she needed all the rest she could get. But he was selfish, wanted to be the one to help her heal, and was getting antsy to see and touch her again. Two days wasn't long at all, but then again it felt like the longest two days of his life.

He pulled the truck into the clubhouse parking lot and killed the engine. Stinger was already climbing out, and Court debated just heading back to his place.

"You coming in for a drink?" Stinger looked at him.

"I don't know. I'm not really in the mood."

Stinger gave him a shocked look. "Not in the mood for a drink? Dude, get your ass out of the truck and come inside. You know all you're going to do to if you go back home is think about your girl, and all the shit you did or didn't do."

The thing with Stinger was he played a part, as they all did to a point. He was there for the club and the members, and although he acted one way on the outside, Court could look in his eyes and see that he wasn't as easygoing as he tried to play. Maybe it was because of the gunshot Stinger had gotten from that bastard Trick? In the end if Stinger wanted to talk they were there, and as long as he didn't put the club in jeopardy they kept out of his business. Court hadn't said anything about what he had or hadn't done, just that they hadn't talked in a while, but Stinger had read him well enough.

"Come on. Some bullshitting will do you some good."

Court ran his hand over the back of his head and sighed. "Yeah, okay." Because Stinger was right, he would have just gone home and thought about a bunch of depressing shit. He climbed out of the truck and headed inside. There wasn't some crazy party going on, but there was a hardcore poker game being played. A lot of cursing and banter were being thrown around, a few of the club whores were hanging on the members, and some of the prospects were keeping the guys hydrated with beer and shots.

"Hey, Court and Stinger are here. Party is about to get started," Drevin yelled out. The blond biker raised his beer, clearly already drunk by the slur in his voice.

"Drevin, shut up, man," Dallas said with a joint hanging from between his lips. Drevin had been MIA during the whole Lilly incident, and although he had been filled in he either didn't know how deep all that shit had been—not likely—or he was too drunk to fully realize how he was acting. But Court wasn't in the mood to correct the asshole on anything, and turned around and headed to the bar. One drink and he would head home. He was tired, couldn't get Lilly out of his head, and just wanted to crash until shit looked a lot better.

****

Lilly lay on her bed and stared at her ceiling. Her mother's home was in an older development of town, and the streetlights were in desperate need to being changed. As it was the globes were foggy and the lights a yellowish color, and when the glow came through her bedroom window it made this piss color stain across her walls and ceiling. Her head chose that moment to throb, but she just closed her eyes and breathed through the discomfort. She had stopped taking the narcotics, and was now only on ibuprofen. It certainly didn't have the same pleasant effect the Percocets had, but she could deal with it.

But it wasn't just the discomfort that was keeping her up. She had also been thinking a lot about Court and everything he had done for her and said. She had spoken to Roan about it, but she hadn't gone into details with him about what exactly had happened between her and Court years ago. More specifically she hadn't told him about them having sex, just that they had shared some time together, and then after that summer they hadn't spoken again. But it didn't take a genius to realize what had gone down, and Roan was no fool. But he hadn't pressed her, and she knew he was either waiting until she was fully healed, or he was going to confront Court first. She wasn't looking forward to either of those scenarios, because surely they couldn't end well.

She pushed herself up in bed and grabbed her duvet to wrap it around herself. The swelling was significantly less, but the bruising was horrendous. Her job at the coffee shop was put on hold, and class was still up in the air. She was so close to being finished with it, but she just couldn't even think about going back there just yet, or traveling down that long, isolated strip of road. Just thinking about it had her shaking and wrapping the blanket around her even tighter. Although it was late, she had a feeling Court would be up. He had always been a night owl back in the day, and she didn't think joining an MC made that change.

Lilly wanted to talk to him and look into his face so much that it startled her. It didn't matter that so much time had passed between them. When he had looked at her when she was at The Brothers of Menace clubhouse, she had known there was no burying her love for him. She stood and grabbed her phone off the nightstand. For a second all she did was stare at the black screen. He had left his number with her mom the night he had helped her inside, but she hadn't tried calling it yet. Roan had told her he had stopped by the last couple of days, but each time she had been asleep. It would have been easy for her to call him, but the last forty-right hours she had been trying to wrap her head around everything that had happened, and clearly everything that was happening between her and Court. There was no fear that the man that had hurt her would come back, because although she had asked Roan what had happened to him, her brother had just told her that Court had handled it. The memory of the blood that had coated them, and then the sight of Roan's knuckles scabbed over told her exactly what had happened.

Not thinking about it anymore, she dialed Court's number and brought the phone to her ear. Her heart was beating so fast she could hardly hear herself think. Someone on the other line picked up, and she heard loud voices, cursing, and female laughter. God, was he with someone right now? It would be so contradictory to the way he had acted toward her and how he told her he had claimed her.

"Lilly."

She was a little shocked to know that he knew it was her, but maybe Roan had given him her number? "Hi. It's not too late to call you, is it?" The loud noises faded away, and she heard a door opening and then closing.

"It's never too late. You call me anytime you want, no matter the hour." His deep voice came through the line like a warm caress, and she smiled at his words.

"You might regret that." She laughed softly, teasing him because she was so sick of this dread and uncertainty she felt inside that she just wanted a moment of peace.

"Lilly, nothing you could do would make me think that."

She swallowed and moved back over to her bed and sat down. "I, uh." She licked her lips and hated that she was so nervous talking to him, but it had been a long time since she was in this situation, and as hard as it was to forget, all she kept thinking about was the last time they had been around each other.

"You're okay?" There was genuine worry in his voice.

"I'm okay, just can't sleep and wanted to talk to you."

"You did?"

She couldn't help but smile at the surprise now in his voice. "Yeah, I did." There was a moment of silence. "I—"

"Since I'm awake, and you can't sleep, maybe I can come see you?"

Okay, that hadn't been what she thought he would say. "Really? It's pretty late."

"I don't care how late it is because I want to see you. I've been trying to for the last two days." There was a desperate note in his voice, and it was so strange because Court had always been in control at all times.

"I don't want to take you away from anything." She still heard the female's laugh close to the phone, and hated that she was self-conscious enough to let that bother her.

"Nah, there isn't anything that could keep me away from you."

Oh. Well. Wow.

"Give me twenty and I'll be over." There was this almost hitch in his voice after he said that. Maybe it meant excitement?

"Okay." There was another round of silence, but this time it wasn't awkward. After they said their goodbye she disconnected the call and just sat there staring at her phone for a few seconds. Finally she forced herself to stand and grabbed an oversized sweater and a pair of leggings. She wasn't about to see Court in her old ass sleeping shirt, even if he was just coming over to talk.

Once she was dressed and it had been about twenty minutes, she started to get really nervous and continuously picked at the edge of her shirt. It was horrible feeling this way, but she couldn't help it. Of course she wanted more with Court, but common sense told her that if it happened that way all those years ago, why would this time be any different? As if her thoughts conjured him she heard the sound of a motorcycle coming closer, and then saw her phone light up with a text.

Court: *I'm outside. Is it okay to come in? Or if you are feeling up to it we can go for a ride?*

A ride? Aside from her ribs being a little sore and her face looking all screwed up she only felt a little discomfort now, and she wondered if she had all this adrenaline pumping through her body because Court was here? She certainly wasn't hurting like she had been before he had called. But getting on the back of his bike probably wasn't the best idea right now, at least not until she was fully healed.

How about you come inside?

She sent the text to him and then set her phone on the bedside table. Her room was on the other side of the house from her mother's room and had a set of sliding glass door that led out to the small bedroom patio. Roan's room was in the basement, so he was far enough away he wouldn't hear them talking. She just didn't want anyone thinking they were doing more than that, not in her mom's house, or after all the shit that had happened the last couple of days.

He hadn't sent a text back, but right before she grabbed her phone and sent another text she heard heavy footsteps on the patio right outside her sliding doors. A second later there was a light tapping on the glass door. Her palms were suddenly so sweaty, and she wiped them on her thighs. She stood and walked over to the door, unlocked it and slid it open. He didn't move inside right away, but they did stand there for several seconds and just stare at each other.. Even with only the light of the moon casting a glow from behind him Lilly could see how muscular and tall he was. Lilly had always been on the thick side, and having a size sixteen frame had made her feel fat all through high school. Now she was comfortable in her curvier frame, but being so close to Court made her feel small and petite. The shadows concealed the front half of him partially, but it didn't cover the clear cut under his eye or the bruises that marred his cheek.

"God, are you okay?" She went to reach up and touch his face, but as fast as lightning he took hold of her wrist, stopping her, and brought her open palm to his lips He kissed the center of her hand, and her heart picked up pace. Maybe she shouldn't feel desire right now, but even with the small wounds he was still so damn attractive, maybe even more so because of them. He looked hardened, so powerful, and like no one could take him down. She hated to see what the other guy looked like. God, her feelings for him were as strong as ever.

"I'm good, Lilly. It's just a little cut." He kissed the center of her palm once more, and she swore he inhaled her wrist before he let her hand go. "You're doing okay?" Even speaking so low that it was almost a whisper his voice was so deep and masculine.

She nodded and stepped back. "I'm okay." Why did she feel so nervous right now? When he didn't move forward she stepped aside and smiled up at him. She didn't miss the dark look that covered his face as he clearly got a look at hers.

"You hurting, baby?" He stepped inside, and she closed the door behind him.

"Just a little, but really, I'm fine." For a moment he just looked at her room, and all she did was inhale the scent of male that came from him. It was everything she remembered and more, and she actually felt herself leaning toward him, as if she just had to get closer. He turned away from her and glanced at her room. When he faced her again the intense heat that came from him had her taking a step forward. She instantly felt her cheeks heat at the fact she had been moving toward him without even realizing it. He was potent and intense in only the best of ways.

He reached out to touch her, but he didn't stop like her mother and Roan had. Instead he very gently cupped her cheek that was uninjured. "I want to kill him all over again for what he did to you." He rubbed his thumb over her cheek bone, back and forth, so very gently. It sounded like he was almost talking to himself, but she didn't respond anyway. Lilly didn't know what to say to that.

For a moment all she did was soak in the feel of Court's fingers on her. It was an innocent touch, but coming from him it meant so much more to her. "You killed him." She didn't phrase it like a question, because it wasn't one. She had known what Court and Roan had done, but she felt no anger or remorse that the asshole that had hurt her was dead. He didn't say anything for a few seconds, but he also didn't let go of her face. Finally, after what seemed like forever of him just brushing her cheek with his thumb, he dropped his hand. Instead of moving away he reached out and pulled her into the warm hardness of his chest.

"Would it change the way you thought of me if I told you I fucking liked killing that prick?"

She rested head rested right over his heart and heard the steady, strong sound of it beating right below her ear. The crazy thing was it didn't upset her that he and Roan had killed that man. She wrapped her arms around him even tighter. "No, it wouldn't." If she just kept her eyes closed and let her mind wander she could imagine that they were five years in the past in some kind of alternate world where she had always been with Court.

"He deserved far worse than I gave him."

Lilly curled her fingers into the back of his shirt and breathed out. She had been missing this for so long, and she hadn't even realized how much she had missed it until this very moment.

"We have a lot to talk about," Court said in that gruff voice of his.

Yeah, they did, but she didn't want to move out of his embrace. Lilly forced herself to move away, though. Her bedroom was small and still had trinkets around that she had collected while in high school. At the time she had collected that stuff it had seemed cute and held memories of a time past, but now it just seemed childish as she stood in the center of her room with Court. He took her hand and led her over to the bed. Once they were seated and she faced him, he reached out and smoothed his hand down the side of her head. For a second he just cupped her head, and then he smoothed that hand over her shoulder and down her arm to rest on her hand once more.

"This seems all so strange, Court." Could he hear her heart beating like a freight train? Could he see how nervous she was? Dammit, could he see the light perspiration that had started to form on her brow because she was aroused and confused, and had about a hundred other emotions moving through her? *Don't be stupid, Lilly. This man is not a man at all, not really. He is a bear shifter, and can probably sense your emotions better than you can.*

"Yeah, I know, baby." He squeezed her hand and smiled down at her. It looked almost ridiculous to have this huge man on her twin sized bed. "It shouldn't have taken all this time for me to realize that pushing you away, distancing my friendship with Roan, and thinking that what we had done would ruin everything because I betrayed my best friend, was the right course of action." He looked down at the ground for a suspended moment. "Because of how I acted I have a broken friendship, five years of missed time with you." He looked at her then. "It is fucked up that it takes me looking at you, knowing that I wasn't with you to protect you, to make me realize that I fucked up big time."

Lilly's pulse was racing at hearing Court's words. She hadn't known where she expected this conversation to go, but she hadn't thought Court would reveal this much. "I knew that what we had done wasn't right because of your friendship with my brother, but I cared for you a lot back them, Court ... still do." She said the last part more on a whisper, but she saw the flare of his nostrils, and for some reason she just knew that he was pleased.

"Did you remember that graduation party your mom threw for you?"

She nodded.

"And that Zack douche was hitting on you?"

Lilly blinked a few times at hearing Court bring that moment up. "Yeah, I remember, but—" She knitted her brows and looked down for a moment. She remembered that day vividly, but what she didn't remember was seeing Court there. "But how did you know Zack was hitting on me? Weren't you working?" She knew Roan had invited him, but to her disappointment he had been working late.

He slowly shook his head. "I was supposed to be working late, but I headed out early. I stopped by and saw you sitting on the deck with a few of your friends around. You were wearing this yellow and blue dress, and you had left your hair down." He lifted his hand, grabbed a piece of her hair, and ran the strands between his thumb and forefinger. "I could smell you even from the distance. It was this soft cotton scent, like freshly laundered clothing that had been dried in the sun." Any other time if someone would have said that she smelled like laundry she would have told them that was a ridiculous description, but hearing it from Court somehow made it sound so erotic. "Up until that moment I had never seen you other than Roan's little sister. You were ten years younger than me, and I knew going after you was wrong on many levels." Hearing Court confess all of this was so surreal. She just wished he would have said something sooner. "And then that Zack kid went up to you, and I could smell how badly he wanted you. This anger rose up in me, and I became so fucking pissed. I was determined that no one would have you but me." His voice was so rough after he said that, and there was this slight growl to his words. He looked away from her for a second, and she could hear him grinding his teeth, as if he were remembering that day and how angry he had been.

Lilly couldn't help herself. She reached out and cupped his cheek and used a slight amount of pressure to turn his head so he was now looking at her. "I wish you would have told me this years ago, Court."

He lifted his hand and covered her hers with it. "It took me this long to realize that I wish I would have. After you and me—" He grew silent for a moment, but she didn't try to rush him. This conversation was a long time in coming. "After I took you in the back of my truck I knew I had fucked up."

Warmth filled her at hearing him say those words, and then at the memory of that night that slammed into her head. A low sound left him, and her nipples hardened instantly. She shouldn't have this reaction right now, because it seemed grossly inappropriate, but it was like her body had a mind of its own.

"I can smell how much you want me, Lilly, and if I don't get this out now I know that I won't be able to later." He leaned in an inch, and she surprised herself by staying right where she was.

"Why won't you be able to talk to me later?" Those words left her on a low rush of air, and she couldn't think of why she would ask him that. He leaned in another inch, so close now that she could smell his warm, minty breath that was lightly laced with the scent of hops.

"Because I'll be taking you like I did all those years ago, but this time I won't run away because I was too fucking afraid of how I felt for you, and worried about what would happen between Roan and me." She sucked in a deep breath and slowly released it. "And I was scared, Lilly, but not just about how I thought it would ruin my friendship with Roan, but because I was afraid of the way my bear wanted you just as much as my human side did." Before she could say anything he had his mouth on hers. He was gentle and coaxing and didn't try to rush her. He cupped the uninjured side of her face once more and tilted her head to the side so he could deepen the kiss. The feeling of him stroking her tongue with his, and moving that thick muscle along the inside of her mouth until she felt like a warm puddle before him, had her softly moaning against his lips. He broke the kiss far too soon, and she forced her eyes open.

"I could kiss you all night, but I want to continue talking, Lilly."

She nodded and licked her lips, tasting him on her mouth. "Okay." He leaned in and softly kissed her this time with no tongue. When he pulled away there was so much emotion on his face that it was hard for her to breathe, given how strongly it filled the air between them.

He smoothed his hand along her cheek, and that spark of arousal was still there, although it was pushed aside when this serious look crossed his face. "After that I immersed myself in fixing anything with wheels. I distanced myself from Roan, feeling like a worthless bastard because I felt I betrayed him by being with you." She had assumed as much. "It was hard staying away, and over time Roan and I just went our separate ways. Your mom got sick, and you both had so much on your plates."

She remembered him coming by when they first found out her mom had cancer. They hadn't spoken, and at that time it had been such a long time since everything had gone down that being in his presence had been just awkward.

"It was hard having you pull away like that, but I knew it was because you thought we had done was wrong. There was a part of me that had felt that I had betrayed Roan, too." She looked down at her lap, about to admit to him what she hadn't told anyone. "I knew doing anything with you would have repercussions, and knew you'd probably never look at me the same way again." She looked at him. "But I never thought it would ruin your relationship with my brother. For that I am truly sorry. It is all my fault, because I could have stopped it, but I didn't. I was selfish, Court."

He shook his head and leaned in to kiss her again.

"No, baby, none of this was your fault. You were so young. I was the one that knew better, but I wanted you so damn badly." He kissed her again, and again, and soon they were locked in an intimate embrace, and the past was pushed aside as their desire for each other rose to an uncontrollable level.

She moved closer and pressed her breasts to the hardness of his muscular chest. She was sore, but he was easy and soft as he ran his hands up her sides, and over her breasts. But there was a hesitance in him, and she just knew that they wouldn't go as far as she wanted them to, at least not tonight. That was okay because after waiting so long she wasn't in a rush to end this. She wanted to go slow and easy, and take her time. But on the heels of that thought she pulled back and looked into his face.

"What's wrong, baby? Am I going too fast? Being too rough?"

She smiled and shook her head. Heck, they weren't going fast enough, but she knew there wasn't any rush in being with him. "No. I just don't know where we stand. I mean, I haven't told Roan about us yet, although I know he isn't stupid and has already figured it out."

"I should have told him the moment it happened, and I should have told him that I cared about you, but my ignorance hurt the both of you. I lost out on time with you and getting to know you on a level that wasn't because you were Roan's little sister." He smiled at her, and it broke her heart at how much he seemed like he was in pain. "But I also lost five years with a man that I care for like a brother. I was blinded by my own selfishness, but I want to rectify that, now." He pulled her into a hug, but she didn't resist. They both needed the comfort.

For several minutes all he did was hold her, and Lilly closed her eyes and enjoyed the feeling of being surrounded by Court. "This is nice."

"Yeah, it really is." He pulled her back enough so that he could look in her face. "I'm going to make this right. I'm going to talk to Roan, explain everything to him, and tell him that you're the one I want." He cupped each side of her face, more gently on the wounded side, and stared right into her eyes. "I want *you*, Lilly, and I don't want to hide behind what I think may or may not happen."

She couldn't agree more, and even though this whole situation and Court's revelation felt like it had just been dropped in her life, she drew comfort in the knowledge that she hadn't been the only one that had been thinking of him all these years.

"I'm not looking to rush into anything, because I have all the time to get back to where things were. My life isn't how it used to be. I live the MC lifestyle, do things that you may not agree with, because others sure as fuck don't, but at the end of all that I want you, baby. I want you by my side. Do you want that, Lilly, to be by my side, to be my old lady?" It didn't take her long to answer, but she knew before she even said the words that he had sensed her intentions by the grin he gave her.

"You know that's what I want, what I've always wanted." She swore she saw the presence of his bear flash across his face, and even watched the way his pupils dilated and his irises turned black. A low rumble left him, and he pulled her into his arms, and then positioned them so they were lying on the bed facing each other. Once situated with her back to his chest and the heavy weight of his arm resting on her thigh, she closed her eyes, and for the first time in what felt like forever, she realized that this was what happiness felt like. She supposed she must not have realized how big the impact of being with the guy she loved was until she had lost out on time with him. It was in the form of a big, bear shifting biker that had been gone from her life for so long, yet at the same time he was so close. It was also the way she felt this inner peace, like she had finally found what she had been missing, and what she had been searching for. Only time would tell on how everything would play out, or how Roan would react. There was the fear that her brother would most definitely be angry and feel betrayed, but not just because of what she and Court had done, but of all the time lost with his once best friend.

"Get some sleep, baby." And it was as if his voice, those words, and the gentle, coaxing feeling of his hand moving up and down her back, had been the trigger she needed. Lilly closed her eyes and let the peacefulness of sleep, and the presence of her big, burly bear biker, lead her into oblivion.

Chapter Seven

Lilly looked at her brother and then turned her attention to Court. They were both sitting in the chairs across from the couch, which was where she was currently sitting. Her mom had insisted on going to a church function, and they wouldn't be picking her up for a few hours, so she thought now was as good a time as any to bring all of this out in the open.

Roan leaned back in the chair and looked between the two of them, and then scrubbed a hand over his jaw. This was the first day he had off in longer than she could remember, and just looking into his face she could see how much he had aged. She saw the dark circles under his eyes because he hadn't gotten enough sleep. There was several day old scruff covering his jaw, and Lilly regretted even bringing any of this up, but it had been kept in the dark for long enough. It had been a couple of days since Court had been to her room and they had talked about their feelings. But she had talked to him every day since then, whether it was on the phone or when he came by the house. It was still a little strange having him in the house, but a lot of that time was him catching up with Roan. Their mother had been around each time he was there, so bringing up the fact Court had taken her virginity all those years ago was a little TMI for her mom, or so Lilly assumed.

"So all of this distance, and slowly moving further away from our friendship was because you slept with Lilly at a field party and thought it was a betrayal to me?"

Court cleared his throat and nodded. He looked stiff and uncomfortable, and exactly how she felt.

"Yeah, but it wasn't just that?"

Roan lifted a brow and stared at Court. "No? You mean there is more? Like maybe how you have feelings for Lilly, but have been too much of a coward to do anything about it?"

Now it was her turn to sit up straighter at Roan's words. There wasn't any anger in her brother's words, but there was a hint of challenge directed at Court. She glanced at the big blond biker that she was falling harder for each and every time she saw him.

"Yeah, that's also a big reason I stayed back. I was confused by my feelings for Lilly, afraid that I had royally fucked up our friendship, and didn't know how to handle it besides running." The room grew silent as Court admitted that to Roan for the first time.

She glanced at her brother, saw that his attention was fully on Court and waited to see what would happen. It seemed like forever before Roan even moved in his chair, but it couldn't have been more than seconds.

"Damn, Court. I have never known you to admit when you were wrong and fucked shit up."

She was sweaty as she glanced back and forth between the two men that she cared about the most. Lilly didn't know if she was waiting for them to attack each other or what, but the room was hot and tension was running high inside of her. Then her brother started chuckling and Court followed suit, and just like that the tension drained and stunned confusion filled her. Roan leaned over and slapped Court on the back.

"Since I've known you there has only been this bad-ass bear that didn't care what anyone thought, kicked asses and asked questions later."

Court glanced away and scrubbed the back of his neck, but she saw the way he grinned. Roan grinned, too, and although everything seemed okay on the outside, she felt strange at how everything had progressed.

"So we're good, man?" Court asked, and although he outweighed Roan by a good fifty pounds of muscle, they were equal in height. Roan had more of a lean, boxer's body, one of toned sinew. Court was just brute strength all the way around.

She glanced down and saw the way Roan clenched his hands. She knew what was coming. But before she could stop it, she saw Court's face harden, and knew the bear shifter was aware of what was about to go down. But he didn't move, and when Roan reared his hand back and slammed his fist into Court's jaw, everything around her stopped. A trail of blood slowly trickled down Court's bottom lip and chin, and he wiped it away with the back of his hand.

"Now we're good," Roan said, and although there was a bite in his words, she didn't feel any animosity coming from her brother.

Would Court attack Roan, and the two of them would be in a full out brawl in her mother's living room? But before she could say anything Court started chuckling and rubbing his jaw.

"I deserved that, and more." He grinned, and thank God Roan did, too. Damn, was this how guys "made up"? She could remember her fights with her girlfriends in high school, and it had always been overly dramatic and drawn-out. There wasn't a punch to the face and things could be smooth again.

"Well, I can't really stay mad at you since you helped me with Lilly, and that goes a long way in my book. But Court, man, you have to have known that if you just came to me and told me how you felt for Lilly I would have been cool with it." But then this look covered Roan's face, as if something just came to him, and his cheeks became red. "Wait, you weren't getting with her before that night, right? You weren't fucking my *underage* little sister, were you?" Roan curled his hands into fists again, but Court was shaking his head.

"Fuck no, man. I didn't even see Lilly as anything but your kid sister until that night at her graduation party."

"I don't understand why that night made the difference?" Roan asked.

Court sat back down, and it took her a second but she followed suit. He looked at Roan, and after a minute he sighed and sat in the chair. "I don't know why it took that moment for me to realize that I wanted Lilly as something more. It was just the time my bear rose up when it saw her and smelled her scent, and I knew I was lost." Court looked over at her, and there was so much raw emotion that it was like she could feel him reaching across the space that separated them and running his fingers over her cheek. "But I knew it was wrong. You and I have a history, Roan, and I love you like a brother. It felt like I was betraying you. And shit, she is ten years younger than me."

"But five fucking years, Court? You pushed me out, turned your back on us all because of some stupid ass notion that I would what, kick a bear shifter's ass for wanting to be with my sister?" When her brother put it that way it did sound ridiculous, but now was not the time to think about any of that.

"Court had his reasons for doing what he did, and I don't think we should harp on why he did what he did. Can't we just think about now and move forward?"

Both men looked at her, and they sighed in unison.

"She's right, Roan. I fucked up, but I did what I thought was right at the time, even though it was far from it. I just want my best friend back in my life." Court turned and looked at her. "And I want to take care of Lilly." Before anyone could say anything Court's cell started vibrating. He pulled it out of his cut, looked at the screen, and stood. "I have to take this. I'm going to step outside."

Lilly watched him leave out the front door, and looked at Roan. Her brother watched her intently, and she knew she was about to get "the talk".

"You have feelings for him, Lilly, like ones that are serious enough that you want to get involved with an outlaw bear shifting biker?" She didn't need to think about Roan's words to know what she felt in her heart.

"I cared for him all those years ago, Roan, but pushed the feelings down after everything went downhill after that night." He ground his teeth, and it sounded overly loud. "I want to see where this goes."

"What if it isn't going where you think it is? What if you get hurt, Lilly?" Roan leaned forward and rested his arms on his thighs.

"Isn't life about getting hurt, dusting yourself off and trying again? And besides, I know how he makes me feel, and I see the way he looks at me."

"Yeah, I see how he looks at you too, like he wants to tear an asshole's head off if they screw with you."

That had her smiling, but not because she found it funny, but because her brother was currently wearing the same expression.

"It's been a long time, Lilly. He's changed from the guy that hung around the house all the time. He's hardened, is involved in a lot of illegal shit and is downright dangerous."

"Yet I know you wouldn't even be giving me these warnings if you didn't already trust him. If you didn't you would have kicked his ass out of the house long ago, and threatened him—bear shifter or not—never to come around me again."

Roan started chuckling and nodded. "Yeah, that's true." He sobered. "I do trust him, I saw the lengths he was willing to go with you that night; and I know that with him no one will ever hurt you again."

Before she could say anything the sound of the front door opening and closing had her turning and watching Court come back into the living room.

"I have to go, club business." He turned to face her. "Can I see you tomorrow?" The smile he gave her was panty dropping, and it was like they were the only two in the room.

Roan cleared his throat and excused himself but before he left Court reached out and embraced him. There were a few muffled words between them, but she couldn't make out what was being said. She didn't want to anyway, because this was their moment of reconciliation.

Roan left, and then it was just the two of them, and all she could do was stare at him. The emotions and feelings she had for this male were consuming but it was the good kind that made her knees weak, her heart race, and everything else feel out of place. Lilly stood and walked over to him. As soon as she was close enough he wrapped an arm around her waist and gently brought her in. She was still sore, but each day she was growing stronger and healing. Court buried his face in the crook of her neck, and she heard him inhale deeply. She grew wet at the sound of him doing that, and then felt him kissing the spot he had just smelled.

"Even after all of these years you still smell the same." He inhaled again and she felt him curl his fingers into her hips, but for such a big, hulking guy he was mindful of how tender she still was. "I want to see you tomorrow, maybe take you out to dinner?" He pulled back, but immediately leaned in and kissed her gently on the lips. "I want to do this right with you." He murmured those words against her lips.

Lilly held onto his biceps and said, "I think I like this side of you." She felt him smile against her. "But I also like the biker you've become, too." He took a step back, but still held onto her hips. No longer did he wear a grin, and she feared she might have said something wrong.

"I want this, want you so fucking badly, but I also want you to know what you're getting yourself into if you decide to be my old lady."

Old lady? Lilly knew that was a powerful title, but it was strange hearing Court say it, and calling her that no less.

"I know all about you, Court, and about the life you lead." She held onto his arms harder when she thought he might move away. "I know about the illegal stuff your club is involved in, maybe not specifics, but that it is illegal." In fact, everyone in town knew. It wasn't like it was a secret. Well, the details were, of course. "I know how dangerous your life is, and how loyal you are to your biker family. We've grown up in this town and I know The Grizzly MC and what they represent."

"It's what *I* represent, Lilly."

"I know." She gave herself a moment to think about what she was going to say. "What I'm saying is that I know about you and what you are, and I still want you more than ever. Trying to live safely got me nowhere except with this." She pointed to her face, and a low growl left him. He had her in his arms once again and cupped the back of her head with his big hand. "I just want to be with you, and you are the one I feel safest with." She felt safe with Roan, but this was a different kind of safe.

They kissed once more. "I'm glad to hear that, because I want all of that and more with you. I'll call you later, baby." One last kiss and then he was striding out of the doors. The sound of his Harley being started could be heard easily.

Well, she knew she was in for one hell of a ride, and it looked like she would need to hold on tight.

Chapter Eight

Court entered the clubhouse with determined strides. Jagger had called him to tell him there was an issue with The Brothers of Menace, and that they had reached out for some extra manpower. He saw everyone in the meeting room and strode forward. Jagger stood at the head of the table, and the rest of the crew were either leaning against the wall, or sitting down. Although everyone looked calm, there was a thick tension in the room.

Jagger looked up at him when he entered. "Good, you're here. I was just about to go over all the details since Lucien called and laid it out."

"Okay, what's up?" Court took a seat and glanced around the table. Everyone was in attendance.

"Lucien called be a little bit ago asking me to round everyone up because they needed some extra muscle. He just called me five minutes ago with more details. Apparently one of the high-profile johns beat up one of his girls bad enough that they were forced to take her to the hospital," Jagger said with a grim voice.

"What's with all these fuckers beating up on females?" Brick said with a hard bite in his voice. The room was starting to grow warmer as everyone's bear was rising up.

"I don't know, but Lucien and his crew are out for blood, and we are going to help him find the fucker," Jagger said and looked around the room. "This guy wasn't properly high-profile, at least not yet. He is the son of a senator, and the kid was only nineteen. The father paid for his son to get his cherry popped, but the kid got away after he nearly killed the girl."

"How the fuck did he escape? Don't they have guys watching over the girls?" Diesel growled out.

"Lucien said they found angel dust in the room he was in. The guy must have gotten high, thought he was Superman, and went after the girl. She couldn't affirm that because when they went in there to get her after the hour was up and neither of them had left the room, she was out cold and half dead. The fucker escaped out the window and out into the woods. Lucien's guess is he was getting rough, and when she went to call out for help from the guys watching over the girls he snapped and starting beating the shit out of her."

There was a collective round of curses, and the tension in the room grew tenfold as bears fought with their human counterparts to escape.

"What's the plan?" Court asked and curled his fingers into his palms. All he could keep thinking of was his Lilly beaten and scared, and how that woman—prostitute or not—had probably felt the same fear and pain as his old lady had.

"The guy is higher than a kite out there, and no way can he navigate in the woods in the darkness or in that condition. Lucien and his men can go after him, and are, but they want our bears to help since we can smell the motherfucker out." Made sense when Lucien and his guys were human and wouldn't be able to find the bastard if he was hiding or had passed out somewhere.

"Well let's get the fuck moving," Diesel said.

Court stood and cracked his knuckles. He didn't know the girl that got hurt, but he didn't care. She was a female, had gotten hurt because some asshole thought to exert his strength on her, and thought he could get away with it. He didn't care if the guy had been high and might not have known what he was doing. None of that mattered because the end result was the same: find him and kill him.

"We are to *find* him, but Lucien will be dishing out the pain, got it?" Jagger specifically looked at Court, but it wasn't a warning, just a piece of information because he knew how pissed Court still was over Lilly getting hurt.

"Yeah, prez, I got it."

Jagger nodded. "Good, now let's get this shit going, find the fucker, and bring some justice to that female."

They headed out of the clubhouse and grabbed a couple of prospects on the way out. The woods that surrounded The Brothers' whorehouse stretched on for miles. It was undeveloped land, and if the kid didn't know shit about the area he was going to have one hell of a time trying to find his way out, especially if he was high.

The mounted their bikes, helmeted up, and started their engines. Court's blood pumped hard through his veins, and his bear was anxious for some violence. He just needed to make sure if he got to the kid first his bear didn't take control. If his animal came through and took control there wouldn't be any stopping the destruction it caused.

****

They had been searching the woods for the last half an hour, but just because The Grizzly MC was in their animal forms didn't mean they could find the fucker in a matter of minutes, especially when it had started raining and washed away recent scents. Now the smells that invaded his nose were of dirt, moss, and rain. He stopped and rose up on his back legs, inhaling deeply. He tried to pick out each individual scent. He scented other Grizzly MC members and heard their steps in the distance. For several minutes he didn't do anything but stand there scenting the air. The human aroma of Lucien and his men surrounded him, as did their rage. He knew those emotions all too well, but his own were not only because another female had gotten hurt, but because *his* female had been hurt, too. He wanted to protect her from the ugliness of the world and from the ugliness of what he was involved in. If he wasn't so selfish he would have let her go, because the violence associated with the MC life were not what he wanted for any female, even if he would protect her with his life.

There was a snap of a twig to his left, and he swung his big head in that direction and inhaled deeply. He caught the scent of toxic waste and made a low sound in his throat. Court moved through the woods until the smell intensified and the light sound of mumbling came through the other sounds of the forest. And then in the distance he saw slight movement. He made his way closer and tried to stay quiet so as not to alert the little prick. When Court finally saw him he realized the drugged out asshole wasn't even aware of his presence. He was busy trying to grab invisible things in the air. His bear was ready to attack and end this miserable human's life, but instead he forced his human side to take control and shifted back to his human form. It had been easier to control himself than he thought, but in all honesty if he was going to deliver a hurting he wanted to feel his fist slam into flesh.

"You fucked up, boy."

The kid turned and looked at Court. "You come here to steal my soul?" the kid asked with wide, seemingly clear eyes. Court had heard about PCP, about the hallucinogenic qualities of the drug, and also of the superhuman strength. The kid stood, but was stark naked. He leaned down and picked up a stick, and brought it down across his chest. His flesh opened up, and blood dripped down his pale body. "You can take my soul, but I'll still have control over the demon dominion."

What. The. Fuck. This kid was off his rocker, but before Court could even respond the kid was charging forward. The stick was still in his hand and raised high above him. He intended to kill Court with a stick? The kid continued forward, but Court held his ground, and when he was an inch away Court reached out and slammed his fist into the side of the kid's head. He fell backward, and although that should have knocked his ass out he was wasted and flying higher than a damn plane. He pulled himself up and weaved on his feet.

"That bitch didn't want to give me her soul, and so I did her over real good. Next time she won't think about whether or not to sacrifice herself for the God of Darkness." He lifted his arms in the air and tilted his head back. The yell that came from him would alert everyone in the surrounding area to where he was.

Court was running on his rage and couldn't control himself. He charged forward and slammed his body into the kid's. They fell to the ground, and Court straddled him, reared his arm back, and connected his fist into the human's head again. But just when he was about to hit him once again, release all his anger on this piece of shit, someone wrapped their arms around his chest and hauled him off. It was a bear shifter because no one else would have had the strength to remove him, but then he smelled Dallas and tore away from the other male.

"Court, this is not our fight. We are just here to find him, not kill him. That is for Lucien and The Brothers of Menace to handle."

Court's chest rose and fell, and although he knew Dallas spoke the truth, trying to control himself was fucking hard. But the sound and scent of the other Grizzly members, and Lucien and his men coming forward, had Court forcing himself to relax. Taking this away from Lucien wasn't right, because if someone had killed the bastard that hurt Lilly—aside from Roan, that is— he would have wanted blood from everyone. He took a step back just as everyone came through the thickness of the woods. Lucien stalked toward, reached down and wrapped his hand around the kid's throat, and hauled his ass up.

"You are about to experience a world of hurt, boy."

The kid started laughing, and it was this crazy sound.

"But don't worry, we will let you sober up before we give you what you deserve for hurting one of our girls," Lucien said and turned to look at Court and the rest of The Grizzly MC. "Thanks for helping out."

Court nodded and watched as The Brothers of Menace made their way out of the forest, dragging that fucker out with them.

"Think they will kill him?" Stinger asked.

Court didn't know, and honestly, if Lucien hadn't come when he did Court probably would have twisted his head off with his bare hands. After all this, and knowing what that kid had done to a female, made Court want to go see Lilly and hold her tight even more than he normally did. But it was late, and he had tomorrow to look forward to. It was funny what love could do to a male, and he loved Lilly with a ferocity that startled even his inner animal.

****

Lilly looked at herself in the mirror and knew this was a bad idea. The bruising in her face was horrendous, and the swelling wasn't completely healed. She also felt like an idiot for the dress she had on—the yellow one with the blue flowers that Court had told her he remembered her wearing all those years ago. But she had wanted to surprise him, and thought it was a good idea until she had the damn thing on and saw her reflection.

She had been a thick girl in high school, but had gained some weight over the past five years. Her tits, especially, were larger, and her cleavage was so prominent it was like her boobs were trying to eat her dress. She turned to the side and glanced at her ass. "Shit, it really has gotten bigger." Yeah, that had grown, too. How in the world had she not realized how big her butt had gotten? There was a knock on the door, and she called out, "Come on in."

"Lilly?" Roan's voice was deep and curious, and when he pushed the door open all the way and stepped inside, she faced him fully. He did a double take, and his eyes grew wide. "Wow. You look great."

She couldn't help but blush. "Thanks."

He knitted his brows.

"What?" She smoothed her hands down her dress and looked at herself in the mirror again.

"Nothing, it's just … I should probably put on the big brother act seeing as you're about to go out with this outlaw biker."

For a second she thought he was serious, and her cheeks heated even further. But then a smile broke out across his face, and she breathed out in relief. Okay, he was so joking with her. "Do I look okay? Is the dress too much?"

He blinked a few times and shook his head. "No. I mean you look great, but don't you think it's a bit revealing?" He cleared his throat and moved his hand over his upper chest. "Like in the northern hemisphere?"

Lilly couldn't help it. She burst out laughing. "Oh my God. I'm embarrassing you by my cleavage."

Roan groaned and closed his eyes. "We are not talking about cleavage or anything else. Court's downstairs." Without looking at her again he turned and left her alone in her room. She looked at her reflection once more, and turned to grab a cardigan from her closet. Her boobs may look good, but that didn't mean she had to walk out there with them hanging out for all to see. Once the blue cardigan was in place and she had the middle button together, she grabbed her purse and headed out.

Court and Roan were by the front door talking, and her mom came out with a glass of lemonade. It was funny to see Court and Roan standing side-by-side, both of them huge, whereas her mother was small and petite.

Maybe it was the sound of her heels clicking on the wood floor, or maybe he could just sense her, but Court snapped his head up and locked his eyes right on her. There was this low noise that came from him and had Roan and her mom looking at him with their brows knitted. Then they turned their attention to her. Okay, so that was awkward, but at the same time Court was giving her this very heated look, one that made her feel like he was on the verge of ripping her dress off when she stopped right in front of him. Her pussy instantly became wet, and her nipples hardened. Thank God she wore the cardigan, because a bra was a no-no with the dress, and she knew the tight peaks would have been visible through the thin material.

"Hi." She was ready to get out of here, because even if Court had plans for them to have a quiet evening talking, she was in the mood for something that she had been craving for the last five years. Was she pretty to look at all bruised up? No, and that might be a deterrent for him, but honestly she also wanted to be with him sexually because she wanted another memory—this one far stronger than them kissing on her bed—to take away the image and feeling of that man above her. "Are you ready?"

Court nodded, but took a sip of the lemonade and watched her over the rim of the glass. Lilly made her way to the front, and right away her mom gave her a hug. This certainly wasn't like she was going away and never coming back, but when she looked her mom in the face and saw the smile there, she knew her mother had hugged her because she was happy for her.

"You look so nice, sweetie." Diera took her hand and squeezed it, and then turned and opened the door for them. "Okay, have fun, and Court? Look after my little girl."

Court turned and looked down at her mom. "With my life, Diera." She patted him on the chest and smiled before ushering them out the door.

Once the door was closed Lilly looked at Court. "So—"

But he didn't let her finish speaking because he had a hold of her hand and was pulling her toward his truck. When they were by the garage, where there were no windows and Roan and her mother couldn't see them, he pulled her toward his chest. Her breasts pressed firmly against him, and he leaned down to take her mouth in a brutally possessive kiss. For several drugging seconds that was all they did. The sun had yet to set, but there was the dusky feeling in the air. Lilly wound her arms around his neck and slipped her hands in his hair. The blond strands were longer, brushing the top of his collar, and giving her just enough length to hold onto.

He broke the kiss and leaned his forehead against hers. "We need to stop, or we will most definitely create a scene in front of the neighborhood."

Lilly pressed her mouth to his again and ran her tongue along the seam of his lips. "Let them watch. I don't care."

Court groaned, but she felt him smile against her mouth. "Baby, you can't say stuff like that." He placed his hands on her hips and rubbed them up and down. "You're still healing, and I don't want to rush this or push you too far."

She shook her head and used as much of her strength as she could to push him back against the garage door. There was a moment of surprise on his face, but he didn't say anything. "I'm healing just fine, but I don't want you to treat me like I'm porcelain and you're afraid I'm going to break." She stared into his light green eyes, willing him to really understand her. "Roan treats me like he is afraid I will go off the deep-end, and I won't." She took a deep breath. "I just want to forget what happened. I want to move on, and I want to do that with you. I want you to replace those god-awful memories with new ones."

He lifted his hands and gently cupped both sides of her face. He stared deeply into her eyes and then slid his gaze to the side of her face that was bruised. He ground his teeth and closed his eyes for several seconds. "I want to help you forget, want to replace that nightmare that you endured, but I'm afraid that I'll make it worse."

She shook her head and smiled up at him even though he still had his eyes closed and couldn't see her doing the acts. "I love that you are this big biker, a bear shifter on top of that, yet you are afraid of going too fast with me." She doubted there were many times he thought about going slow in his life.

"Lilly, there is a lot I missed out on with you, and a lot I want to experience with you. I'm not in a rush." He pressed his lips to hers, and just when she would have taken control of the kiss he pulled back. "Make no mistake I want you." To emphasize his point he took hold of her wrist and brought between their bodies. Pressing her hand to his crotch told her he was hard as steel. "So, yeah. I want you really fucking badly, Lilly."

Her heart slammed fiercely against her ribs, and if she had her way she would have let him take her right here against the garage. But she wanted privacy, and certainly wasn't going to get that right here.

"Come on, I have plans for us." He led her to the truck, the same one that he had taken her virginity in, and it felt almost surreal and nostalgic in a strange way. After he helped her inside and was in the driver's side seat, he started the engine and pulled out of the driveway. Trees passed by on either side of them as he headed out of Steel Corner, and she was curious as to where he was taking her.

"Where exactly are we going?"

He looked over at her and grinned but didn't respond to her question.

Lilly used that moment to take in his appearance. She could have when she had seen him standing in the entryway of her mother's home, and could have when they were outside, but she had been focused on his face and had tunnel vision because of her desire for him. But now she had as much time to look at him as she pleased. With that strong, square jaw, lightly stubbled cheeks, and light green eyes, he wasn't handsome in a clean cut, classic way, but more so in a brutally hardcore manner. He made her think of sinfully wicked things.

He reached over and turned the radio on, but to her surprise he didn't blast classic rock. That had been his favorite music of choice back in the day, but instead he put on an oldies station. He adjusted the volume so it was barely audible, making it more background noise than a filler.

Lilly looked at the thickness of his biceps. They were huge, and his t-shirt was formed perfectly to the smooth flesh and hard muscle. He wore his cut, but she liked that he always had it on. It made him look dangerous, and what girl didn't want a man that looked like Court, that poured potent masculinity, and didn't have to even say anything for people to know that he was deadly? His jeans were loose, but still showed off the thickness of his thighs, ones that looked powerful, like trunks of massive trees. When she moved her eyes back up to his face her cheeks instantly heated when she saw that he looked at her.

He glanced back at the road, but the corner of his mouth kicked up. "You know how to make a male feel wanted, Lilly."

She scoffed, but couldn't help but smile. "Don't act like you aren't used to women looking at you the way I just was." Although she was embarrassed that he had caught her checking him out, there was this familiarity between them, and it made the air lighter.

"I'm used to it." The tone of his voice wasn't arrogant as he spoke. He looked at her. "But I've never gotten pleasure from it until you did it."

Wow. Gritty biker and a smooth talker, too. She cleared her throat and stared out the front windshield. Lilly couldn't look at him, not when just staring into his eyes had her feeling she was back in high school and unable to control her hormones. "So, where are we going?"

"I thought we could have a picnic."

That had her turned to face him and lifting a brow in surprise. "A picnic? Won't it be getting dark soon?"

He nodded and reached over to take her hand in his. "Yeah, but the picnic we are having isn't outside." They drove for another five minutes before he pulled off of the main road and moved up an incline. Finally he pulled to a stop in front of a small house on a cleared out strip of land. There were trees on all sides of them, but they weren't too far out from town, and not deep into the woods. This place was just a small house in its own little sanctuary. It was perfect.

"Is this your place?" It might have seemed obvious that it was, but then again nothing in Steel Corner should be considered obvious. She looked over at him.

"Yeah, bought it a couple of years ago." He stared at the house, but then looked at her. "It was really nothing more than a corpse of a building, but I had a lot of help from the club in fixing it up. It's small, with two tiny as shit bedrooms, but it works for me." He leaned in, and she knew he was going to kiss her, but the sound of an approaching car had him pulling away from her and looking over at the driveway. "Perfect timing." He spoke to himself, but before he got out he leaned in, gave her a quick peck on the lips, and headed out of the truck.

A small and rusted Toyota made a U-turn in the gravel driveway, but the way he stopped had the headlights flashing right in her face. There were some murmured voices, but she couldn't hear what was being said over the heavy bass coming from the car, or see who Court was talking to because of the headlights. After a few minutes the car left the property. Before Lilly could get out Court was opening the door for her. He held two brown bags in his arm, and the scent of chicken filled her nose. "You ordered food for our picnic?"

He grinned and didn't look sheepish at all. "Believe me, you do not want me cooking for you. I manage to burn toast."

That had her laughing. She grabbed his hand he held out and got out of the car. They made their way toward the front door, and once he had it unlocked and opened he allowed her to enter first. He turned the light on, and she heard him close the door. Inside was what she would have expected for a bachelor in terms of furnishings. It was clean, but it smelled of lemon, and she had a feeling he had cleaned it before she came over. That had her chuckling. He hadn't been lying when he said the place was small. There was one couch that looked the worse for wear, but the TV was big and looked expensive.

"I'm going to get this shit together. Make yourself at home." He had an eloquent way with words.

She turned to face him. He was in the kitchen, and the entryway allowed her to see only partially, but she saw stainless steel appliances and a black and white décor. The sound of him grabbing some plates and of the dishes clanking together could be heard. She didn't see any decorations aside from a few framed pictures of motorcycles, and even one with a half-naked chick on it. Lilly moved closer to that one and saw that it was actually a painting—a very realistic painting, but one nonetheless.

Minutes later and Court was coming back into the living room. She grabbed the dishes from him, but didn't know exactly what his plans were, so she stood there and took cues from him.

He grabbed a blanket off of the couch and set the bags of food on the coffee table. "I hope you're ready for some home cooking." He gave her this devilish grin and motioned for her to come closer. Once they were seated on the blanket and he had the food out and dished onto the plates, they ate for a few minutes in silence. Court grabbed a bottle of champagne from beside her that she hadn't even seen him carrying, and produced two glasses.

"You're full of surprises." She took one of the wine glasses and brought it to her mouth. Taking a sip of the light yellow liquid, she let the bubbles dance along her tongue "So, home cooking to you is fried chicken and sides that are delivered to your door?" She was teasing, and fortunately he grinned.

"Baby, compared to what I could have cooked for you, this is gold."

"Maybe one of these days I'll cook a real meal for you?"

He stopped eating, and there was this strange expression on his face.

"What's wrong?" She set her food down, too.

He shook his head. "Nothing. It's just having you cook for me is a pretty special fucking thing." They stared at each other for a moment, and although there was silence between them it didn't seem uncomfortable or strange given the intensity with which he had just said those words.

"Well, I never thought someone would think my cooking would be that special. You must not have tasted it before." It was like this man could look at her and she felt like no one else mattered in the world to him but her.

"No one does."

Had she said those damn words aloud?

"For me, there is only you, Lilly."

Suddenly she didn't want any food. All she wanted was Court, and seeing the way she could make out the long, thick length of his erection as his pressed against his jeans, told her that food wasn't on his mind either. "I was afraid of going out tonight because of my face." She lifted her hand and touched the tender spot right under her eye.

"I wouldn't have taken you anywhere public, because I could sense that you were uncomfortable. Besides," he leaned in until their breaths mingled together.

She smelled the slightly fruity flavor of the champagne on his breath, and her pulse pounded hard and fast between her legs. She wanted him desperately, wanted to feel his callused hands slide along her body as he took off her dress. She wasn't wearing a bra, but her panties were nothing more than a strip of fabric right up the center of her ass. She felt the material move along her now soaked pussy lips, and nearly closed her eyes as her pulse beat heavily right in her clit. It felt like she had two hearts, one in her chest and another between her thighs.

"I saw you wearing this dress and instantly got so fucking hard." His mouth was so close to hers that she felt his lips brush along hers with every word he formed. "All I could think about was taking you back to my house, stripping this dress off of your body, and feasting on you." He tilted his head and ran the very tip of his tongue along her jawline. "And I'm starving, baby, so damn hungry for you that if I'm not careful there wouldn't be anything left of you when I get finished."

Chapter Nine

Court was having a hard time keeping his bear under control. The beast wanted out, wanted to claim Lilly right now. But he needed to remind himself that she was still healing, and that although she told him she wanted this, if he took her in the way he really wanted to, he might hurt her further. Court liked the rough kind of sex, the one where he kept a female's hand pinned at the base of her spine. He liked to push the hair off of her shoulder so he could see the long, smooth column of her throat, and plunged his dick into her tight, warm heat. No, that was a lie. He didn't do that to anyone he fucked. In fact, this was the first time he had thought about looking at the smooth arch of Lilly's neck as he fucked her deep and hard and claimed her the way a male did his female. And she was *his* female, irrevocably.

"Court?"

"Yeah, baby?" He continued to run his tongue along her jawline and groaned at the sweet flavor of her skin. His cock throbbed behind the zipper of his jeans, and his bear paced right below the surface of his skin. He was feral, territorial, and wanted to possess every inch of this female until she acknowledged that she was his, and that she always would be.

"Take me to your bed, remind me how powerful you can be." She pulled back and looked in his face. "Remind me of how powerful you can be between my legs."

A low, needy growl left him, and in a matter of seconds he had her in his arms and was striding to his bedroom. Forget about dinner, because he was about to eat her alive until she came so fucking hard his ears would ring from her screams and his bear would be able to sample the nectar that would surely flow from her lush, curvy body. He set her on the center of his bed and took a step back and just stared at her. Her dress had risen up, and the majority of her thighs were visible. They were smooth and creamy in color, and all he kept thinking about was parting them and watching as her pussy lips spread wide so he could see her wetness. Court's mouth literally watered when that image slammed into his brain. He reached down and pressed his hand right over his dick, applying pressure and trying to ease the ache in his shaft.

"The way you're looking at me is a little frightening." She said this on a whisper.

Court inhaled, but didn't smell any fear. In fact, all he smelled from her was arousal and the need to be with him. "You should be frightened of what I want to do to you." He removed his cut and set it on the dresser, and grabbed the hem of his shirt. Once he had the t-shirt off and tossed it to the floor, he went for his belt and undid it, and once his zipper was down he took off his pants. Was he rushing this along? Maybe, but he had never wanted a female as much as he wanted her. To be honest, ever since he had taken her at that field party it had been hard to be with anyone else. She was all he thought about, all he pictured when he closed his eyes. He should have taken that as a big fucking red sign that he was being a dumbass in staying away.

"Court?"

He blinked and realized that he had been thinking about the past, and there was no more time for that. Now all he wanted to focus on was this hot fucking female right in front of him. "Take off the dress and sweater, Lilly." Court could hear his bear in his voice. It had a rough, harsh quality to it, one that was slightly distorted and on edge. Even through the blue material of her cardigan he saw her hardened nipples. They were so fucking erect that he wanted to bury his face between her breasts and rub his cheeks on the stiff peaks.

She sat up and went for the lone button that was keeping the two halves of the cardigan together. Once that was removed and tossed aside her stared at the huge mounds that were all but spilling from her the top of her dress. She had always been a thicker girl while growing up, and once she hit high school that baby fat had turned into womanly curves. But it wasn't until that damn graduation party that he fully appreciated the fullness of her thighs, or the way her tits were well over a handful.

"Although I am all about you teasing me and removing the dress slowly, right now I am pushing my will to stay in control." Fortunately, she didn't try to be a little seductress, although he knew she could do that without even trying.

When the straps of her dress were off her shoulder, she reached behind her back and he heard a zipper being lowered. She looked up at him with her big blue eyes, and swallowed. Keeping her gaze right on him, she pushed the top of her dress down. Her breasts bounced free of their confinement, and Court couldn't stop himself from grabbing the base of his cock and stroking himself from root to tip.

"Touch yourself, Lilly. I want to see you grab those big tits and roll them around." His chest rose and fell violently, and he couldn't help it. "Imagine it's me touching you, baby." A drop of pre-cum lined the tip of his dick, and he spread it around his head, adding lubrication as he jerked himself off and watched Lilly. He could have easily gone over there and touched her himself, but watching her lift her hands and grab the mounds like she was doing right now was a much better visual, and arousing all on its own. He would go over there and touch every inch of her, lick every part of her body, and feel her writhe beneath him, but he wanted this visual temptation first.

"Like this?" Her voice was low, and he watched as a blush stole her cheeks and covered her chest. She ran her palms up and down her breasts, and then curled her fingers into the giving flesh.

"Yeah, baby, just like that." That was it. He couldn't take any more of this delicious torture, and although he wanted to be really fucking rough with her, wanted to feel her surrender as he took her, they had many, many more times for that. He climbed up on the bed and reached for the straps of her panties on either side of her hips. Slowly bringing the thin material down, he stared at her chest as she continued to touch herself. The scent of her arousal slammed into his nose once the underwear was gone, but he didn't need to tell her what he wanted. She was already lying back and spreading her thighs, Then again this was what she wanted, too. That much was clear, and it still stunned the hell out of him that he was lucky enough to have her as his female.

"I want this, Court. God, I want this so badly." She had her hands off her breasts and her fingers digging into the mattress.

"Lilly, if you had any idea how much I want you right now it would scare the fuck out of you." Placing a hand on both of her thighs and slowly moving his fingers toward her pussy, he exerted pressure until she spread even wider for him. Court watched with a primal hunger as her labia spread open, and her darker pink, soaked flesh was revealed. He had been the first one to have that, to claim her, and nothing would ever take that away from him. He slowly moved his gaze over her ribs, saw the bruises, but forced himself to stay calm. He continued his appraisal of rounded stomach, but when he saw more bruising on her thighs his rage boiled within him at a fast and intense rate. But before he could get any angrier he felt her hands on either side of his face, and the pressure she used to lift his head so he was looking into her eyes. His rage lessened, and all he felt was calm as he stared into her face. Even his bear eased marginally, and Court knew that this woman had a lot of fucking control over him.

"Don't go there. I know I'm not right now." She smiled and pushed herself up so she could kiss him.

Court broke the kiss and moved between her thighs once more. With his wide shoulders between them there was no way she could close them—if she wanted to—and block herself from what he was going to do. The scent of her pussy was musky and sweet, and it felt like his tongue swelled with the need to run the length through the center of her body. But he didn't deny either of them any longer. There had been enough time elapsed between them to last a lifetime. Placing a thumb on either side of her pussy, he pulled apart her flesh even further and covered her entire slit with his mouth. He worked his tongue in her hole, moved it in and out, and then flattened it and slid it all the way up her cleft and closed his mouth around her clit. The breathy sound she made was like adding fuel to the fire of his need to make her come in his mouth. Over and over, he licked and sucked at her, keeping her open with his thumbs and making sure to memorize every inch of her cunt. The bastard within him wanted out, wanted to tear Lilly up in only the best of ways, but this was Court's time with his girl, and no way was the animal he held within taking that from him. But that didn't stop his bear from still trying. His nails turned into claws, and he felt his incisors elongate. The gasp that came from her when she clearly felt the sharpness of them had his cock jerking in response.

"Court, God, Court, I can see your bear trying to get through." She didn't sound afraid or disgusted, and by the warm gush of cream that spilled from her and the scent of her lust Court knew she liked it.

He lifted his head from between her thighs and felt the product of her arousal cover his mouth. He knew his bear was right there, despite him trying desperately to keep him back. Not answering because he didn't know if he could form a coherent word right now, he covered her pussy with his mouth again and sucked on her clit harder than before. He needed her to come, needed to her cry out her orgasm and beg for more. And then she was tensing and reaching out to tangle her hands in his hair.

"Oh God, Court. Yes, right there."

He sucked faster and slipped his hand lower so he could shove a finger deep inside of her. Instantly her inner muscles clenched around the digit, and he added another one right when she came. "You're so hot and tight, and all this wetness is for me, baby."

She groaned out loudly and pulled at his hair hard enough that the sting went down his spine. But he wanted more from her.

He pulled away when he sensed her orgasm waning, and got off of the bed only long enough to grab a condom from his wallet and sheath himself. Court moved back between her legs, smoothed his hands over her thighs and up her belly, and then molded his palms right over the huge mounds of her breasts. Her areolas were a dark rose color, and he couldn't help himself from leaning down and sucking on the stiff peaks for a few seconds. He would have gone longer, feasted on her succulent flesh, but his dick was roaring out to be buried inside of her. Court allowed himself just a second longer to look at her wet cunt. Taking hold of the base of his dick, he aligned the tip of his shaft with her small opening and started to push inside.

She gasped and tried to close her legs as if on instinct.

The head of his cock broke through the opening, and a groan left him when she clenched around him. "*Christ*, Lilly." Court closed his eyes and groaned out deeply at the incredible tightness of her body. "You're so fucking primed for me, baby."

"Yeah, I am." She panted out those words.

Court continued to push inside of her, deep and slow until his balls rested against the big, soft and fleshy mounds of her ass. They both made a low sound in their throats, and Court opened his eyes, not realizing he had kept them shut this entire time. He looked down at where his body was connected with her, saw the way her pink flesh was stretched around him wide, and felt his pulse shoot up as he looked at all the glistening wetness coating her. It was all for him. Court pulled out almost all the way, and then pushed back in slowly. Over and over, he thrust deep inside of her, loving the sound of their wet flesh slapping together every time he slammed into her. He started to increase his speed and trained his gaze on her tits, which were bouncing wildly from his actions. His hold on her hips was firm, but the force with which he was fucking her had her body sliding up the bed. Reaching up and curling his hand around her shoulder, Court anchored her and continued to slide his dick in and out of her fast and hard until the only things that filled his head was her heavy breathing, her soft mewls, and the erotic sounds of their bodies meeting.

"It's so good, Court." She had her hands on her breasts and to his surprise and pleasure started tugging at her nipples.

"That's fucking it, Lilly. Pull on your nipples until it hurts so good."

A gasp left her. She closed her eyes and her lips parted, and he sensed another orgasm about to break free from her. She arched her neck and cried out long and softly, and he increased his speed. His bear broke free enough that the asshole could enjoy this as well, and shit were they both enjoying it. It was like watching a masterpiece being created as she came right below him. The rhythmic pulls of her inner muscles along his shaft would have had him coming right along with her, but he held himself back. He wasn't ready to let this end just yet, not when there were more parts of her body he wanted to taste.

She relaxed on the bed and breathed out roughly. "God, Court."

A light sheen of sweat covered her chest, and Court leaned down and ran his tongue along the tiny beads of wetness. The salty sweetness that invaded his taste buds had him wanting more. Before the little tremors that shook her body waned, he pulled out of her, heard her gasp, and flipped her onto her belly gently, so as not to hurt her side. Grabbing a pillow from beside her head, Court placed it under her hips. Her ass was popped up, and he immediately grabbed a cheek in each hand and spread her wide. Hidden beneath the full mounds was the tight, pink hole of her anus. He had always been an ass man, and Lilly had one that went on for miles. It made his cock go even harder, and had been the image that he had jerked himself off to.

"What are you doing?" Her voice held a breathy quality to it. She looked over her shoulder, and there was a hazy quality in her expression. Her eyes were half-lidded from her multiple orgasms, but he planned on making her come once more.

"Doing something I have been thinking about for a long damn time, baby."

She licked her lips. "Back there?" There was a touch of hesitancy in her voice, but no fear or reluctance.

Without answering, but still holding her gaze with his own, Court leaned in and ran his tongue right up the center of her ass. He pressed his tongue to her anus, moved it around the tight hole, and then gently pressed in.

"Court…" She closed her eyes again, and that had a groan leaving him and pleasure filling him.

Humming around her anus, he continued to lick at her, slowly at first as to get her used to what was certainly something new to her, but then he started to feel his control slip. She tasted good, slightly salty from her sweat, but still having the sweetness to her. Then his actions started getting more demanding, more forceful. He squeezed her ass cheeks, growled against her now soaked flesh, and needed to feel her let go this way.

Lilly moaned, and it was fucking music to his ears. "I've never felt anything like that."

It was almost like she spoke to herself, and so he renewed his efforts. Slipping a hand between her legs, he found the hard little nub of her clit and rubbed it back and forth at the same time he licked her asshole. Court pulled back and used his other hand to press a finger to the tight ring of muscle. Gently inserting into her ass, he never stopped rubbing her clit in the process. Court watched as she shook uncontrollably and as she curled her hands into the mattress and bunched the sheets in her fists. "Come on, baby girl. Give me one more." Court pressed his finger harder on her clit and rubbed it back and forth faster and harder. He pushed another digit into her ass, but she was nice and slick from him working his mouth all over her, and the finger slid in smoothly.

"I feel so full."

She hadn't felt anything yet. Just as she started to come, he removed his hand from her clit, positioned his dick at her pussy hole, and shoved in deep and hard and in one long stroke. The scream that came from her had Court picking up his speed. With his fingers still buried in her ass, and his cock stuffing her pussy full, he started moving his hips back and forth. But it was too much for him to handle, and when her inner muscles started milking his dick he had to take his fingers out of her bottom, hold onto her waist, and slam into her repeatedly until he was also coming right along with her. He started to get off hard, felt the hard jets of his cum fill the tip of the condom, and worked himself into her more fiercely. "That's it, Lilly, you are squeezing my cock so damn good, baby."

"Ohhh," she gasped out.

He slammed into her again, knew he was hitting something sweet inside of her by the sounds she made, and did it again and again. Sweat lined his temples and spine, but he didn't stop pumping into her until he saw the way her arms shook as she held herself up and heard her breathing start to slow. Court pulled out of her with a grunt and collapsed beside her. She was already on her belly, her face toward him, and her eyes closed. Lifting his hand and brushing away a strand of her dark hair that was damp from her sweat, he then leaned in and kissed her forehead.

"I love you, Court." She opened her eyes, and the blueness of her irises was a startling shade. "I have loved you for a really long time."

Court cupped her cheek and just stared into her face for several seconds.

"I don't expect you to say it back or anything. That wasn't why I told you." She placed her hand over his and closed her eyes. "I just needed to tell you."

He moved closer, wrapped his arms around her, and pulled her up so her upper body was on his chest. For a moment he didn't do anything but hold her, and listen to the sound of their hearts beating the same rhythm. His bear was content, his human was sated, and he cared about this female more than anything else in the world.

"I didn't make this an awkward after sex thing, did I?" There was a teasing note in her voice, but there was also a touch of uncertainty. He squeezed her tighter against him.

"I love you, too, Lilly." He felt her press her face to his chest. "I have since that night at the field party. I wanted you before that, but being with you that way, being the first guy to have that part of you, had my bear already staking his claim."

She lifted her head and stared at him. "Really?"

She was so young, ten years younger than he was, but none of that mattered. She was his, would always be his, and there was nothing that could change that. "My world is crazy, intense, dangerous, and not pretty most of the time."

"I know, Court. I've lived in Steel Corner my whole life, remember?" She smirked at him.

He smoothed his hand along her cheek. "I know, baby, but I just want you to know what you're getting into if you really want me."

"Court, I will always want you, have always wanted you." Now it was her turn to smooth her hands along his face. "I know about the biker life, know that The Grizzly MC is more animal than human, but I don't care, Court. I just want *you*." She rested her head on his chest again.

Despite the grimness of his lifestyle and the years that had passed between them because of his stubborn stupidity, at the end having Lilly wrapped around him, made it seem like all of that was miniscule compared to what he had with his female. And Court wasn't about to fuck that up again, or let anyone take that happiness from him.

****

Her mother all but squealed after Lilly told her that she and Court were giving a relationship a shot. Would it work out? Lilly sure as hell hoped so, and loved him enough that she was willing to work out things if they got hairy. Was his life an easy one, or one that she could be comfortable with? Honestly, she didn't know. Knowing about an MC, and seeing how they lived from the outside was not the same thing as actually living within those walls. And that was what she was doing now. Court probably lived one of the grittiest lives she had ever been around, but he took care of what was his, made sure that the people he cared about knew that, and she couldn't have asked for a better man to love.

"What does Roan think?" Her mother was at the sink and dried the plate she had used for lunch.

Lilly was sitting at the kitchen table. She shrugged even though her mother's back was to her now. "We actually talked to him about this earlier, but things between Court and me weren't certain until recently."

Her mother turned and had a smile on her face. "I'm glad you're happy, Lilly. Now we just have to get your brother to settle down." Diera walked over and sat down in the seat across from her. "I want to make sure the two of you are at a good place in your life."

Lilly knew what her mother was referring to without her having to say it. "I wish you wouldn't do that."

"Do what, sweetheart?" Her mom looked at the table as if she couldn't meet Lilly's gaze.

"Think about death, and then talk about it like you won't be around for much longer."

Her mom lifted her head and reached across the table to take her hand in hers. "Lilly, we all have only a limited amount of time on this planet. Some of us are blessed to spend far longer with their loved ones than others. It is heartbreaking, but a fact of life, and something we have to embrace instead of rebel against." Her mom rubbed her hand along hers. "Death isn't the end, honey, at least in my eyes it isn't. It is just a new beginning to something different."

"I know, but I don't want to think about stuff like that."

"I know. I've come to accept what path my life is going down, but nothing is set in stone. All I can do is live every day to the fullest, and let my loved ones know what they mean to me." She smiled at Lilly. "And I love you and your brother very much. Without you two this journey would have been unbearable."

Tears started to well in Lilly's eyes.

Her mother shook her head. "No tears, Lilly. We enjoy each day, be grateful for the things that have blessed our lives, and just be happy." Diera sighed and smiled wider. "Now, you go see Court, tell him how much you love him, and see if he wants to come over for a family dinner tonight."

Lilly smiled and nodded. "Okay, Mom." Lilly stood, and she walked over and gave her mom a hug. "I love you, too." She didn't want to think about death and her mother not being around.

Diera patted her on the back and gave her a kiss on the cheek. "Go on, honey, and let me know about dinner."

Lilly gave her mom one more hug and left the house. Once in her car she headed toward The Grizzly clubhouse, and wondered if she should have called Court first. They had spoken this morning, and she knew he was working on some bikes with a few of the other members. Lilly wanted to see him, but she would use the fact her mother wanted him over for dinner as the excuse as to why she stopped by. She shook her head and chuckled at her thoughts.

Pulling her car into the parking lot, she immediately saw Court standing around a broken down motorcycle with a few other tough looking bear shifting bikers. The damn man was shirtless, and the sweat that gleamed off his chest was hot enough that she actually contemplated running her tongue all over him, grease and all. She pulled her car into an empty spot and climbed out.

Court turned toward her, and the grin that spread across his face had her heart slamming hard in her chest. The tattoo that covered one pectoral muscle was The Grizzly MC logo. The dark motorcycle that was over the blood red claw marks was deadly as much as it was artistic. The top rocker read GRIZZLY, and the bottom one said COLORADO.

He moved toward her, and the guys that had been standing by him all hooted and hollered. Court lifted his hand and flipped them all off, not breaking his stride as he made his way toward her. "Hey, baby." He had her in his arms as soon as he reached her and lifted her easily off the ground. His claiming her mouth with his own had Lilly moaning. The flavor that assaulted her was salty and all male, and the scent of his clean sweat and grease filled her nose and had her pussy becoming wet. He growled against her lips and pulled back slightly. "I could take you right now and make that pussy even wetter, Lilly."

She smiled, tempted to tell him to stop with the threats and just do it. But that wasn't why she had come here, not really. "My mom wants you to come over for dinner tonight."

He kissed her again. "Is that why you came here?"

She shook her head, and now she was the one to take his mouth in a kiss, and to sweep her tongue between his lips. They kissed for a few seconds, but she didn't care that the MC was watching. "No." She felt him smile against her mouth.

"Yeah, I didn't think that was the reason. Well, I was hoping my girl didn't come out here to ask me to go to dinner."

She chuckled and shook her head.

"You know I'll be there, but afterward you're all mine." He moved his mouth to her ear and whispered, "And the things I want to do to you are so fucking filthy you'll need a shower afterward."

God, she was so looking forward to that.

THE GRIZZLY MC: VOLUME TWO

Epilogue

Six months later

Lilly helped Maggie, Darra, and Sonya clean up after the family meal they had had at the clubhouse. There were children from other members running around, their laughter having Lilly smile.

"I swear I need to have this baby now." Maggie sat in one of the barstools beside where Lilly stood.

"You look great."

Maggie looked over at Lilly and grimaced. "Thanks, but I look like a house."

Lilly just smiled and rubbed Maggie's back. Although Maggie's belly was rounded, there was no doubt that the little boy inside of her would be just as large as his father, Diesel.

"Well, it's time for me to get home and convince Diesel that he wants to rub my swollen feet." Maggie started laughing, and then was off the barstool and wobbling over to The Grizzly MC VP. Wobbling was a pretty good description of how she was walking, and all Lilly could do was smile at how cute she looked.

"You ready, baby?" Court came up to her and wrapped his arms around her waist.

She rested her head on his chest and listened to his heart beating. "Tonight was nice." Over the last six months she had really gotten to know the members of The Grizzly MC, and their old ladies. They might be rough, brutal in a lot of aspects, but they were also so very caring and loving when it concerned people in their circle of protection.

"Yeah, it really was. We need to have these family dinners more often. It's good for everyone." He continued to hold her, and she just let herself enjoy the feeling of being cherished. "Your mom still having Sunday dinner tomorrow?"

She nodded. Her mom was still sick, but she was a strong and stubborn woman, and wouldn't let anything get her down, not even cancer. Lilly didn't know how much longer her mom would be with them, but she didn't take one day for granted and cherished every moment.

Court pulled back and cupped her cheek. He leaned down and kissed her softly on the lips. "Come on. I need to be inside of you. I've been watching you, and trying to hide this fucking hard-on you gave me."

"The hard-on I gave you?" She smiled, but her heart started racing. She licked her lips and nodded. "Let's go home." Even six months later she was insatiable when it came to Court, and it seemed he was the same way concerning her.

He led them out of the clubhouse after they said their goodbyes to everyone. Once on the back of his Harley with their helmets on, they were headed on the road and toward the home they shared. She was wet, ready, and needed him liked she needed to breathe. It was a twenty minute ride to their home, and she swore they were off that bike and inside in a matter of seconds. As soon as the front door was shut behind them Court had his mouth on hers and his hands in her hair. He kissed her like he hadn't seen her in years, like he was desperate for her touch, and she couldn't help but moan against his mouth. He took a step back from her, and she swallowed the lump that had suddenly formed in her throat. Lilly didn't move as Court went for his cut and removed it. She couldn't tear her eyes from him as he gripped the edge of his shirt and pulled it up and over his head. Lilly took in the tanned, hard, and tatted up flesh that was revealed. She'd never get sick of looking at the ridges of muscles that made up his six-pack, his defined pecs, and his bulging biceps.

God, but was she turned on.

Court stood there, his jeans now unbuttoned and hanging off his lean hips. "Lilly. Strip for me."

Hearing him say those three words after her name had her pulse throbbing between her thighs. It was as if his words alone elicited something deep inside of her, drawing out her needs and wants and combining it all in one hard package that represented Court.

"Baby, I'm dying over here with the need to fuck you, but I want to go slow."

His dirty words excited her. Her hands shook as she lifted them and gripped the hem of her shirt, slowly peeling it up and over her head. What she wanted was hard and fast, but she liked this side of Court, too. And then her shirt was off and the cool air brushed along her exposed nipples. *Why did you forego wearing a bra?*

"Fucking hell, Lilly. You are playing dangerously by not wearing a bra for those big, mouthwatering breasts." A moment of silence passed between them. "Now the pants and panties, Lilly." The way he spoke had her lifting her eyes to his. His voice hitched, and she could see his chest rising and falling a bit faster as he looked at her breasts. As if his gaze alone could draw the tissue taut, she felt her skin pull even tighter, felt the blood rush just below the surface of her skin. Hands now on the button of her jeans, she slid it through the buttonhole and drew the zipper down. She hooked her fingers under the edge of her pants and panties and started to push them down her thighs. Even though the chilled air hit every part of her, the very knowledge that he was staring at her had her body hot.

When she kicked the garments free she stood there, eyes locked on his, trying to decipher what was going through his head. She let her gaze travel down the length of his body again, stayed a little longer admiring the tight *V* of muscles that disappeared beneath his jeans, and then swallowed hard when she saw his erection pressing against the material. Her mouth watered, and her pussy clenched. She knew how big his cock was and how stretched she would be once he shoved all those thick, hard inches into her.

"Come here." Voice low and deep, Court crooked his finger at her.

She swore he could hear her heart beating, could see it slamming against her ribcage. That first step toward him was the hardest, and soon she found herself right before him, her breath coming in short, hard pants. They both wanted this fiercely, yet they were almost being cautious. His gaze seemed to be riveted to her chest, but she saw him lower them until she knew exactly what he was looking at. Just knowing that he was looking at her pussy had a shudder leaving her. She felt soaked and squeezed her legs together.

"I'm going to fuck you so thoroughly, baby." He sounded out of breath.

She looked down at his bulge once more, but Court lifted her head up with a finger under her chin. There was this low rumble that left him, and she knew his bear was close to the surface, as it always was when they had sex. It was like the beast had to be with her, too. Their combined breathing was harsh, and she knew that there would never be anyone she wanted more than she wanted Court.

"On your knees." His hand landed on her shoulders, and he gently pushed her down. Lilly couldn't lie and say his demand didn't make her even wetter. Court knew what he wanted, and what he wanted was her. That thought alone was empowering.

The cold, hard wood beneath her knees sent a flash of discomfort and pleasure up her body. His erection was right in front of her face, straining against the material, insistent on being free. Good God, she wanted his cock in her mouth, wanted to taste the pre-cum at the tip that she would know would be covering the bulbous head.

"Christ, Lilly. I could come just looking at you on your knees right now." He cleared his throat and dropped his hands so they hung at his sides. "Go on, baby. Take my cock out and suck it. Suck it like you're fucking starving for it."

She lifted her hands and undid the rest of his jeans until the material fell off of his lean hips and pooled around his feet. His cock sprang free, and she was so close that the slickened tip actually brushed along her mouth. Lilly licked her lips, and Court groaned above her. His gaze was heavy lidded, and his face was a little flushed. His pupils were fully dilated, and she swore she saw the flash of his inner animal right there below the surface.

"Go on, baby, hold onto the root of my dick and suck it into that lush little mouth of yours."

Her pussy so soaked that her cream slid down her inner thighs, Lilly did exactly that. He grunted when she gripped him around the base of his cock. When his erection was free and she got the first look at it, she knew her look was one of surprise. "God, can we skip the foreplay and go right to the fucking?" The words tumbled out of her mouth. Court grabbed a chunk of her hair behind her head and yanked her head back. A gasp left her at the pleasure/pain that radiated within her.

His cock was just as tanned as the rest of him, and the bulbous head was flushed red with a drop of pre-cum dotting the slit at the tip. Her mouth watered, and she leaned forward and engulfed the crown into her mouth. She moaned at the salty, musky flavor that covered her taste buds. He groaned and tightened his hand in her hair, his nails digging into her scalp. She sucked in more of his length and ran her tongue along the underside of his cock. Lilly tried to get even more of him into her mouth until she felt the tip of him hit the back of her throat. The gag reflex was there, but she didn't care. She continued to take as much as she could, bobbed her head back and forth until her eyes watered, and held onto his thighs as he started fucking himself in her mouth.

"*Christ*, Lilly." Court groaned and jerked in her mouth until he hit the back of her throat once more. He fucked her mouth slow and easy at first, and she found herself moving her tongue along his flesh, tasting a burst of saltiness as his semen coated her tongue. She wanted him to come in her mouth, wanted to swallow every last drop until she smelled and tasted like him.

"Yes. Oh fuck, yes." His hold on her hair tightened, and he started thrusting hips more franticly in his need for release. "Take it all, baby. Take all of my fucking cock and drink my cum."

"Mmm." Closing her eyes she focused on getting him off. They could have sex later, Right now was about pleasing her biker.

She still gripped his strong thighs, and she then moved her hands behind him until she felt the firm, taut cheeks of his ass. They flexed while he pumped his hips back and forth. Lilly knew when he was close, and she dug her nails into his flesh. He pumped forward once, twice, and stilled on the third time. He buried his cock all the way in her mouth until she felt his balls bump her chin and his cum slide down the back of her throat. She could smell the residual scent of grease from when he had been working on Harleys at the clubhouse, smelled the faint aroma of clean sweat on him, and moved her hand down between her thighs. Rubbing her clit with her finger back and forth while Court still pumped shallowly inside of her, she knew she would get off in a matter of seconds.

His orgasm had been powerful, and it had all been because of her. But right before she came Court had his cock pulled free from her mouth and was helping her to stand. Her legs were wobbly, and this sense of euphoria gripped her tightly.

"I'm going to be the one that makes you come, Lilly." He had her in his arms and was striding toward their bedroom. Once inside he strode to the massive bed and set her on it, but before she could move he gripped her legs and pulled her so her ass was hanging off the mattress. There was no waiting with Court. He pushed her legs apart almost forcefully and buried his face between her thighs.

The pleasure was instant, and she knew she wouldn't last. Gritting her teeth, she bunched the sheet in her hands as he pulled her labia apart and sucked and nipped at her sensitive flesh. When he sucked her already oversensitive clit into his mouth and shoved a thick finger into her, twisting and curing it inside of her so he hit her G-spot, she came hard and fast. The cry that left her was intense, and she bit her lip hard enough that the tangy metallic flavor of her blood coated her tongue. He didn't stop eating her out until tremors worked through her and she was gently pushing at his chest.

Court moved up the bed and pressed his mouth right on hers. He was almost brutal as he shoved his tongue into her mouth and made her taste herself on him. He moved his hands behind her and cupped her ass. His cock was starting to harden again between their bodies, and she lifted her hips, needing the contact. She may have just gotten off, but she would always want him, and always need Court like this. He was the only one for her, and had been since she was a teenager.

"I love you, Lilly," he murmured against her mouth, and moved one of his hands away from her ass to between their bodies. And then he was pressing the tip into her opening and sliding all the way in. "You're mine, Lilly." He pulled out and slammed into her. "All fucking mine."

"Yes." And that was all she could say, because Court was fucking her like neither of them had just gotten off. If she died from the pleasure Court gave her, it would be one hell of a way to go.

The End

www.jenikasnow.com

Evernight Publishing

www.evernightpublishing.com